Keep telling yourself – it's just a game… it's just a game.

Tyler MacCandless can't focus, even when he takes his medication. He can't focus on much of anything except caring for his older brother, Brandon, who's in rehab. Just when it seems like his future is on a collision course with a life sentence at McDonald's, his mentor Rick asks him to test an incredible new video game. If his score's high enough, it could earn him a place in flight school. But then Brandon goes MIA and Tyler discovers that the game is far more than it seems…

D1643373

Powys

37218 00497924 6

TL COSTA

Playing Tyler

STRANGE CHEMISTRY
An Angry Robot imprint
and a member of the Osprey Group

Lace Market House
54-56 High Pavement
Nottingham NG1 1HW
UK

www.strangechemistrybooks.com
Strange Chemistry #12

A Strange Chemistry paperback original 2013
1

Copyright © T L Costa 2013

T L Costa asserts the moral right to be
identified as the author of this work.

ISBN: 978 1 90884 460 6
Ebook ISBN: 978 1 90884 462 0

Set in Sabon by EPubServices

All rights reserved. No part of this publication may be reproduced,
stored in a retrieval system, or transmitted, in any form or by any
means, electronic, mechanical, photocopying, recording or
otherwise, without the prior permission of the publishers.

This book is sold subject to the condition that it shall not, by
way of trade or otherwise, be lent, re-sold, hired out or
otherwise circulated without the publisher's prior consent in
any form of binding or cover other than that in which it is
published and without a similar condition including this
condition being imposed on the subsequent purchaser.

This novel is entirely a work of fiction. The names, characters and
incidents portrayed in it are the work of the author's imagination.
Any resemblance to actual persons, living or dead, events or
localities is entirely coincidental.

*To my Grandmother, who gave up everything to raise
me as her own. I miss her every day.*

*And to my mom and dad, for making the years we had
together filled with joy and dreaming*

CHAPTER 1

WEDNESDAY, SEPTEMBER 12

TYLER

My fingers drum into the desktop, beating out the rhythm of my hammering thoughts. Have to go. Have to move. Have to leave.

"The area of one square face of a cube is equal to sixty-four centimeters squared. What's the volume of the cube?"

Mr Beard is a moron. Hate Geometry. Don't care. Need to go. I'm missing stick time.

The girl in front of me coughs. Her back shakes beneath her sweater. Her tight sweater. What's her name again? Sheryl? Amber?

"Tyler, dammit, can you stop that please!" she hisses, turning from the seat in front of me.

"What?"

"That drumming. Just because you forgot to take your Ritalin today or whatever doesn't mean you can bang on your desk all the time." She stares at me. Face all tight. Smug. She adds, "I mean, if Ritalin doesn't work, you can always try Adderall or whatever it is they give you freaks."

My cheeks burn. She giggles. I hate it when girls giggle. Wonder if she giggles at everyone or just at me. Ashleigh. I think her name is Ashleigh.

"Does anyone know how to solve the volume of the cube?"

This sucks. Last period's an hour and a half. Sucks. Should have cut. Could have been at home gaming. I drum harder, foot going. My friend Alpha's in the back row sleeping. Don't know why he gets on me for cutting when all he does at school is sleep. Need gum. Do I have any gum? I could swear I put a pack in my pocket this morning.

"Sam, do you know what the answer is, or how we can find it?"

Sam's shoulders straighten, get all stiff. Like he's scared. He should be scared. Sam has been barely passing Math since first grade. Some kids just can't do it. Not his fault. It can be hard.

"Sam?" Mr Beard asks again.

Sam's face pinches up. If he pinches it any harder all those zits are going to go bursting off. "Leave him alone, he doesn't know," I say. I hate it when teachers pick on kids. Kids who they know never have the answer. Sam never has the answers. Not here, not in Math, not ever.

"And you do, Mr MacCandless?" He turns his grubby eyes on me, now, all sneery.

"Can I go to the bathroom?" Have to get out of here. Have to go. My leg bangs into the desk and I lean forward, ready to go.

"Sure, after you answer the question." He sidles around to the front of his podium, lips pulling back into a wicked grin. "Or is it that you can't answer because you haven't been to class in, what is it now, seven days? You have to go to at least part of your senior year to get into college, you know."

I look at the whiteboard marker he holds out towards me, like a challenge, like he's daring me to take it. Jackass. I look at Sam, who is looking down at his desk. Shit. Why did I open my mouth? "I'm here now, right?" But it doesn't matter, I can't go to college. Rick will give me a shot, though. A chance at a future.

"Three absences in twenty days of class is hardly a great start." Mr Beard walks through the rows of desks, holding the marker like a knife. "Now, can you please solve the problem for us?"

Right. Screw this. "Five hundred and twelve centimeters." I get out of the desk and walk up the row to the front wall.

Beard looks like I slapped him.

"Cubed," I add. Yeah. I've got ADHD, but I'm not stupid. Not at Math, anyway.

"Can you show us your work?" His eyes sharp, like a bird.

"No." The pass is a broken triangle-shaped ruler that Beard scribbled LAV PASS over like fifty times with a black Sharpie.

The hall's empty, so I hold out my hand and scrape the pass over the top of the lockers, feeling each space, each divot reverberating through my arm as I make my way down the hall. The sound of plastic skimming over metal echoes through the empty passage. Sounds good. Sounds like I'm not in class.

I don't stop at the lav though, why would I? School sucks, it's too quiet, too hard to focus with all that quiet. Makes me jumpy. I keep walking, right through the front doors of the school.

Ride. Pushing my feet into the pedals, burning, my lungs swallow the crisp air, feels good, like inhaling Lysol or something. Pedal faster, almost there. Cars come close. Music blaring, something good, something heavy and hard, I cut off a car and turn into the parking lot of the center.

The building, an old Victorian mansion with "grounds" or whatever they call a sweet yard that the junkies get to look at but not really use.

I throw the mountain bike off to the side of the porch on top of some flowers. Crap. I should pick that up, the flowers might die. No, they should put in a bike rack. I take the first stair. I look down at my shoes. I go back down, pick up the bike, lift it up the stairs and prop it to the right of the front door. Flowers are nice. I ring the bell. They should put in a bike rack, though. Not everybody can drive.

I wave to the camera. The door clicks and I pull it open. The place smells old, like a closet without the mothballs, but with a lot of artificial cleaners dumped on top of it to hide the fact that it's old. Knesha's at the desk. She's wearing one of those nurse shirts. A pink, unflattering, stiff thing with little blue birds all over it. Makes her look even bigger. Why do they make her wear shirts like that? She's not a nurse. Can't make nice women wear ugly shirts like that. It's not right. I give her a smile and let her lead me back through the ugly green halls.

Brandon's waiting in one of those over-sized wicker chairs, painted bright white. So bright it makes the green AstroTurf floor of the sunroom look dingy. His cheeks are fuller, eyes a little sharper. Heroin does that, they say, makes you get all skinny and gross with hollow eyes... but he looks good, well, better. More like Brandon.

His grin is the same. "Ty, man, you look like shit."

That's the thing about Brandon. His voice is like music. Like crazy music, like anything he says is true. He used to have this internet radio show and that voice got him listeners from all over the world. He had a popular blog, too. Everybody said he was the left's rising new star, but now, well, that's not what they're saying. He can't broadcast from in here. Can barely get any time to email. "You're a dick, you know that?" I say. I pull over a metal chair and sit. Hate metal chairs.

He laughs. "That's why I'm here, right?" Brandon's voice is a little tight, a little strained. "How's school?"

"Sucks." My eyes go to his arm. It's habit, now, I guess.

Of course he's OK, he'd tell me if he wasn't. He doesn't lie, not to me. Not anymore. He's wearing jeans. That's good. They'd keep him in those robes if he wasn't doing good. Must be improving, be close to getting out. He asks, "Have you applied to the Academy yet?"

"I'm not going to the Academy."

"What?" Brandon leans forward, gray-green eyes drilling me. "I thought you sent in the form to get nominated like months ago."

I lied, Brandon. "Like the Air Force would take me, B."

"What do you mean? Of course they'll take you. Dad went to the Academy, you lettered in Wrestling. You just haven't heard back yet."

"Stopped Wrestling." Can't go. I can't leave you. "And I'm failing Math."

I messed up once, didn't see him slide. Too focused on school, on getting into the Academy, on myself. I dropped the ball and he disappeared. *Poof.*

"What?" He looks pissed. He sits up. "How the hell are you failing Math?"

"I don't go." Last period, three days a week, makes me miss too much stick time. "It's boring."

"Well, of course it's boring, but you still have to go. What about the Air Brigade thing?"

"The Civil Air Patrol?" He always messes up the name. "Yeah, I go sometimes. I see Rick a lot, though. He takes me up, gives me lessons." Flying is all I want to do anymore.

"Rick?" he says. I look up. He can't forget who Rick is. "Oh, right, the mentor guy."

My mentor. My drug-free, Civil Air Patrol male role model. Role model's a loose term, really. Last time Rick and I got together we went to one of those grown-up arcade places and played air hockey and skeeball for like six hours. "He's more like a friend now, really."

"What's he say about your chances for the Academy? He can write that congressman for you, explain things, maybe."

"I don't think that there's much he can do, B. Between the Math and History, I'm hit." And you. I can't leave you.

"Didn't you say once that Rick consults for Sikorsky or something? Maybe he can get you a job there while you get your shit together. Just don't give up, Ty."

"I won't." Lie, lie, lie. Sikorsky, a local helicopter manufacturer, would never hire a kid who didn't graduate. Even with Rick's recommendation.

"How's Jessie?"

Jessie, Brandon's ex-girlfriend, isn't doing so great. Every time I see her I remember the way she was, the cheerleader, the cute smile and great tits, the way she would glow at Brandon while we watched him broadcast his vlog. He was going to be famous. Huge following and all that.

Now she works at Dunkin' Donuts. She got knocked up by Jimmy Rothstein, had the baby and is stuck. Last time I saw her she had gained like twenty pounds and even those great tits of hers looked tired. "She's OK."

He takes a sip of water, eyes off somewhere else. "I'm supposed to call her and apologize." He smiles weakly. Like it hurts him. "Part of my therapy."

That's so not a good idea.

I say, "You know, Rick gave me this game. It sucks, kinda, really boring. But if my score is high enough on the game, then he'll let me test this new gaming platform that his company is trying to develop for the military as some sort of pilot training system."

"What does that get you, though?"

"Well, if I help him find the bugs in the upgraded system, then he says he'll get me into a flight school he has connections with."

"Part of the Air Force?"

"No, some private company. It's OK. As long as I can fly."

"What about school?"

"What about it?" College obviously worked out really well for you, B.

"You should go." His eyes get dark. Sandy hair hangs like strands of twine around his eyes, making everything about him seem old, used up. "Don't stay here just because of me."

He's tired. I can tell. His eyelids look like sandbags, but there's a spark there. In his voice. Is this really the same guy who used to kayak circles around me when we'd vacation in Vermont? Who used to read all my books for English out loud to me so my grade in English wouldn't suck ass? Reading's hard. It's like the letters are all over the place. The teacher would get pissed and tell me all the letters were in neat little lines. They weren't. Not for me. Brandon understood. Brandon tried to help. Worked with me on every essay or report I ever had to write. And I let him down. The one time he actually needed me, I had no idea anything was wrong. I missed it.

I look up at the clock. Why don't they have digital clocks?

"It's OK, B, I gotta go." I don't want to leave. Don't want him out of my sight. "Later." I choke out before my damn eyes burn up again.

"Yeah, man, tell Mom I said hi."

She won't come. Mom can't ever come. Can't face the fact that her boy is here.

I just hope that she'll be around when he gets out.

CHAPTER 2

WEDNESDAY, SEPTEMBER 12

ANI

Have I been having fun at college so far? Not so much. The only thing worse than being the only sixteen year-old freshman at Yale is being a sixteen year-old freshman *girl* at Yale. Every time I walk into class I feel like I have a big red *Sixteen* stamped across my forehead. I wish I looked at least a little bit older, so not everyone would look at me and assume I'm some kind of girl genius. It makes meeting people next-to-impossible: no one likes to think that they might not be the smartest person in the room. Little do they know how much I'm going to suck at Philosophy. If only I could paint that across my forehead, too, then maybe someone would actually *say* something. Instead, they give me awkward, halting smiles and look away.

Just like in high school.

Yale's campus sits inside the city of New Haven, Yale's beautiful old architecture secreted away in a city ravaged by urban decay. Stray too far off campus and the streets become a jumble of abandoned storefronts and forgotten towers. It would make a cool backdrop for a level of *Behemoths of War* but not such a great place for, say, an unarmed girl to take a stroll. I hold out my phone, double-checking the address of the building in front of me. The restaurant's sleek lines and soaring windows exude everything modern and chic on a street that walks the line between the acceptable and the derelict.

I swallow and tuck my phone back into my backpack, rubbing my palms down the sides of my jeans. I'm not dressed for this; when I got the text from my boss I came straight over after class. What a fantastic impression I'm going to make.

I've only met him in person a few times. Once was during my job interview, and the other time was when he came to my house to make the offer. I heard from the other members on my team at my summer internship at Althea back in LA that he had come around to ask about me, but I wasn't there at the time.

I haven't even heard from my boss at all since the day I sent him the program. He sent me a quick message saying that the prototypes are ready for testing and to wish me luck at school. No word from him for over a month.

Which isn't so bad, actually, since it looks like classes here are going to be insane. I have to read two novels a week for freshman Lit? Who can read that fast? Not to mention take four other classes and hold down a job. Why am I even trying to make friends? I'm not going to have any time to leave my dorm room for the next four years.

Pushing the door open, I see him at one of the tables over by the window. He smiles and raises his hand in a gesture that I suppose is meant to be friendly but looks a bit stiff. "Miss Bagdorian, it's lovely to see you."

"Hi, Mr Anderson." I nod and swing the backpack off my shoulders. Should I try and stuff it under the chair or leave it in the aisle? It's not like there's that many people eating dinner this early, but there are a few tables full of business-types swilling glasses of whiskey in front of piles of papers and plates of fried calamari. I stuff the bag under my chair and sit. He watches me like an analyst, scanning my face so that he picks up every twitch of every muscle. I squeeze the sides of the water glass. "So, am I in trouble? Did the software not work?" I ask. I've never written that complicated a program before, took me about a month. It was really similar to what I did on my internship, and that helped, but it's the first time I ever got paid to do something so massive by myself. I hate it, having all the pressure of the success or the failure coming down on my head. But it's only fair, I guess.

Having a job that covers most of my tuition for Yale is definitely better than what could have happened if I chose not to work for Haranco. I shiver.

He tilts his head to the side and I look away, focusing on the smell of the calamari. I'm so hungry I could probably gnaw on the tablecloth. I read the class schedule wrong and missed lunch.

"No, no the program is working perfectly," he says, giving me that smile again. I don't like his smile, I can't get a good read on its intent. "Wait until you see the final product, I think you'll be impressed."

The hardware we got to use over the summer was fierce, so I can only imagine. I wish we were at the office looking at the final product now instead of hanging out in a place like this. "So why are we here?"

The waitress comes over and he orders a plate of calamari and some sort of appetizer pizza to share.

"How are classes?" he asks, his voice soft.

"Fine."

"Making any friends? I remember my first year of college was quite the learning experience. Whole dorm full of people I didn't know."

My throat tightens. I don't need this, I don't need someone trying to pretend that they care. Especially not my boss. "Look, if there's some kind of problem with something I've written or you need me to test something out, just tell me and I'll do it."

He sits back in his chair. "The system is fine. We're here to celebrate, to talk about how school is going. I want you to know that you can come to me with any sort of problem you may have."

Lots of old guys saying that line would make it sound creepy. But not him. He has this aura about him like he came out of his mother in a uniform of one sort or another. When he came to talk to Mom about hiring me, he mentioned the word "honor" no less than fifty-six times. *It would be an honor to have her on staff. I would be honored to check up on her progress at Yale.* My stomach clenches. Mom just ate it up. Lapped up every word like he was some kind of fatherly-inclined superhero. But I *have* a father, something that I wish that she would remember.

"I'm not sure the start of the semester is really a cause for celebration," I say.

"Maybe not." He leans back in his chair as the waitress sets down steaming trays of incredible-smelling food in front of us. "Miss Bagdorian, I've been stationed overseas for ten of the past twelve years. If being away from home has taught me anything, it's to celebrate each new starting point, no matter how insignificant it may seem at the time."

"Why is that?"

"Because endings can break a man." His eyes drift off, shaded for a moment. He raises his glass. "So at Haranco, we choose to focus on beginnings."

Is that Christy doing shots? At least she doesn't stop and stare at me when I walk in the room like everyone else does. It takes all of three seconds before they give me the collective sweep, assess and dismiss. "Christy!" I call out and she tips her head back in unison with two other girls. The floor seems to pulse along to the death metal blasting from the sound dock as I shuffle through the crowd. The boys move out of my way, like if they even accidentally bump into me they'll be jailed for statutory rape or something. The girls are just as bad: standing around all perfectly preppy and pretending that I'm not even there. Even the other power nerds ignore me.

I push to the table with the drinks, but Christy has disappeared. I need her; I somehow managed to lock myself out of our room. Hordes of sweaty jocks talking finance and beer pong are in one corner, arms wrapped tightly around smart girls wearing very flimsy, very expensive clothes.

Have I been having fun at college so far? Not so much. It's different and filled with unexpected problems. A last-minute party on my floor on a school night? Didn't really see this coming. Keeping track of my keys? Not so good at that, apparently. I mean, *keys*. Who even *uses* keys anymore? Even Mom changed the house over to a keypad. And then there are the more disgusting problems, too, like finding a used condom in my slipper this morning.

"Hey, you, kid." A guy, tall, skinny, preppy-ish and really drunk, by the looks of him, calls to me from the frame of an open door. "You're like that super-genius girl, right? The one who's like ten?"

I sigh, my hands wrapping around my soda. "Sixteen," I say.

"Right, cool. Come on in here." He giggles, cheeks red and his eyes clouding over as they move up and down my body. I shiver. So does he, oddly enough. "Yeah, you should like totally come in here."

I take a step back, but his hands wrap around my waist and he's pulling me into his room.

"We need someone for our friend, Frank, here." I look over to Frank. I assume he's the really skinny guy over in the corner with the thick black glasses and bag of pork rinds.

"Someone to do what with Frank, exactly?" I ask, missing Julie, my sister, who is really, really good with situations like this. Mainly by helping me not get into them.

"You know." He leers. Leers at me. Frank smiles a smile that only the truly stoned can give while waving around a PS3 controller.

"I can show you the secret level." Frank giggles. Holding onto the word *level* like it's a new vocabulary word.

"Level for what? *Age of the Demigods*? No such thing." The first guy pulls me into him, reeking of pot and man-fumed body wash. "Let go."

"Please, like you could possibly know more about *Age of the Demigods* than our Frank, here. He's the best in the dorm."

"I doubt it," I say, shoulders tightening, voice falling.

"Why don't you go over there and prove it?" They laugh.

Cheeks burning, I need to get out of here. "Get off!" I push him away. The other guys in the room laugh as their friend hits drywall.

He smiles at me. Smiles! Then says, "Relax, babydoll, I was just playing with you."

Idiots. Drunk, stupid, horny idiots. I grit my teeth, eyeing the other guys in the corner as they giggle.

"Oh, wait, you're that, like, super-gamer, right?" Frank dissolves into a puddle of laugher. "What was your handle, again? SexKitten20? Jailbait15? Damn, you gotta come over here and play. Show me how it's done."

I walk out of the room, not wanting to hear him, not wanting to be here. I push past the mobs of kids laughing and making friends and enjoying themselves, flying down the cramped old stairwell and burst out of the front door and into the night. I put my hands on my knees and breathe, hoping no one sees me.

Wiping my eyes with the bottom of my sleeve, I stand up and look around campus. It's not such a bad night for a walk, really, it's warm, with a nice breeze. It's definitely better than being back in there. I do a few laps around campus, hoping to run myself clean.

CHAPTER 3

WEDNESDAY, SEPTEMBER 19

TYLER

Rick's here. We're watching the movers. You can totally tell that Rick used to be in the military. Looks like one of my old GI Joes. Standing in the kitchen. Wearing jeans.

Think I still have some of my old GI Joes in the basement. Bet I could sell them on eBay. Or give them to some kid.

The men come in carrying all sorts of boxes into my room. Good thing Mom's not here. She'd freak.

They pile in, the men. They don't look like movers, not really. But they're loaded down with boxes. Men in khaki pants and white polos carrying box after box into my room. Some of the boxes are damn big, too.

Two guys come in, each holding one end of some oblong black package covered in plastic wrap. "Good thing you have a ranch," Rick mutters, checking the time as he takes a bite out of the Pizza Pocket I gave him. Watching me, he asks, "Something wrong?"

I shrug. "Went to see Brandon. No big deal." Another guy walks in carrying a long, skinny box that is almost as tall as I am.

Rick puts his hand on my shoulder, like he wants to comfort me but he doesn't really know what to say that will make it better. Or maybe it's just that he knows that there isn't really anything he can say that will make it better. But he tries. "You're doing everything that you can for him, Ty. No one can ask more than that."

I let the heavy feel of his hand on my shoulder give what comfort it can, then wipe my hands on a napkin I grab from the countertop. Motioning to the boxes, I say, "Looks expensive."

He meets my eyes for a minute, sighs and says, "There's no shame in loving your brother, you know."

I look down at the tile floor. Damn, I need something to drink. Where'd I put that bottle of Mountain Dew?

"A brother is definitely worth the concern. Now, if you had a rotten ex-wife like mine, well, somebody like *that* sure isn't worth all the time or the pain… and definitely not worth all the damn money."

Finding the extra bottle at the back of the fridge, I pour a glass of Dew. "How much are they spending giving me this thing?"

"As a rough guess I would say a hell of a lot. Did you know that you're one of only five people in the country to qualify for it?" His thin lips pull into a genuine smile and he shakes my shoulder a little before letting go. Like he's proud. Of what? Of me? Well, at least somebody is.

"Out of how many kids?" I ask. I shouldn't ask. I know it's not really important.

"Thousands." He stands and grabs his briefcase, digging out a file and glancing at his watch.

"Why do you keep looking at your watch?" I ask as I open the freezer and dig out another Pizza Pocket. "They not moving the stuff in fast enough for you?"

His eyes are bright, sharp, like an owl's... only not as yellow. Rick's are more of a green, but still, owl-like. Maybe it's his hair, sort of shapes his head in an owl-like way. "No, they are doing a fine job. I'm just waiting for our installer, the person that designed the unit. She goes to Yale, her classes ended over an hour ago and she should be here by now."

"Unit?" I shake my leg as I wait for the ding of the microwave and the next round of Pizza Pockets.

"Yes, unit. It's smaller and hopefully more user-friendly than the flight simulators we've used in the past. We're hoping that your feedback will help us figure out how to make the design better, find any kind of bugs, that sort of thing before we put the unit into production."

"Hope it's more exciting than the PC game you gave me."

"Maybe. The game that you've been playing is a flight-simulation game. We've integrated a gaming platform with a system known as the USC, the Universal Control System. Whereas before you were flying a computer-generated combat theater, the UCS uses satellite maps of approximately seventy-five thousand miles of South Asian airspace."

"So you've written a game into Google Earth?"

"More like a 3D, Haranco version of Google Earth, but yes. Not to mention the hardware. Lots of screens and gadgets and things you'll love. You'll simulate the missions of multiple UAVs, Predators and the like, and we'll use your experiences to test comfort factors, enhance the usability for pilots, stuff like that. My department wanted to come up with a way for our boys to be more at home behind the controls of a drone. Make it a one-man operation based on the game and the equipment we're having you test."

"Cool."

He smiles. "It's a great game, Tyler, you'll love it. Just write down any problems you find with it."

I grab the Pizza Pocket. Damn, it's hot. Now the whole kitchen smells like cardboard pizza.

"How high do I have to score on this sim to qualify for your flight school?" I don't want to be stuck. I want to go to that flight school. It's right down the road. I could stay close to Brandon.

He smiles, a good, open smile. "Just play it, Tyler." He winks. "And who knows? The Air Force is like anything else."

I raise my eyebrow.

"Sometimes you get to sneak in the back door."

The doorbell rings. It's one of those modern bells in a long case next to the door, manufactured special so that it sounds old. Sounds like you're hearing an actual bell. I hacked its code so that it rang "Happy Birthday" on Mom's birthday once. She laughed. That was a long time ago. I don't think she'd laugh now.

I shuffle on the shag as I reach the paneled doors. I open the door.

Holy shit. The cold air slaps me in the face like a sock full of quarters and my mouth goes dry. It's her.

"Hi. I'm here to set up your system."

My tongue goes numb. Freaking numb. Can't move it. Shit. It's SlayerGrrl! Designer of *World Of Fire*, three-time ILG champion. Until she stopped playing. Why did she stop playing? The International League Gaming championship is the biggest competition around. Her nose is smaller than it looks in the picture. Terrible picture. She's totally hot. Say something, Ty. Something witty. Something smart. She looks around the porch. I'm losing her, say something quick. Witty, clever... Now, Tyler, now. Speak.

"Hey," I say.

She nods and twists her awesome lips into a tight smile...

Dammit! That was so not suave. Tell her you know who she is. That you've always wanted to meet her, a girl who games to game, not to impress a boyfriend or because it sounds like something fun to do when stoned. A girl who designed a game so badass that supposedly people have actually died while playing it because they didn't want to walk away from the console. Quick. Now, Ty, witty, clever. "Your nose doesn't look so big in real life." Shit. Her eyes widen in surprise. Her cheeks turn bright red. Like neon red. Shit! "I mean, your profile picture is just awful."

Her eyes narrow and her shoulders square.

I so suck at this.

Rick smiles slightly as he opens the door. "Miss Jones, please come in."

"Hi, Mr Anderson, sorry if I'm a little late," she says.

"Not at all." He shoots me a sly look. "Miss Jones, this is Tyler, the young man you will be assisting with the simulator."

She looks like she's not really happy to be here, and as she comes into the house she trips, stumbles.

"I know who she is." Stop talking, Ty. Just stop. "She had the highest scores ever in a few combat games." She looks up at me, like I might be saying something right. Wow. She is so pretty, face even looks like a heart. Lips that dark pink. "Till I beat them."

Now her look is closed again. What? Girls make no sense sometimes.

"Miss Jones here is a student at Yale. She works in our UCS design department."

Yale. No wonder she hasn't been online in a while. She's so cute. Standing in my house. Dressed nice. I mean, her jeans sorta hug her hips a little, and cling in all the right places, but she's wearing an old *Akira* T-shirt, like she knows she doesn't have to dress up to look good. She does look good, though. Real good.

"Now, Tyler." Rick walks across the shag. I like her hair. Dark brown except for one streak near the front bleached blond. "Tyler!" Rick says. I jump. He laughs, leading SlayerGrrl past me and into the house. Just wait till I tell the clan. Peanut and Alpha will never believe that I met SlayerGrrl. Rick's phone buzzes and he reads a text. "Dammit. I have to run. Tyler, can you go with Miss Jones and let her give you the rundown on the unit? I'll call and check in with you later."

Hell yeah, I'll go with SlayerGrrl. I'd follow her anywhere.

The upgrade is sweet. Not as sweet as SlayerGrrl, though. She sits in the console chair and looks like a goddess. The chair itself is pretty impressive. Like an office chair, only it's specially designed to mold to your ass or something.

The whole contraption's shaped like a big half-shell. You sit facing a high-def screen in five panels, stretching up and a little over where your head goes when you're sitting in the thing. She's in front of the central keyboard, and there are two controllers. One for the altitude and angle of the flight, and the other is this big ball that sits under your palm. It has little touch pads around it for finger commands.

The top part of the screen has a panoramic setting in crazy-high definition. You can pull any of the simulated drones' cameras up on any screen except for the one that sits just above the keyboard. The screen over the keyboard is like a standard gaming map-panel. Only here it's a GPS-specified map of your waypoints and target locations and some info on weather, wind speed and direction and other basic flight data.

The game looks about the same in its most basic components as the PC version, only where the original game had pixelated terrain, like an Xbox game or something, this one looks more like a movie. Graphics are epic.

"Tyler." SlayerGrrl looks me in the eye. My heart jumps. "Are you listening?"

"No." I look at the screens. "I just want to try it."

"Yeah." She purses her lips. Like she's not used to telling people what to do. Or telling people anything, for that matter. "Please listen to what I'm trying to tell you, OK?"

She doesn't look too happy with me. Her nose, which is sort of cute even though it might be considered a little big, is all wrinkled up like she's frustrated. It's really cute, actually. Except it means that she's pissed, probably. Focus. I look down at her shirt. "You know that they're playing *Akira* down at Criterion in a few weeks. Midnight movie. Wanna go?"

"Yes, no, I mean, yes, I know that it's playing and no, I'm not going with you. Can you just listen?"

"Sure." That. Sucks. She doesn't move, though, doesn't get further away. Maybe I should start slow, like with her phone number.

"When you sit down, make sure to put on the cuff first." She holds out a floppy circle of blue Velcro. "Just roll up your sleeve."

She slides the cuff up my arm. Damn, her hands are soft. Like, I don't know, something nice. Something I want to feel more of. She hits a few keys and the cuff tightens. "It's measuring my blood pressure?"

"You have to be wearing the cuff to log on." She looks at the screen on the bottom right that has all the flight stats, and a small icon for my blood pressure readout pops up onto the screen. "The joystick will also be measuring your pulse as you go."

I frown. She stands and gets out of the chair. "Please sit," she says.

I do. The chair is nice, big, like an armchair, except for the stupid cuff around my arm. "OK, well, what's the sign-in procedure? Do I get to enter a gamertag or something?"

She looks at me like I just shit myself. "This isn't *Call of Duty*."

I look at the setup around me: multiple screens controlling multiple drones, fancy chair, me, Tyler MacCandless, beta testing equipment that's probably going to be sold to the Air Force. "Yeah, well, no, actually," I look her in the eyes, "It kinda is."

I move over in the seat. She should sit. Doesn't need a lot of room. She's tiny. And if she sits she'll be close. I tilt my head to point out the empty space next to me in the chair. "Wanna play?"

ANI

Did it have to be him? Tyler MacCandless, the boy who beat my record? It had to be him? It's not like we actually played against each other that year, so he didn't technically beat me, just my record, but still. Seeing him makes me miss gaming even more.

I just have to take a deep breath and plow through this demo. The way he looks at me makes my heart beat in a new, quick little rhythm. No boy has ever looked at me that way, like I'm just a girl, not some genetic aberration.

In fact, he's looking at me like I'm actually worth seeing and I'm not so certain that I like it. He is cute, though. Most gamer boys are either gangly or, well, large-ish. But Tyler's built, not too big, but he has great arms and has deer-like eyes that are focused entirely on me.

And he wants me to play?

Part of me still can't believe I stopped competing; that science fair project sort of eclipsed everything. But competing was all I used to live for, giving me a break from Mom, keeping my mind off of Dad back when he was deployed.

I look at the empty space. Should I do it? Is it like, unprofessional or something? I played the thing for hours and hours every day in between classes after meeting Mr Anderson in that restaurant last week. I wish Mr Anderson had let me make the game more exciting; I don't know if I really want Tyler to play. If he's expecting it to be as cool as *World of Fire* then he's going to be disappointed.

Tyler's eyes are dark and sweet and desperate and I sit, trying to rub away the warmth that's rushing to my cheeks before he notices.

TYLER

"I shouldn't. Check your login one more time, make sure that you hit the code in the right sequence so you can get onto the system after I leave." SlayerGrrl points as she leans in over my shoulder. I like her here. Next to me. Her hair sorta skims over my shoulder. She smells like, I don't know, flowers and things. Good things. Girly things.

"Login's fine," I say. "Wanna play *Haven*? I could hook it up to the UCS pretty easy."

"No, I can't." She stops, like she's holding another word in her mouth. "Sorry."

I grab a bag of chips, hold some out to her. "Why don't they just ask you to beta test their system?" She stands up and arches her back. She looks good. Real good.

"I designed it." She shrugs. "So I guess I'm biased."

She's so pretty. And she's in my room. Shit. Should I have hid that magazine? Maybe take those posters off the wall? I don't know. Sort of messy, my room. I get up and kick some dirty clothes under the bed. She smiles. Pretends to look at the screen.

"You miss it?" I hold the bag as she takes a few chips. "Gaming?"

Her eyes cloud over a little, go all distant. "Sometimes."

"Why'd you stop?" I ask.

"It's complicated." Her cheeks are like this shade of pink, pink like cotton candy.

Damn, for the first time in my life I wish I went to Yale. Or maybe at least wasn't failing Math.

SlayerGrrl touches my shoulder. My heart leaps. Oh shit. She touched me, what does that mean? Dammit. I really should have cleaned my room. Bet those guys at Yale remember to clean up their rooms before a girl comes over. I dig under the piles of crap on the floor and grab a few games. She's gonna try and leave if I don't think of something.

"Do you have any more of these chips?" she asks, moving to sit on the corner of my bed. My heart flies. Like, well, maybe explodes, just... quietly.

I should say something cool. I mean, there's a girl. A hot girl. A smart, hot, gamer girl, sitting on my bed in tight jeans and a T-shirt.

Seeing her there, perched on a sea of mismatched sheets, face haloed by a wall full of band posters, makes me want to, well, redecorate, I guess. Not hole up in such a dump. Shit, wait, do I have more chips? I better. "I don't know."

"Oh." She looks at the empty bag. Do I ask her to come with me to the store? No. Can't do that, I don't have a car.

Be brave, Ty, bold. "Let's call for pizza."

She puts down the bag. Her face is a mask. Shit. I can't read it. She says, "I should get back. There's a meal plan."

"No!" I jump out of the seat. "We're just getting started and you're going to leave?"

She looks odd, tilting her head. Maybe that was the wrong thing to say. I probably sound like a cave man compared to the guys at Yale. I suck at this. But she has to stay. I look at my feet. Boyfriend. She's got a boyfriend. Too pretty not to. "Boyfriend waiting?"

"No." She looks like she's been slapped. I really suck at this. "No one's waiting. I just have a lot of work to do."

No one's waiting? For her? That I just can't believe. "Well, you gotta eat."

"I have to go."

"OK, so." I catch her eye. My hand shakes. I hold out a controller. Damn, she's hot. Her eyes dance and I just want to jump right in. She needs to stay. Needs to come back. "Next time you can preach all about proper–"

"There is no next time, Tyler." Her face clouds, like someone came along with a big eraser and just took all feeling right off of it. She doesn't take the controller. "I'm not coming back."

What? "Why not?"

"Mr Anderson's rules." She shrugs her shoulders. Her eyes look at the floor when she talks about Rick. She turns. She walks out the door. "Thanks for the chips. Good luck with the sim."

I'm not worried about the sim. That I can handle. It's the girl I can't handle. I finally get to meet the girl. This girl. This girl who is sweet and who games and who's smart as hell and I'm not supposed to see her again? My heart races. Catches in my throat.

That. Fucking. Sucks.

I walk out the door after her.

And I hear it. The thud, thud, thud in the distance. SlayerGrrl looks at me. I like it when she looks at me.

Stupid Sikorsky. My throat's caught in that vice again. Sikorsky running their test flights over my house. Over the whole town. It rings in my ears. Thud, thud, thud.

"Can you tell what kind of chopper that is?" SlayerGrrl raises her hand up over her eyes.

"It's a Black Hawk," I say. Say through the thud that beats against the back of my teeth. Through the thud pulsing against the back of my skin. Through everything.

Dad used to fly a Black Hawk. He was in the Air Force, part of a rescue squadron, then the Coast Guard. It used to be a great sound, until some drunk driver hit him and B on the way home from a soccer game. Leaving Dad underground and B with broken ribs. Slipped discs. And a prescription for oxy for the pain. But the doctors forgot to tell him that oxy can't kill the pain of losing your dad. Can't make you forget that your dad used to fly a Black Hawk every time one passes over your house.

Push it down, focus. ADHD sucks sometimes. Focus, dammit. Get her number. Get SlayerGrrl's number. "Can I have your number?" I ask. Please say yes.

"No. The rules, remember? Look, any issues you find with the sim have to be recorded in the report file. If you talk to me, then it's sort of like tech support."

"I want your number, but not to talk about the sim," I say.

"I can't." Quiet. But something on her face. Something in the way she holds her face tells me that she wants to.

Shit. Do I push it? "You want to give me your number, though." She blushes. Blushes. Over me. Awesome.

"Not really," she says. But her voice is weak. Like she doesn't really mean it. I hope she doesn't really mean it.

She turns and gives me a questioning look. As she walks away, down towards the bus stop, I feel light. Finally, I've met a girl who gets gaming, gets *me*, and she's smoking hot. I pull out my phone and send Alpha and Peanut a quick message telling them that I actually met SlayerGrrl.

Then I start my search.

CHAPTER 4

FRIDAY, SEPTEMBER 21

TYLER

Mom jumps when she sees me in the hall. Coming out of the bathroom in my pajamas.

"Tyler, oh, I didn't realize you were home," she says. She's always surprised to see me. Even at midnight.

"I brought you a sandwich for dinner like five hours ago, Mom," I say.

"Oh." Her eyes fix on some speck of dust or something on the wall. Looking past me. Again. "That's right, you did. I was finishing up some work on this case and, well, thanks."

She's still in her power suit from work. Makes her look like a woman who is kickass. She is kickass. At work, anyway. Always traveling for some big thing. At midnight, she just looks weird. "You should get changed Mom, it's late."

She looks back to me again. Like she's already forgotten that I'm there. She smiles, that smile that doesn't reach anywhere but her lips. The smile that isn't really a smile. More of a muscle memory thing. "Right."

I hug her. Hold her small body in close, careful not to get her blond hair stuck in the buttons of my shirt. She needs to be hugged sometimes. To remember that I'm here and that I love her and sometimes, sometimes when she hugs me back, when she cries, I think that she's Mom again. That she's who she was before. The mom that would take Brandon and me roller-skating every weekend in winter, who held my hand when we did the hokey-pokey, who would lift the limbo bar up higher so I could get under and feel like one of the big kids. "Love you, Mom. Go to sleep, OK?"

Her eyes are cloudy. Distant. Someplace else. "Love you too, Tyler." She says the words. Soft, hollow, sad. And I know that she wants to mean them, but doesn't remember how.

I guess I should go check and make sure she actually ate the sandwich that I made for her. Sometimes she takes it and just leaves it on her desk. She forgets. That's why she's so thin. Not good, being so thin. Not healthy.

I hear Mom close the door to her room. No. Not going to check. I can check to make sure she eats breakfast before school. Throwing myself down on the bed, I stretch. Nice bed. Soft.

Brandon and I would take this mattress off of the bed, drag it over to his room and build forts. We'd grab every blanket in the house. Raid the linen closet. We'd make these crazy-big forts, with secret passages and libraries stocked with pillows and flashlight and comic books. Mom never got mad, she used to stomp on the floor and pretend to be a big bad wolf, shake the sides of the fort. Brandon and I would scream and laugh and beg her not to blow our house down. She would laugh. Brandon would laugh. Sometimes when I close my eyes I can remember the sound.

I was thirteen the first time I found Brandon.

Unconscious. On the floor of the bathroom. He wouldn't wake up. I kept shaking him, listening to see if he was breathing. Then there was that noise. That noise Mom made. The one that was low in her throat as she pulled his head into her chest and started rocking. Running her hands through his hair and crying. Crying for help. Crying for God, and rocking. She couldn't do anything but hold him and cry and lie to him. Tell him he would be fine. I picked up the phone, called 911. I waited. Waited while they loaded him in the ambulance. Waited as they loaded Mom in there, too. Mom who was glued to Brandon, who couldn't stop begging everyone around her for help, grabbing their shirts and pulling, even as they tried to shoo her away so they could work on him. I was too young to drive. So I watched the lights and the sirens leave me standing on the driveway, alone.

Waiting.

ANI

What's with the avocados here in Connecticut? All of the avocados I've seen here look like they've been thrown all the way from California. What I wouldn't give for a fresh avocado with a little bit of lime. Instead, I have to settle for a grilled cheese and scoop of guacamole that looks like it was made with cornstarch and green food dye.

I grab my tray and sit next to Christy, who's on her cell. The guy next to her is texting someone so I pull out my ereader. Might as well start on one of those novels for freshman Lit.

"Hey, Ani?" Christy puts the face of her phone down on the table next to her untouched salad. "You want to come with us tonight? We're going to go over to Ted's tonight to see Bill's band. They're like this mix of thrash and dubstep but it could be fun."

"Bill?" the guy next to her asks.

"Yeah, he's in our Bio lab, remember? Long hair. Comes to class on a long board."

The guy next to her nods and then continues to text.

I say, "I'm not sure I could get in." I passed Ted's the other day on the way back from the bookstore. It's pretty clearly a bar. Even if I had an ID that said I was twenty-one, no one would look at me and believe it.

"That's crazy, you only have to be like eighteen. C'mon, Ani." She clasps her hand together and leans over the table. "It'll be fun."

"I'm only sixteen, remember?" I look down at my plate so I don't have to look her in the face. She's sweet and supposedly really good at academics like English and History, but she seems to forget a lot of things. Sort of important things like buying her own shampoo or that her roommate is only sixteen. I could make a fake ID that says I'm eighteen, but it would take a while.

"Oh, honey." She reaches across the table and squeezes my wrist. "I totally forgot. Well, you should try and sneak in, then."

"I can't, can't really get in trouble," I say.

"Oh my God, you have one of those dads, don't you?" She shakes her head at the guy sitting next to her, who's following her every movement like it's ballet. "One of those you-mess-up-I'm-dragging-you-back-home dads. Shannon has one of those, too. Totally sucks."

My throat dries and I open my mouth to scream, but nothing comes out. I just shake my head no and squeeze my eyes shut, ignoring the burn. Ignoring the image of Dad's eyes and the way they looked through the glass.

"You have to promise to come out with us soon, though, OK?" she chirps.

Christy has this way about her, a sweet, wide-eyed sort of charm that helps me to look past the fact that she uses all of my toothpaste and leaves her clothes strewn across the floor. When she's around it's like someone placed a TV in the middle of the room at full volume. Her brilliant orange curls and smile demand to be noticed. She's entertaining and lively and fun, but it's as if it's a non-interactive experience. Everything seems so one-sided. I doubt she'd recognize my voice if I called to her across a hall. She invites me out with her and her burgeoning circle of friends almost every single morning, but she forgets by the end of classes and just leaves without waiting. Living with her makes me miss Julie even more.

"Yeah, OK," I say and look back at my book as she calls someone else on the phone.

I remember what it was like to be a champion. The rush I got as I beat everyone, everything that was thrown in front of me. I could conquer any game, any opponent, and fast. A little girl in a dark room packed with gamers watching me slaughter their friends in 3D and surround sound. They all hated me, too. They tried to hide it, but after everyone figured out that I designed *World of Fire*, the fact that I was also kicking ass at a national level didn't strike people as fair, I guess. Any conversation I tried to start ended immediately after "hello."

I wish I could have kept playing at that level.

But I sort of became obsessed with SkyPet. SkyPet was going to be a hardware component to my *World of Fire* game. Basically I took one of those drones that you can control with your cell phone and switched it up a bit. I took out the inner workings of the existing drone and replaced them with better components. The most important being a cell-camera with a pivoting head, so instead of only looking straight ahead, the drone would be able to capture an all-terrain, street-level view of wherever it flew. Then the video from SkyPet would be imported into the game and the player could use it as a backdrop for a free-play level. It would be something totally new that only *World of Fire* could do: offer the player the opportunity to play on his or her own street, or favorite park, or wherever. They could make as many personalized levels as they wanted. I tried to write something using existing satellite imagery, but the ability for full-range, first-person-shooter vision wasn't really possible with the aerial view. SkyPet worked beautifully. I entered *World of Fire* with SkyPet in the state science fair. SkyPet's what got me the internship at Althea, and that's what got me the job at Haranco, which is how I'm able to go to Yale. So it's not like I wasn't right to let competing in ILG go, but I do miss it.

In the three years that I dominated the gamer scene, my mom tormented me, begging me to stop. Even Julie, the sister I practically worshipped, didn't understand, and would sit by and watch her friends mock me. Hate mail flooded my inbox on a daily basis; some people were jealous and others wanted pointers and secrets. Only one was ever sort of nice, sort of sincere. It was six words long, from a boy who I beat in one of the semi-final rounds the last year I played. It came about ten minutes after the game ended. It said:

Good Game.

–Tyler MacCandless (aka Tyrade)

And now that I've met him, now that I've seen how nice he is, well, it doesn't make Mr Anderson's rules about not having any further contact with him any easier to swallow. I didn't think I would mind when I signed the contract, but now that the rule applies to Tyler it seems so wrong.

The season I left gaming, Tyler beat all of my records and took the national title. It was the only congratulatory email I ever got. Now he's right here, cute and just down the road, playing my brainchild, and Mr Anderson doesn't want me to even talk to him.

I nibble on the sandwich as I pull out my phone and check my email. Fourteen new messages, most of them crap, but there's one from him. Tyler. I drop my fry and look around before opening it:

Hey SlayerGrrl, Rick only said you can't *talk* to me, right? He's cooler than you think. Wouldn't really care.

You should come over, play a quick game of *RAGE* or something. Won't talk about the *thing* at all, promise.
–Ty

I stare at the phone, shaking a little in my hand, and slip it back into my pocket. Reaching for my drink, I wish I never had checked my email.

CHAPTER 5

MONDAY, SEPTEMBER 24

TYLER

"Come over tonight, I got the new *Prisoner of Echelon 3*. Totally going to school your ass." Peanut's well-padded shoulder hits me as I take a bite of my granola bar.

"You suck at *Echelon*, man, there's no way," I say and drag my chair over to make room for Alpha and his tray full of green stuff. "Can't tonight, anyway."

Peanut wrinkles his nose at Alpha's lunch, making him look like a freckled rabbit. He shoves a fry into his mouth. "Why? You're sure as hell not doing your home-work."

Alpha laughs and squeezes ranch dressing out of a tube. Hope he doesn't get any stuck in his beard this time. He's doing good. Trying to eat right. Wants to like tone up or something. Two days in a row he's gone for the salad. "Bet it's got something to do with SlayerGrrl, right? She call you back yet?"

My foot shakes. I take a swig of Dr Pepper. "Naw, man, but it's just a matter of time."

Peanut wags his head back and forth. Half-eaten fries spill over the table. "There's no way. Your aura just isn't right for that kind of girl. No way someone like SlayerGrrl ever calls a guy like you, Ty."

"Fuck you." I take a handful of fries from his basket. Peanut thinks he can read auras. Not sure he knows what an aura is. "She's going to call, she like, I don't know, we had something. I could feel it."

"It's called a boner, and I'm pretty sure that was all you, bud," Peanut says.

"You're dead wrong, man, dead wrong," Alpha says. "She designed that game you're testing for your friend, right? That pilot guy or whatever?"

"Yeah," I say. Need something else to drink. Screw Peanut. He doesn't know. He wasn't there.

"Then she'll call you back." Alpha takes a fork to his salad, squirting gelatinous tomato seeds onto the table. Looking like a sea of little eyeballs. "She's going to be too damn curious. One of the best gamers in the country is playing her new system? Hell yeah she's calling. Remember all those feedback forums she set up after she released *World of Fire*?"

"Yeah," I say. I do remember. That girl's all about quality control.

"She's calling. She checked those things every day till that game was like flawless." Alpha smiles, his whole face seeming to grow.

"In your dreams." Peanut takes a swig of his Dew. "Face it, guys, it doesn't matter. A girl like SlayerGrrl is never calling one of us. Ever. For any reason. Tyler, man, you know that I love you like a brother. But don't get your hopes up."

I open up another granola bar. He's wrong. She's gonna get back to me. I can feel it.

The first few missions are cool. Well, no, they're dull as hell. But they make me feel like I'm doing something important, like one day some pilot is going to actually be doing something just like this, for real. And I helped make that happen. And that's kind of a good feeling. Like I'm not just a waste of space. Like I'm doing something for my country.

Beta testing some new flight simulator twenty-five hours a week isn't exactly what I planned on doing with my life, but it's a start to some kind of a future, I guess.

The sim mimics real drone missions. The back-story says that a bunch of insurgents plant the explosives along the road, and then innocent civilians or coalition forces drive over the road and detonate the explosives. You have to like fly for a billion hours over some road and check for people who are trying to plant IEDs in the culverts underneath it. All I do is just patrol miles and miles of empty road. It's good, though, cause I'm starting to get the hang of the program. Lots of math. Lots of calculations and recalculations of speed and adjusting for wind resistance and things. In the earlier version you don't have to worry about takeoffs and landings, because ground crew take care of that for you, you just pick up the mission at the start of the flight, or plug in somewhere midway. But in this one the takeoffs and landings are on you, which means that there's that much more to do in the game, so that's something, at least.

The sim gives me four drones to control at a time. Each has two missiles. I haven't gotten to hit anything yet, I just designate waypoints and mark the locations of any suspicious activity. In real life, those points would be texted to troops on the ground who could intercept the people in question.

So far my feedback has been that it's boring. Like drive-you-insane kind of boring. If Rick's company wants to get kids interested in being pilots, or pilots interested in sitting and staring at a screen instead of actually taking a plane up in the air themselves, then he has to liven this shit up.

I can't stop thinking about SlayerGrrl. Maybe I should tell her. She'll get it. It's been almost a week. Wish she were here. Wish she would come back. The way her cheeks moved when she chewed. The way she wiped the salt off of her hands onto the back of her jeans. Totally hot. I like a woman who can drink soda and eat chips and not bitch about calories. She's sort of quiet. Shy? I don't know. I liked it when she talked, even when she didn't. It was cool. Sitting next to me, talking about flying... gaming. I like her. I mean, well, yeah.

I look back to the top screen. All drones online. All focused on one mission. Nothing going on. Nothing on the sim. Nothing with my social life. I sent her three emails and she hasn't returned even one.

"Tyler." Rick's voice sounds like a dog chasing off a puppy trying to steal its food. Shit, I totally forgot that he's here. "Focus. Get through this and we'll go out, OK? I bought tickets to see the late showing of *Rise of the Juggernauts* in IMAX 3D, but first we have to do this."

"What?" I take a swig of Mountain Dew, smiling, rubbing at the stupid blood pressure cuff. Last time Rick and I went to the movies it was epic, spent hours together afterward in the arcade. He's cool, Rick, even though he can be a tightass. My eyes follow the road. Shit. Wait. Something is happening. "Two unfriendlies spotted at culvert 347 at latitude north 32.7 longitude east 70.1. Two trucks moving north-northwest." Finally get to tail something.

He looks down at the lower monitor. "See the numbers flashing in red at the bottom right hand of the screen?"

504 and 503. "Yup," I say, keeping my eyes mostly trained on the trucks. Heart picking up speed.

"The flashing numbers in red mean that central command wants you to take drones 504 and 503 off of primary mission and engage."

"Finally." I check the time. Real time. Ten hours ahead of Eastern Standard. Dark there. Drones should be invisible to the fake people in the trucks. Kind of like that WWII game where you got to fly bomb strikes over Germany. Only more current. Less exciting. But still.

"Here, put on your headset, record your moves once the commands are called."

I slip it on. Finally we are getting to do something in this game. Finally I get to see the little red guys on screen that indicate the "unfriendlies." "Taking drones 504 and 503 off primary mission." I punch in the codes and direct the two drones to follow the trucks.

A computer-generated voice in my ear calls the directions, flat and emotionless. I look at Rick. His face is stretched tight like a drum. He pulls a flask out of his pocket, takes a sip.

"So I just do what he says and confirm in the mic?"

"You got it." He smiles. The smile doesn't reach his eyes.

"They record it towards my score?"

"Just do what it says."

I listen to the call. "Drones 675 and 231 on auto. 504 and 503 in pursuit of target one."

Rick leans over my shoulder. Smells like Bengay. Bengay and the stuff in the flask. What's up with the drinking? He never drinks. "Confirm MTS autotrack on target one, Ty."

"You OK, man?" My left hand pulls off the camera controls and I bring it to the keyboard to type in the code.

"Dammit, Tyler, you need to focus."

What the fuck? I say, "MTS autotrack on target one confirmed." MTS autotrack is cool. Apparently the government can track anyone they want as long as they have a cell phone. "If something's wrong, Rick, you can just tell me."

"Check weapon readiness." Rick takes another sip and puts his hand on my shoulder. "Sorry, Ty, I just want you to do well here. I care about you, about your future, and right here, right now you can put yourself on the right track, get ahead. You understand?"

"Yeah, I get it, just relax, man, I'll be OK. I got this." I push my lips together to try and give him a weak smile.

I know he worries about me, but he shouldn't, not with this, anyway. I focus on the screens. Tail 231 is a Predator drone and it has two missiles. I lock up target one with tail 231.

I type in a code that turns on the laser. I read the screen. Arming the weapons. Waiting… The green light blinks. "We have power."

I read the screen and punch in the code that enlarges my view from the tiny tail 231 box. Each drone has a window that shows its camera view on monitor one and I make it so that I have a three-screen view of the camera from tail 231.

"Good." He squeezes my shoulder tight. "Now set the laser." His eyes are riveted on everything at once, just like mine.

I pull up the laser screen, check the code then say into the headset, "Laser ready." Green light one. "Laser armed." Blinking… that's the go. "Lasing," I say and hit target one with the laser that will guide the missile.

Then I flip up the safety on the joystick that controls the weapon. Rick holds his breath. This is kinda exciting. Finally getting to blow something up in this damned game. The go light blinks for the weapon. "Three… two… one… rifle."

I wait, I see the truck moving across the screen, a tiny white ant racing across miles of brown nothingness, and then count down: "Three… two… one… impact."

The truck explodes. The explosion doesn't have sound effects or anything, like what watching an explosion on Google Earth would be like. Just doesn't have the same zing. Too bad. The graphics are tight but you'd think if you're signing up for the Air Force they'd give the sim better audio.

"Good job, son."

"Told you not to worry." I look up at him and he smiles, for real this time, one that shows all those wrinkles on his face, only in like a good way. "We still on for that movie?"

He looks past me at the sim, his smile fading into this weird, intense sort of expression. He takes another drink.

CHAPTER 6

TUESDAY, SEPTEMBER 25

ANI

Cartesian dualism? I throw down my pencil, disgusted. Why on earth do I have to know this? Philosophy may just kill me. Christy is up front, actually talking with the professor, and I wonder what would happen to me if I went to the dean to drop the class. What would they threaten me with, losing credit? Having to take a big W for withdraw on my record? I could always replace it with something less Philosophy-like – Art, for instance, or even Creative Writing. I had to write a storyline for *World of Fire*, it can't be *that* different. Still, a W might not be so bad, as long as the dean doesn't have to call my mom.

Mom would lose her mind. I wonder what she'd threaten me with, though, now that I'm in college. Once I got a B in gym and she forbid me from talking on the phone with Dad when he was able to call from Afghanistan. I cried for a week. The only good thing about skipping grades was getting away from Mom that much sooner. Not even perfect Julie can calm her down when she goes into her snits. Especially after what happened the last time Dad came home.

Every time I think of her I hear Mom's words in my head: *Truth is, Your Honor, that he frightens me now, I just don't know if me and my girls are safe with him in the house.*

I'll never forget the look in his eyes as she spoke. The last fatal cracks in the shell of the man who so desperately wanted to hold himself together.

She was silent when they sentenced him.

My jaw clenches at the thought of my mother. I don't know why she hates Dad so much. Lots of soldiers have PTSD when they come home; he didn't mean the things he said, the things he did. If I can understand that, that he's sick and he can get better, then so should she. She hated my gaming, too, dismissed it as a pastime for the "junkies and the jobless." When I won the state science fair, she didn't even come to the awards ceremony. She had a headache. I had to get a ride from Julie's boyfriend. My phone rings. Oh no.

The phone buzzes in my pocket and I stand up and gather my books and push them towards my bag so I can leave, but then my binder falls. The phones buzzes again. I have to get it, looking at the papers scattered all over the floor around my desk, I wince as the professor looks over at me. I leave the books on the floor and rush out into the hall, bolting towards the stairs so no one will be able to hear me talking.

Kicking the block in front of the stairwell doors out of the way, I wait for the click of latch before I say, "Hello?"

"Ani." The voice is low, Mr Anderson.

"Hey," I start.

"How are things going at school?"

"Fine." Should I do it? Should I ask? My heart races as I think of Tyler, moving over in the chair, looking up at me with those eyes, those eyelashes that seem to go on forever. The memory of the way he looked at me, reverent and fearful and awestruck, has been on instant replay in my head for days. I can't delete it. I know I should eventually, but I just don't want to let it go. "But, um, about the project. I may have to go back over to Tyler's, I'd like to update the…"

"No, Ani. That won't be necessary. I have complete trust in the integrity of the system. I know you're anxious about potential errors since this is your first project on such a large scale, but don't worry. Nerves are completely natural, and there are going to be errors and things that need updating in every system. Don't let this keep you up at night." He pauses. "Besides, you know the rules, you're not going to have contact with any of the beta testers after you set up the system."

No. I want to see him again. "But if there is an error and we don't catch it–"

"There, you see? You're worrying. If there's a problem, we'll deal with it. If you were older I'd tell you to have a beer and try and relax. Since you're not, I think maybe a good walk around campus might do the trick." He sighs. "Besides, Mr MacCandless is our most qualified beta tester, he has at least two years of actual piloting experience. I've taught him most of what he knows myself. If anyone can work around initial bugs in the system, it's him. That kid was born to fly, he'll figure it out." The pride in his voice is unmistakable, and a sliver of jealousy slides in beneath my ribs.

"But–"

"You don't find the rules guiding this project unfair, do you?" His voice is cold: a mortuary door slamming shut. Fear wedges in my throat. Oh God, what Mr Anderson could do to me if I mess this up. He knows what I did back in California, and I don't want to go to jail.

"No, not at all." Hating the way the words feel in my mouth as I speak, I think of the way Tyler looked at me, like I was strong, like I was *there*. My stomach clenches.

"The next system is set for delivery Thursday at 1600 hours, right?" His voice lifts again, but the threat underlying his previous statement stains my consciousness. I can't ever relax around Mr Anderson, I can't ever forget what he can do.

"Yeah, I just need a few hours to work out the bugs and it will be ready. I can probably get into the office tomorrow, I don't have class on Wednesday afternoons."

"Perfect. See you then." The line goes dead.

I stare at the phone in my hand, studying it for a minute, and then shove it back into my pocket. Why is he insisting on acting as a go-between?

WEDNESDAY, SEPTEMBER 26

ANI

Who has time to join a club? Tables brimming with fliers and free water bottles litter the quad as the students at large try to sell their clubs to the freshmen.

"Hi there!" The girl looking at me is tall and classically beautiful, you know, long hair and lots of makeup and perfectly plucked brows. She shoves a leaflet into my hand and my feet crunch through a pile of leaves as I take a step back. She says, "I'm Stacy and you should meet up with me and the girls on Thursday nights. We go into an inner-city school here in New Haven to help tutor kids in need three afternoons a week. It's a really great cause and we cover any subject you like, and–"

"Sorry." I look at my feet. That does sound like a great thing to do but: "I have to work."

Her nose twitches up just a little as her eyes scroll down to check out my clothes. My cheeks burn. Yeah, that's right, I have to work. Unlike you, apparently. I look at her face, perfectly bronzed and set off by little pearl studs.

She smiles, that plastic little half-turn of the lip that I think we invented out in California, and just like that, I disappear from her line of vision. Forever.

I was an idiot for thinking that the East Coast would be different.

Swallowing, I raise my bag up a little higher on my shoulder and walk over towards the dorm, passing the table for the anime club with something that feels a little like regret.

CHAPTER 7

THURSDAY, SEPTEMBER 27

TYLER

Nothing gets a direct response from SlayerGrrl. For each question I have, Rick answers. He might ask her, but it's him that texts me. If she sent me a text, even if she blocked the number, I could trace it. She doesn't return my emails. Maybe I should use more emoticons. Girls like emoticons, right? Smiley faces and shit.

Sucks. I knew they gave me a fake name when she came to my house, which is fine. No contact or whatever, I get it. So I checked her gamer record. When she hit one of the high scores at some LA Comic-Con, they made her sign for her prize with her real name and not just her gamertag. Used the gamertag and tracked it back and got her name... Ani Bagdorian.

Pronounced "ahh-knee." It's an Armenian name, or at least that's what Google says. She's from LA. I know nothing about LA. Except that's where they make movies. And it's supposed to be hot. I shake my foot. Need to think. I yank open the door to class. Need to think. Should be playing the sim. Not here. Not in school. Need to think.

Do girls walk around in bikinis in LA? They do in the movies. Blondes with big tits and roller skates hanging out under palm trees. Ani would look great in a bikini. Wish she'd at least accept my Facebook friend request.

Test. There's a test today? Shit. Right. No, it's cool. It's History. I can do this. Only failing because I'm never here for the tests. Never make them up when I miss them. Nodding at Alpha in the back of the class, I shove my books under the desk. Alpha's got this black hair that covers most of his face, and a beard that takes care of the rest. He raises his hand in greeting. Looks back at his desk.

Get the paper. Why is the classroom always so quiet? Don't they have a radio they can turn on or something? Even crappy music would be better than nothing. I look down at the test. OK. Well, maybe I can't do this.

Look at the clock. An hour and a half. Look at the test. Names and dates and laws and wow this is going to be a really long ninety minutes.

I read question number one. I don't know who signed the Treaty of Versailles. I should have read the chapters at least. Reading is hard, though. Takes time and energy and concentration and it's just so much easier to not do it. Lines and letters everywhere, fighting to make sense but mostly just don't. Takes forever just to get through a page.

Essay questions. Good. Do those first. Get to choose. Gross domestic product driving decisions about rebuilding after the war. Shit. OK. Back to question one. Is it hot? I move. Focus. Read the question. Has to be some guys that I know. Perfume? Is Jack in front of me wearing cologne or something? Smells awful. OK, twist around again. Look out the window. Is the sun going down yet? How long is ninety minutes? Can't do this. No, focus. Read question two, you can go back to number one. Shit. Takes forever to read, the question is really long and has a lot of different people in it and I don't know who any of them are. Can't do this. I grind my back into the hard plastic of the chair, slamming my feet into the ground. Good, got question two. OK, focus. Question three. Need to leave. But the letters aren't coming together and that cologne is going to make me sneeze and I can almost hear that clock, that clock that's meaningless because the ninety minutes is just for everyone else, and for me, with extra time, it's a life-sentence. I have to stay here until I'm done. Forever and ever and ever and now the clock is ringing in my ears and the lines are jumping all over the page and the smell, oh God the smell of that cologne is riding up my nose and rotting my brain from the inside out.

I push up from the desk. The feet of the chair scratching at the tile floor is the only sound in the room. Walking to the front of the room, I put the test down on the teacher's desk. "I'm done."

"But it's only been fifteen minutes," she says. Her eyes look sad, worried, almost. "Take it back to the desk, Tyler. Give it another try, you can sit in the hall if you want."

"Later." I wave as I walk out the door, sneakers wrecking the perfect silence of the empty hall, drowning out the clear notes of sorrow in her protests.

Where's Mom? She's supposed to be home by now. I sent her a text. OK, three texts. She can't forget. She has to drive me. The Department of Motor Vehicles closes at five. It's 4.15 and if I don't get there soon I won't have time to take the test and won't get my license. Need my license. Need it today.

I call her cell and walk up the driveway. Don't see her car. Don't see her coming. Third ring. No answer. Where the hell is she? Why does she always flake out like this? Fifth ring. No car. No answer.

I pace. Up and down and up and down the driveway. Voicemail. Again. I hang up. Dial her work number. Pick up pick up pick up. Have to get there. She can't forget, she can't. Reminded her every day for the past week. Hell, probably two weeks.

Third ring. No answer. Not at her desk. I text her again. Dammit, Mom! She can't just forget like this. She can't but she will. She totally will. I kick the side of the house. Kick it again. And again.

The phone buzzes. I look down. Mom. She sends me a text:

Sorry, I completely forgot. But things are really busy here, I have to work on this case. Be back late tonight. Maybe we can get your license next week? <3

Why can't just for one day I have a normal freaking life with a normal mom who...

"Tyler!" A car pulls into the driveway. Rick. Thank God. "Aren't you supposed to be getting your license today?"

"Yeah" – I hold up my phone – "Think mom forgot, though."

"I thought that she might. Get in, if we hurry we can still make it to the one in North Haven before they close." He smiles, motions with his head for me to get into the car. I rush around to the passenger side. Throw open the door. Hop in.

"Thanks, man." I adjust the seat so that it slides back and I can stretch my legs. Grateful with every breath I take that at least Rick is functional. At least Rick gives a damn. "You really just saved my ass."

"Anytime." He backs up and we're off. Just hope we can make it before they close.

ANI

Why is he so determined to talk to me? I lay on my bed, running through a mental list of possible answers, my mind hovers around one:

He must like me.

How do I feel about that? Giddy? Excited? Terrified? Stretching out on top of my comforter, I pull my philosophy text up onto my lap. No one has ever sought me out. Not if they didn't need me to do something for them. Even Julie, and she's my sister.

And he's cute, too. Really cute. My heart flitters around right behind my ears and I push my arm into my forehead. I need to think. Maybe he just needs something, or has a question about the sim. Checking to make sure Christy is out of the room, I pull out my laptop and call up the tracers I put on all the sim systems. Access to this new technology, or at least the technology that it's based on, is highly classified. Mr Anderson's department came up with very specific parameters for its use. It's part of the reason why he doesn't want me to talk to the kids after I set up their systems. I may not be able to talk to Tyler, but I guess I can make sure his system isn't buggy from here. Staring at lines of code, searching for patterns, for anything off, my mind narrows, focuses, comes to life.

Wait a minute, there's a line I didn't write. Looks like nothing more than a linking program but I back it all up anyway, in case I'm missing something. Mr Anderson would be pissed to know that I have my own private log record of his program. But nothing will end a career faster than not having sufficient backup.

My cell rings. I kick my roommate's jeans out of my way as I go over to my coat and pull out the phone. "Julie?"

"Hey babe, what's up?" Her voice is bouncy, like her curls, like her smile, like, well, her. You'd never know that it was past eleven out in California, not with Julie. She's never tired.

"Um, nothing." Maybe I should ask her about Tyler. She's dated enough guys to know whether or not I should write him back or forget him.

"Any Ivy League hotties out there to tell me about?" She's so up, all the time. UCLA is perfect for her, she even made the cheerleading team.

I scoff. "No, but there is this guy…"

"Does he go to Yale?"

"Well, no, he's–"

"Ani, ditch him. Every relationship I've ever seen where the guy goes to one school and the girl goes to another never works out. They might pretend that it does for a while but then the next thing you know you're walking downtown with your girlfriends and see your guy sucking face with some girl he told you was just his cousin. Anyway, moving on, I need your help."

Of course she does. "Um, OK, which class?"

"Psychology 101, section three, with Professor Hernandez."

"Psych? I thought you wanted to major in Psych?" I ask, not as surprised as I expected to be.

"Ugh. I did, until I got shoved in that moron's class. Did you know that he actually gave me a D on my test? A D! Doesn't he know that this school needs me?"

"Did you study?" I try and cut off the usual tirade.

"Of course… mostly… he just hates women, Ani." She loves to play up to my feminist side. *Loves* it.

"Alright. When are grades due?"

"The profs put them in by midnight on the ninth."

"Got it, consider it a C." I scribble down the info. I'll do it after class.

"Love you, Ani! And ditch the guy from the other school, it's a waste of time!"

She makes kiss-smacking noises into the phone and I give her a half-hearted goodbye. Ditch the guy. She's right, of course, I have to just forget him. I can't break my contract with Mr Anderson. I can't. He helped me out of an impossible situation. He not only helped me out of it but also offered me a job, a way to pay for a college as amazing as Yale.

Fingers seeming to move on their own, I stare at Tyler's latest email:

SlayerGrrl, you out there somewhere?

My fingers hover over the keys.

CHAPTER 8

SATURDAY, SEPTEMBER 29

TYLER

Saybrook College isn't really a college. It's a lie. I guess saying "dorm" is just too lowbrow for Yale. They even each have their own dining halls and shit. Probably separated by income bracket. Like the George W Bushes and the John Kerrys are kept on one side of the campus and the kids of the doctors and lawyers and the Asian kids on scholarship are kept on the other.

I kick a pile of dead leaves. Check out the fliers on one of the poles in Saybrook College's courtyard. Blowing air into my hands to warm them. I should have worn gloves, man, it's cold.

Scanning the rain-beaten multicolored fliers tacked up on the post I see nothing, nothing that looks like SlayerGrrl would be a part of. Foreign film festivals and fundraisers. Guess they don't advertise the secret societies, huh? Too bad, would have been fun if I snagged one of their fliers for B. He likes that stuff.

I shove my hands into my pockets and walk over to a bench. Guess I'm gonna wait here. I sit. My ass is cold. Stupid jeans. Stupid fall. Stupid Tyler thinking that the whole stalker routine is gonna work. Peanut and Alpha told me not to come, maybe they were right.

"Hey." A guy walking as he talks on his cell stops, comes over to me on the bench. "Hey, man, I know you! You're that guy, MacIvrish, no, wait, MacCandless, right? With the show... the vlog? I loved it, man, what was it called, *Divergence*? Why'd you stop?" He looks so happy. Black hair and thick black glasses and short leather coat contrasting with the wild yellow of the leaves on the tree behind him. Like a black spot on the sun, almost. His eyes are wide, like I'm somebody.

I get even colder. "Nah, man, that's my brother, Brandon."

"Oh, man, sorry." His eyes narrow, just a bit. His enthusiasm leaks away. "Hey, where is he going to school, does he still have a vlog?"

My fingers clench into a little ball and try to find the right words, the nice words, the words that will be nice to this poor guy and to Brandon. But I can't. What would Brandon say? Damn, he's good at this stuff. Everything was always so easy. Especially with words. I say, "Nah, he doesn't do that anymore. He's" – think, Ty, think – "on sabbatical." Totally a word B would use.

"Oh." His face softens, and he shuffles his feet, breath leaving cotton-ball puffs in the air. "Well, if he ever starts one up again, let me know, just post it on the Yale message board, OK?"

"Yeah, sure." God, please let that happen. He walks away, and I wonder what it would be like for Brandon to have been here. He would love it here. He would love all of this. His grades were good, too, man. He belongs here, not… not where he is now.

I should sit outside the buildings that have the classes. No. They have class all over New Haven. Could be anywhere. Damn. I don't even know what she's studying. I don't even know why I'm here, really. It's not like Ani's answering any of my emails. Rick always talks about persistence paying off, a real soldier never accepting defeat. And I know in gaming, if you go at a level enough, you'll beat it. So hopefully the same rules apply to girls. Well, to this girl, anyway. The conversation about Brandon's messing me up. Can't think. Why did I come down here? This is stupid. I should have printed out a copy of her class schedule or something. I am such a moron sometimes.

I grab a flier off of one of the poles on my way out. Upcoming events. Perfect.

CHAPTER 9

TUESDAY, OCTOBER 2

TYLER

PPT? Why do I need another PPT? Planning and Placement Team? What a joke. I hate these things. I have to sit here while they list off this long string of issues. ADHD, apraxia, all that crap. An overgrown parent-teacher conference where I have to sit here and listen to all the stuff that's wrong with me. I'm sure I have all the problems going on that they say that I do, but it's me, it's all that I know how to be. Why are we here? "Mom." I pull out the chair for her. It's the right thing to do, help your mother. Mom's cool. Works a lot, tries really hard. Not easy to pay bills. She sits. She smells good. Mom always smells good, like some perfume she's always worn, she smells like home.

"Mrs MacCandless, Tyler, we're so happy that you could join us today." The second Dempsey hits the door he sends those marble-like little eyes rolling all over my mother. I hate him. I sit beside Mom. I lean in close to her. Want to look imposing. "Would you like some water? We just have to wait for the school psychologist."

Ugh. I'm seventeen now, do I really have to sit here and deal with Dempsey and his crap?

My foot starts under the table. I hate this, hate waiting. There's nothing to do when you wait. Except lose time that could have been spent actually accomplishing something. It's like dying. Only I imagine that dying is nicer because if you're dead then at least you won't be bored. Or worried about the way Dempsey's eyes are hanging on my Mom's rack like an overcoat. Sick bastard.

Look at her, all clearing her throat, he doesn't get it, just keeps staring at her chest. Damn. Can I throw something at him? It's not like she's wearing anything tight even, just a dress shirt.

I hate him. Hate him even more now. My foot goes crazy under the table and I shift in my chair again so I won't just leap across the table. Smack that leer right off his face.

Mom reaches her hand over, grabs mine. Be cool, Ty.

I love Mom, and she wants me to be here, so I'm here.

The school psychologist, Ms Kinney, walks into the room. It's about time. Hate Kinney. She's almost less cool than Dempsey. She's always asking these questions like she cares and tells you that everything you tell her is confidential but it's not. She tells Dempsey, my mom, anyone who will listen.

"Tyler, so nice to see you!" she greets as she pulls out a chair. Concern oozes from her like honey-covered pus.

I shift in my chair again. At least Dempsey doesn't pretend, just sits and pulls out his notes. "As I mentioned in my email, Tyler has been missing a lot of school lately. In fact, he has only been to school four times in the past two and a half weeks." Dempsey eyes just freaking glow when he looks at my mother's face.

"Yes, you did mention that." She looks at me. Thrusting my feet into the floor, I brace myself. Her soft voice, asking, "Tyler, is that true?"

Can't look at her face, there is more than enough disappointment there normally, don't need to see any more of it now. I nod.

"What have you been doing?"

The fear. The fear in her voice. It tears me right through the middle.

"Nothing, Mom." How do I make this clear to her? "Nothing bad, just hanging out."

I look into her eyes. Wide. Blue. Pained. I'll tell you later, Mom, I promise.

Ms Kinney clears her throat. "Also," her voice filled with sweetness so intense it sounds like rot, "Tyler mentioned that he hasn't been taking his prescribed medication, and I felt that it was best to make sure that you are aware of the situation."

Why do I keep talking to her? Why do I tell that woman anything? I am such an idiot. Grinding my feet into the tile I lean back so that I'm looking at the ceiling and not at her. I know I shouldn't trust her. Why does it piss me off every time? Can't trust anyone. Ever. Should know that by now. Well, maybe Mom. Maybe Rick.

"Has the doctor suggested anything to help Tyler, Mrs MacCandless?" Dempsey now, voice low, playing the part of vice principal who gives a damn. Just wants to come off that way so he can get into Mom's pants. I should punch him. So smug.

"Medication, but Tyler doesn't like the way it makes him feel." Mom, voice like a cord wrapping its way around my middle. She can't say that B used to steal it. Leaving me with an empty bottle and a prescription that I could only fill once a month. So I just gave up filling it. Had to deal without it. Like things better without it now, anyway. Used to it.

"Yes, well, we're afraid that his recent string of absences may be the symptom of a deeper problem." Drugs. He doesn't say the words. But he leaves the thought. Leaves the thought right there. On the table. Playing on Mom's worst fears in the world. That sick fuck. I am going to kill him. "Statistically, students who have ADHD are more likely to... experiment with other things."

"That's bullshit, there's no deeper problem and you know it," I say, leaning forward across the table.

"Tyler, your language." Ms Kinney shakes her head. "And we never insinuated that you–"

"Fuck you, Kinney. You say all that stuff is confidential and here you are lying to my mom." Words flying around my head a thousand miles an hour. All of them fighting.

"I'm not lying, Tyler. We are just making your mother aware that your behavior is consistent with certain patterns..."

Thoughts pound at the back of my skull. Can't grab them. They're trying to come out but all I can do is look at my mom.

Her face is like ice. Like glass. Cold and numb and broken. I want to scream, want to kill them for hurting my mom. They don't know me. Don't know that I would never do that to my mom and now they're telling her that I'm doing drugs and I'm not. Why are they doing this to her now? They are all idiots. All of them. Brutal. Freaking. Idiots.

They keep talking, accusations flying around me. "Always late." "Distracted." "Disrespectful." "Displaying some of the same behaviors as his brother."

Each word they say hits me like a club, beating me down until there is nothing left. There is one thing in life I would never do and it's drugs. Ever. I can't even get the words out to say anything. I just sit there like a punching bag and listen to my trial. Witnesses lined up condemning me in front of my mom. And it's not true. Do they know that I can't defend myself? They know.

All of them trying to ruin my life. They need to leave Mom alone I will hurt them if they hurt her how could they hurt her? How could they hurt her now? I can't believe I trusted Kinney. I'm a moron.

"Tyler." Mom's voice breaks through the chaos inside my head and tugs at my heart. She reaches out and holds my hand. "Focus for me, baby. Look at me. Just at me."

The whirlwind quiets. I don't know if everybody else stops talking. If they finally shut up. All I see is Mom. She used to do this. Holds my hand and tell me to squeeze, hard, to help me focus, to help bring the thoughts into order and be able to get them out. I turn her hand over in mine. God, it's so small, her hand. Soft skin drawn tight over little bones, like a bird. My hand is massive, like I could hurt her if I held it too hard. My heart pounds. I am so pissed right now.

The blue of Mom's eyes melt together like an ocean I just want to drown in. Her lips curl up at the edges and she puts her other hand on top of the one already holding hers. She knows how hard it is for me. She knows. Damn, I love her.

Dempsey's voice stays low, like a jaguar waiting for the kill. "As it is, he'll have to do summer school to get enough credit to graduate."

I stand up, pulling Mom up by the hand beside me. Standing feels good. Not good enough, though, I wish the ground would push back on me sometimes. Make things easier. I ram my chair back into the table. The movement feels good. Need more. I push Mom's back in, too, and she stands beside me. I grab her hand, again. Yes, I hold my mom's hand. Love my mom. My words come in short, frantic bursts now that I'm up. "I'm seventeen, right? Well, I want to withdraw from school."

"But–" Mom starts.

I look at her. "I can take the GED, it'll be fine."

Ms Kinney, that voice going all sticky sweet again, "Tyler, the test is very difficult, I'm not sure you understand–"

"I'm not stupid," I say. Voice sharp. Not stupid. Just scattered. "Besides, I get extra time."

I pull Mom out of the door behind me and slam the door as their voices rise up in protest. We march right through the office. Down the hall. Across the entryway and right out of the front door.

We walk, not saying anything. Silent. Still holding hands. We get to the car. Walking to Mom's side to open the door for her, she meets my eyes. Pain and hurt and worry all mash around at once. They think I'm a moron, a druggie, a loser. The words. So much I want to say and just can't put into the right order and I am a moron if I can't even tell Mom that I love her and wouldn't do that to her and that I'm not stupid and that I can pass the GED but that sometimes I feel stupid and I can't stop this pain inside of me that eats at me like a rat in the pit of my stomach every time I think of B and I want to just...

She sees. She wraps her arms around me and I bend down to hug her. I want to speak. Really want to. But I can't. So I hold onto her as tight as I can and let her love me any way that she can.

CHAPTER 10

THURSDAY, OCTOBER 4

ANI

So what if I'm totally obsessed with checking my email? I know that it's wrong, on a certain level, and I should concentrate on the lecture Professor Jimenez is giving about the Golden Age of Spanish Literature. I'm sure that Gongora's poetry is fascinating, but it's really just nowhere near as fun as checking to see if Tyler's sent me another email.

I look up at the SMART Board, red circles surrounding the bits of the poem and the metaphors that I should be taking notes on, and open my Gmail. Three new messages, one from Tyler.

SlayerGrrl, Sometimes I wonder if all this is worth it, you know? School. Worrying about the "future." How bad can it be, really? I mean, my cousin never graduated and owns his own bike shop, he does alright. This probably sounds stupid to someone at Yale. Never mind. Meet me at Criterion on Saturday, please?

God, I want to, even though I hate that movie. His emails started to get like this a few days ago, still short, but personal. Odd, considering that I only ever spent an hour or two with him, but the turn these emails have been taking touch me, somehow. He sounds almost as lonely as I've always been.

I Google ADHD. I read a lot of things about inability to sit still and difficulty focusing. But sadly, they don't list "hot" and "may incite normally reasonable girls to think way too much about certain boys who suffer from it" as common qualifiers.

Professor Jimenez clears his throat and reads the poem out loud for the third time.

After glancing up to make sure that he's not looking my way, I lean forward and send Julie a quick email.

Hey Julie, it's me. What's going on? How's class? So far I'm not loving Spanish Literature. Are you taking Spanish at all? Love you, –Ani

This is the third email I've sent her in as many days. She's my sister and my best friend, and yet she never writes back. Never texts, even. She calls sometimes, though. Mostly when she's stuck on her Geometry or Chem homework, but still. That counts, right?

OK, Ani, time to get serious. You need a B average over all of your classes or that scholarship will disappear, so you better get into Gongora.

Typing notes on my laptop, analyzing love poetry somehow does very little to keep my mind from drifting to Tyler. What's his problem? I mean, he's really cute; I have a hard time believing that he wouldn't be able to get any girl at his school if he put his mind to it. Probably does have another girl at school, actually. Maybe he's just a player and wants to get a Yalie, or a gamer girl or whatever under his belt. Dammit.

I open a window with Tyler's latest message. Doesn't seem like much of a player, though, does he?

"Dad?" It's hard to hear with the mad rush of people around me at the change of classes. "Can you hear me?"

"Yeah, honey. What's up? How's the Ivy League treating my baby girl?" His voice is distant. I can't tell if it's the connection or not. Sounds so different than the man that would take me to the park to feed the ducks.

"It's OK. Classes are good, I guess," I say. My eyes stray to all the smiling faces around me. It's hard to know what to talk about now that he's in jail. "How are things for you?"

"The counselor says things are coming along. There's a whole group of us vets in here, so I'm not alone."

"Mom come visit yet?" I have to know. Mom used to write him every day while he was deployed, saying that he had to know that we were still here and that we loved him. She was so superstitious, said that if he didn't feel like he had something to come home to that he'd get killed. I would try and tell her that it's the luck of the draw, but she'd never listen. Then when he came home, when he wasn't right, she basically tossed him out. They're still married, though, and I know she loves him. Well, I hope she still loves him.

"Oh, honey, you know your mother."

So that would be a no, then. "Do they think that you'll be paroled anytime soon?" My voice wobbles a little. "I mean, they have to know that this isn't fair."

"Don't you worry about me, baby. I'm going to be just fine. Tell me all about school."

"I don't know if I like it all that much, honestly."

"Making any new friends?"

I think of Tyler. Damn. "No, not all that many."

"Give it time, baby, it's still early. You've got four years ahead of you and you've only been there a month. Friendships don't happen overnight, right?"

"Julie had tons of friends in her first month at UCLA."

"Now, honey. Julie is... well, Julie. You choose your friends more carefully, so in the end you may not have as many, but they'll be good ones. Julie loses as many friends as she makes, you know that."

I open my email, staring at Tyler's latest message. "Dad, do you think that I should be OK with my boss telling me who I can and can't talk to?"

CHAPTER 11

FRIDAY, OCTOBER 5

TYLER

Rick's waiting at the field. The airstrip. Borrowed Mom's car to get out here, she's working from home today. Should probably text her and let her know I have the car. Does she even know that I finally got my license? I filled out the form to add myself to her insurance, but she probably didn't notice. She just signs stuff when I put it in front of her. I set up all the bills for the house so they come out of her account automatically. Learned to do that when they cut off our electric. It's not that she doesn't have the money, it's just that she forgets to pay. I shoot her a quick text and walk over to where Rick's waiting.

Normally I would feel a little bad coming out here since I've been blowing off all the Civil Air Patrol meetings. But it's sunny and warm and the trees add bright shocks of red and yellows and oranges to the green of the field and well, I have a hard time feeling guilty on such a nice day, I guess. Rick saunters up to me with that smile. I like that smile. Lately he's been looking like he'd only be happy if leaping from a helicopter fully armed, but today he looks tired, old. But nice.

"Glad you could make it." He puts his hand on my shoulder, firmly, intently, then turns his eyes up to the cloudless sky. "Wanna go up?"

"Hell yeah," I say without thinking. Rick has a plane. A small propeller plane that he probably bought way back in the Nineties, but it still flies like a dream. We used to go up a lot, when I first started going to the Civil Air Patrol meetings. Usually, mentors are randomly paired, but Rick came to a bunch of meetings, watched us at the controls, studied our files. Creeped me out at first, this guy in uniform who was sort of part of the meetings and sort of not. Then like two years ago he told me that he was going to be my mentor. Most of the other kids already had them, usually a bunch of middle-aged guys who flew a lot of model planes or who liked to play soldier. Rick couldn't be more different than those guys. He totally sold me on the whole mentoring thing the second he handed me the controls of his plane. It was like he could see right inside of me and just knew. We stopped hanging out with the group, have been doing our own thing ever since.

He's a hero, Rick. A real American hero, not some rock star or some politician or shit, someone who actually put his life on the line and just keeps on doing it. He was in the Air Force, has these great stories. And even though he pretty much is Haranco, he never makes me feel like he'd rather be doing something else when we hang out.

The first time B went missing and Mom freaked out, Rick was the one who was there. He drove me to hundreds of different shelters all over the state, called police stations and hospitals, held me up when I wanted to turn off the way Mom did. The mornings I didn't want to move, didn't want to get out of bed. Some days I felt like the world was just too loud and I would shut myself away, cover my head and scream to try and make everything stop hurting. Rick was there, always, pulling me up. Getting me out of the house, taking me for epic trail runs or even just out for a coffee. Mostly we talked. I talked. When I could.

He smiles, small wrinkles spreading out on his tanned face as we walk over to the prop. The day smells like burning leaves and hamburgers from the airport grill, and sounds from small engines flying somewhere overhead all blend together to make music in my head. Love it here. Now that B's back, though, getting better, maybe I can start getting out here more, getting my life back together again.

The leather bucket seats feel so good, so sleek as we slip into them and put on the headsets, the real headsets, not the fake ones like in a game. It's so different. In the game the fields look sort of gray, life through a lens. Here, with the windows of the plane open and the real, full tremble of the steering wheel in your hand, the hum becoming a roar as you barrel down the runway, the sinking feeling in the pit of your stomach as you lift into the air, the wind nipping at your hair and the smell of fuel, this is nothing like the sim. Nothing at all. This is real. This is a thing of glory.

Rick looks like a kid. I mean, not a real kid, but he gets this loopy grin when he flies. Always. Like a pervert at a porn convention. This is why we get along, Rick and I, because there is nothing either of us would rather do than this. Than fly.

The fields stretch out wide beneath us, and the rhythm of the engine buzzes up along my spine, like I can feel it in my soul.

Rick gets all nostalgic when he's airborne. "If you think flying these things is cool, Tyler, wait till you get to fly a Warthog, man. Those things just go, dropping cluster bombs everywhere. When you see the surface of the earth rise up in a cloud of dust behind you, man, it's just the best." Rick smiles. "You know what the peaks of the Hindu Kush look like in the morning sun? Mountains set on fire by the sun as you fly over, it's just amazing. You'll see."

"I hope so," I say. Rick has this thing for speed. The A-10s he used to fly have a lot more power than this old thing does, I'm sure.

"It will be, you just have to visualize it, hold it tight in your mind, and you'll get there." Rick swallows. "The ex-wife, she had no concept of what could be, no vision. You believe it and you'll find a way to make it happen." It took a year or so before he even mentioned his ex-wife. He had a son, too. Ex-wife took the son to some party while Rick was gone. His son fell into the pool and drowned. Three years old. He had to fly back from wherever he was stationed to go to the funeral. When he got home from his deployment for good, she was gone. Took everything from him. I know it still hurts him every time he thinks of his son, of her. Just like it hurts every time I think about Dad. About Brandon.

I press my lips tight.

"Here, keep her steady." Rick lets go of the wheel, and I check the stats, hold her up, hold her even, feeling like my arms are just another piece of machinery.

"Is the flight pattern registered?" I ask.

"This is so easy for you, isn't it?"

"What?" I ask, eyes on the gas gauge, the elevation, the azimuth, the window, the ground below.

"You know, when they asked me to be a mentor, they tried to steer me away from you. They told me that you lost your father, your brother was going off to college, and that you had ADHD so bad that it would probably keep you from going anywhere," he says, all matter of fact. "Told me I should pick somebody else."

"They said that?" Azimuth good. Turbulence, though. I bring her up a little. Kinda pissed that the Civil Air Patrol people would say that about me.

"Yup." He smiles, leaning back in his chair. He reaches into the cooler and grabs a beer. I've never seen Rick drink when he flies. "But look at you, Tyler. No medication, look how easy it is for you to do this, to control everything at once, to focus on everything, everything around you with precision, to execute good decisions even when you are focused on five other things."

The turbulence eases up. New altitude steady. "Yeah, well, tell that to my Social Studies teacher." Former Social Studies teacher. Have to remember that. Have to sign up for that GED.

"No. See, that's their problem, Tyler. They're teaching to the past. Trying to force kids to conform to a system that's already dead. You're at an advantage. It's the human body taking the next step, changing to meet the needs of the future." He takes a sip of beer.

I hold the plane, pressure from its resistance firm beneath my fingers. "What?"

"Evolution, Tyler. Your gift, you're an asset, not a liability. You know that, too. Somewhere, deep down, you knew when they told you to take those drugs, to make you fit into their archaic, dying system, you knew. You didn't take the drugs, you knew they'd make you weak. I like that. A man who recognizes strength for what it is."

"Yeah," I say. He's wrong. Not taking the drugs has nothing to do with that. Just every time I filled the script B would take all the pills. Sell them, take them himself, whatever. I could never squeeze in more than one or two days' worth before the pills were gone. Just didn't seem like it was worth it. So I stopped. Been fine. Mostly fine. Nice that he thinks it makes me strong, though.

He leans over, "I could see then, even, your potential."

I look at him, smiling at me, and my chest feels big all of a sudden, good. "You think I'm gonna score high enough on the sim to get into that flight school? Cause I really want to do this, fly for real and all."

He leans back, sipping his beer. "I don't know, the world is changing, Tyler. Moving away from all this." He motions to the open sky around us. "But there might be alternatives."

"Like what?"

He sips his beer and looks out the window.

Why is he drinking so much? Been back from the airstrip for hours now and it just won't let me rest. Whatever it is that Rick does for a living, that's what I want to do. Except if that's what's making him drink so much. Have to try and talk to him about that. Find out what's making him drink. Find out if it could be something going on with his job. Then talk. Help him out like he helped me.

I look up Haranco, see if there are any press releases about mergers or something that would piss him off.

Tick tick tick... what's ticking? Right. Set the clock on my phone to tick. Thought it would be fun. I change it a lot. Slam it off, keep searching.

Wait, what's this? I stop at a document on some French wiki site that features a list of Tidewater subsidiary companies. I look at the sim, check the stats on my drones on the big screens as I hit the link on my laptop that I put to my right. Nothing going on with the drones today anyway. Quiet. Boring.

Huh, Haranco has a parent company, Tidewater. Tidewater opens different branches to run different parts of their operation, then gives those branches separate registry information. That way, each sub-company can qualify for government funding on its own. Smart. Like Rick.

Blip blip blip... I try and read faster. Stupid drones pick something up. I punch in the code to set a tail on the suspicious truck.

Haranco bases. One here in Connecticut. Two are in the Balochistan province of Pakistan and one is in the United Arab Emirates. Lots of smaller offices, though, spread all over the world. What the hell? I click.

Blip blip blip. Stupid truck. Looking up at the sim monitors, I have to put the laptop down and pick up the headset to get the call for the intercept of the truck.

It's cool that Rick's the head of some company that does good things. That helps keep soldiers safe. But something gnaws at me, at my stomach, as I turn back to give my full attention to the sim. What's bothering him, though? I don't see any news, any changes made to the company structure or anything. I keep clicking. My fingers freeze.

There is no record of Haranco having any kind of flight school.

"Balochistan? I mean, why there?"

B shakes his head. Wonder if they let him eat more. He looks good. Gaining weight. Not like he's getting fat, but like, normal-looking. "Did you check to see who funds the Haranco operations?"

I shrug. He thinks it's obviously not Haranco shareholders or he wouldn't be asking. I hand him my phone. He can search it quick. He grabs it and his hands start flying.

"JSOC." His eyes light up like this should mean something to me. It doesn't. "Joint Special Operations Command."

Still got nothing. "B, what are you getting at?"

"Looks like your boy Rick runs some sort of program for the government. And if it's funded by JSOC, then it doesn't have any congressional oversight. Hell, Congress may not even know Haranco exists." His fingers keep pounding on the keys. Then his eyes get wide in a rush. The muscles on his face freeze, then fall. "You said that Haranco is a subsidiary of Tidewater, Tyler."

"So?"

"Did Rick tell you any of this?" B's face is bright, excited, angry.

"Why would he tell me any of this?" B doesn't make any damned sense sometimes.

"The guy brings some crazy piece of equipment built by one of the largest independent defense contractors in the nation into your house, Tyler, to give to you to 'test' for him and you didn't even ask him exactly who he works for and what it is that he does?"

Brandon seems to take up three times as much space as the little wicker chair that he's sitting on.

"No, B." I look at my feet. Worn boots on the concrete floor. B's face looks hard, like the concrete. Like I'm an idiot.

"Look, you have to talk to my friend Todd about him. He wrote a whole book about Tidewater. They're no good."

"I trust him." Rick's been there for me. Kept me going when all Mom could do was cry and when you were doing nothing but putting more track marks on your arm in some ditch or crack house or wherever the hell it was that you went.

"Then why did you look all this stuff up?" B asks.

"Because Rick's the only functional person in my life right now and if he's acting weird, I want to know why," I say. It's true. Drinking. Hate the drinking.

B leans over, puts his elbows on his knees and runs his hands through his shaggy hair. His face looks like a balloon slowly deflating. I'm not supposed to bring up the past when I visit, guilt makes recovery harder, I guess. Right in front of me the color that was in his cheeks, that was in his voice when he was talking, disappears. I should be more careful with what I say.

"Shit, B, I didn't mean it like that. I looked it up because I was bored."

"Watch yourself." The words, his voice, sounds thin, breakable, like glass.

"Sure."

"No, I mean it, Ty. Don't put too much faith in the guy. These big companies can be into all kinds of crazy things, things you don't want to get involved with." Paranoia comes with the drugs, but really, B was paranoid long before he got into H. Rick's cool, I'm sure of it, his ex-wife must be bugging him for more money or something. That causes a lot of guys to drink. Drink more than usual, anyway.

We sit. I stare out the window. Barren, twisted trees outside looking a lot like I feel. I dig out the paper, soft, folded, opened and folded again like three thousand times. I open it, look down, read it, close it, put it back into my pocket.

"What's that?" B asks, pointing to the softened paper.

"Nothing."

B's eyes run over me and I try to keep it cool. He smiles. "So who is she, exactly?"

Shit. What do I say? This chick that I'm stalking? Best gamer in the country? Yalie who should have nothing to do with me?

He snatches the paper.

"Hey!"

"What's this, Ty? List of upcoming events at Yale? Who do you know who goes to Yale?" His voice is stronger now.

"This girl... she... she set up the sim in the house. She did this summer internship at Althea or something. Works for Rick now."

"Why do you have this?" He holds up the paper, with that smile traveling up into his blue eyes, like a teacher, like an ass, like my brother.

Don't get too excited. Just cause he has moments like this doesn't mean he'll be back, doesn't mean he'll beat it. "Her name is Ani, and I took it off some bulletin board thing on campus."

"An older woman, Ty?" That smile turns his whole damn face high voltage. He laughs. "A Yalie? Shootin' high, huh?"

"Shut up. I don't think she's older." I reach for the paper and he holds it just out of reach. I lunge for it and crash into him. We tussle back into the chair as I grab for it again, careful not to hurt him, and he laughs as I twist his arm back behind him. "You're such an ass sometimes."

I grab the paper out of his hand and we both keep wrestling, laughing. He twists me around and digs his knee into my back. I yelp. He's breathing hard, like it hurts. He says, "We better stop or they're gonna think we're being serious or something."

He lets go. I move back to my chair, looking down at the crumpled paper in my hand. "I'm trying to figure out if she's gonna go to any of these things."

"A Yalie?" He sits. Takes a sip of water from the one plastic cup still standing on the table. "She's gonna be at chess club for sure."

I laugh. "She's not really a chess club kind of girl."

"No? Glee club, maybe?"

"Fuck you." I run my fingers over the list of student-sponsored activities, some on-campus, some off. "I'm thinking she might go to the midnight showing of *Akira* at Criterion with the anime club."

"*Akira*? Anime club? That's pretty power-nerd right there," he says with a sigh. His face falls and he crosses his legs and leans back into the chair slowly. Like he's getting tired. I should go.

I stand up. Can't tire him out when he's doing this well. I tuck the paper back into the pocket of my baggy jeans. "See you tomorrow?"

He scoffs, reaches his arms out over the top ledge of the chair. "Yeah, man, I'll be here."

Picking up my coat and pulling it in over my arms, I say, "Later."

Just as I'm walking out of the door, I hear his voice. "Hey, Tyler."

"Yeah?" I turn. He's smiling like Satan in Vegas.

"If it goes anywhere with that girl, remember" – he leans forward, eyes throwing sparks – "please her first."

Shit. Did he really just say that? My blood seems to pop and my stomach fills with gasoline. "What?"

"Face it, man, you're seventeen, you're a virgin, you'd last all of three seconds. All I'm saying is, you please her first, and she'll be more likely to let you try it again." Smiling son of a bitch.

"B," I say. Shit. He thinks I'm going to have sex with SlayerGrrl? With Ani? I. Freaking. Wish. "There's like no chance."

Miles and miles of empty road. Need more Mountain Dew. Need something. My eyes are red and my ass hurts and my sight is all blurry. Stupid sim, man.

The drones are all stuck on different flight patterns over different highways. Though in this game, by "highway" you're really talking about a dirt road best used by sheep. I'm looking for anything suspicious. Mostly this is the sim. Boring sim. Awesome sim. Can't really make up my mind about it sometimes. What is this getting me? What's the freaking point?

My eyes are hot. Head dips into my chest. Then up. Shit, what time is it? 8am. Damn. Maybe I should log off and get some sleep. Then I see it. Pickup truck. Bottom of screen four. Finally. My heart picks up. I tap into the voice control on the headset to call the central command of the game unit, SKY. Don't remember what it stands for.

I set the drone 407 on its tail and zoom in. "I've picked up an unidentified truck moving north-northeast at approximately forty-five miles per hour."

SKY says to set the tail in that monotonous computer voice. I pull drone 407 off auto and set it to track the truck. Pickup truck. Zoom in closer. Old truck, half-rusted, like out of some zombie apocalypse flick. "Speed decreasing, set tail 407."

"Confirm tail." I don't know why the voice from SKY has to come through a headset. I'm gonna tell them that they should change that. It's sort of annoying having some voice cutting into your tunes to tell you what to do all the time. Like the stupid GPS in the car.

The truck blows past some shack. Nothing much in the desert. Lots of dirt, lots of road, sometimes the computer even gives me sheep, but not today. Just some rusted-out truck and broke-ass gas station.

A puff of dust temporarily blocks the lens of the camera as the truck pulls off the side of the road. Shit. Driver just probably needs to piss. Do they program that into videogames? They shouldn't. Totally shouldn't. I check the mapping screen and overlay the truck location to the potential vulnerable culverts beneath the road. Good places to put an IED.

I make the match. "Vehicle parked at culvert 56."

"Clear to target," SKY indicates and I set the targeting device on tail 407. Two people get out of the truck. Carrying backpacks… to the culvert beneath the road.

"Two men leaving vehicle and heading south-southeast into culvert 56."

"Weapons ready on tail 407?"

"Two Hellfires." I'm gonna take them out. "Lasing."

"All clear. Targets engaged?"

I grab the joystick and flip off the safety. Hitting in the key code to arm the machine guns on the drone, I fly it in low. "Targets locked." The drone lowers, so low along the road I swear I can see each pothole and oil stain. "Engaging."

I fire. The men, which the computer overlays with red to help assist in targeting, go down. The whole segment of road blows. Too bad I can't see the shock on their faces. The dudes in most games always look so surprised when you kill them. I pull the drone around.

"Targets eliminated." I say into the mic, circling the drone around for the clean-up sweep. Truck is far enough away from the road that it escaped most of the blast. "Approved for clean-up?"

"Heat signature in truck?"

I scan the truck. Don't think there's anybody else in there. If so, that's too bad for them. "Normal. Wait. Yeah. Got one more in the truck."

"Clear for cleanup."

I sweep the drone around and target the truck, dropping one hundred pounds of Hellfire on its ass. Circle for a bit, waiting for the heat signature to go cold. Not such a bad game, really. Putting the drone back into the auto route with the others, I note that my kill count in the upper left-hand corner of the screen is now up from seven to ten. Low kill count, of course, compared to most other games. Don't care, though, this one feels real.

Maybe too real.

CHAPTER 12

SATURDAY, OCTOBER 6

ANI

I turn back to the computer, briefly glancing at the people in the other booths. They keep an active log of all sites visited by guests at the library, but it doesn't matter, I just need to do this from a public ISP. There will be no log when I'm done; public computers like these are easy to clean. Libraries have the worst firewalls ever since the good ones cost too much money. Gotta love public funding.

Moving my head from shoulder to shoulder, I stretch the tense muscles of my neck and take a deep breath. The library smells like a sad mix of dust and industrial carpet cleaners, but I love it all the same. The way the quiet amplifies the sound of my heartbeat as it rises, like an audience hushing as the curtains rise before them on a stage.

Shooting the lady behind the reference desk my best sweet little girl smile, I get to work.

Getting past UCLA's security is too easy, really. All it takes is some time and a few bucks that I bummed from

Julie before she even started there so we could have an easy way in before she set one of her polished toenails through the door. I started a "rate my professor" type website, which is free to use, but requires a working email address. Then we posted a link to the site on her Facebook page so all of her eight hundred friends, many of whom are now with her at UCLA, can see it.

It never takes long before a professor finds out about such pages and tells their friends in outrage, and they can see what all the kids are saying about them as long as they, too, have a working email. I set up the site in August of last year, and by October of last year I had at least ten UCLA professors check the site from their work addy. From there, I sent them each a meaningful email along the lines of:

Professor Jones.

We are currently in the process of updating our account setup. Please click here to make certain our records our up to date.

Then all I did was sign the name of the system administrator, put their street address and cut and paste the university logo and I had something like six of the ten professors actually do it. Which means I can do everything they can do… only better.

So it takes all of maybe five minutes to get in, change my sister's grade to a C, and get out. Three quick little clicks more and all the computer log shows is that I was on Amazon.com and MTV. Should I be risking jail to change my sister's grades? She always looked out for me, let me hide behind her and her cheerleader friends when all the other kids at school would have been happy to stomp all over me. And I owe her for that. She's always loved her freakish little sister, and isn't that worth something?

And besides… this is fun.

I feel good, actually. I go back to my email, open Tyler's latest message and read it again. I've been thinking about it, and Mr Anderson would have nothing to gain by sending one of his employees to jail. My science fair project, SkyPet, is what made Althea and Haranco both notice me. It was so easy to do, to change the drone I bought at the store and make it do what I wanted it to. It was just a matter of plugging the chips into the computer and rearranging the subroutines. So simple it was brilliant. Timed to take pictures every seven seconds, I flew it undetected over the red carpet at the Oscars ceremony, so I could make my demo level for *World of Fire* be a free-play set on the red carpet. I could weave in and around movie stars and limos and it was going to be amazing. It was amazing, actually, writing that level, and showing it off at the demo at the science fair was great.

But something went wrong during SkyPet's first flight. Unfortunately, I planned for a maximum wind speed of up to five miles an hour. I wasn't expecting the thirty-five mile an hour wind gusts. SkyPet was thrown off course and flew over a corner of the Los Angeles Air Force Base, still taking pictures every seven seconds. I sort of ended my report for the fair before that bit, glossing over it by saying that it was blown off-course and I tracked it to where it eventually landed just outside of El Segundo.

World of Fire's Oscar level went viral, it seemed like the whole world was talking about it and SkyPet. Althea offered me the summer internship, helping them update their Universal Control System. Althea's model is based on having two pilots sitting at the controls and one supervisor, and I didn't really have to do much.

Then Mr Anderson knocked on my door. He wanted me to make a game based on Althea's UCS. But he wanted a single-pilot machine that would then be used to train the pilots for the UCS that Althea was set to sell to the Air Force. He mentioned all these wonderful things about a job with Haranco: the ability to work close to Yale, enough money to be able to cover almost all of Yale's tuition, the chance to graduate from college with four years of relevant work experience to put on my resume, a chance to help my country.

But that's when the job interview became strange. It's like he was reading my face, seeing that my first choice for college wasn't Yale, it was MIT. And working for Althea was great in that it would almost guarantee admission to any school I wanted, but I wanted to design videogames, not work for some branch of the military-industrial complex. He watched me as my mind disengaged from the interview, and he asked my mother if she could get him a glass of water. As soon as Mom left the room, he showed me the pictures.

Pictures from SkyPet's cameras as it flew over the Los Angeles base. He used words like *restricted air space* and *criminal trespass* and *federal offense*. If I worked for Haranco, he could make sure that I avoided prosecution.

I was fifteen, it was my first real job interview, and it was an offer that I couldn't refuse.

Cheeks burning, I still can't believe that I forgot to factor in the potential for such high wind gusts. It was stupid.

But I've been thinking a lot about it over the past week and I don't think that Mr Anderson would bring it up again. I mean, he would look even worse than me in court because he *knew* that I violated restricted space and hired me anyway. By turning me in, he would be turning himself in, and he doesn't strike me as the type of guy who would do that just because I sent an email to Tyler. Tyler's promised not to even talk about the sim, so I just don't think it will be that big of a deal. Maybe. Hopefully.

Staring at Tyler's email, I hit reply:

Hey Tyler,

Sorry I haven't written you back…

No, that sounds completely pathetic. I delete and try again:

Hey Tyler,

How are you?

No, I know how he is, he emails me like every day. God! I delete, try again:

Hey Tyler,

How are things going? Got your emails, but I've been busy.

Argh! That makes me sound mean. I'm not going for mean. Why is this so hard?

Tyler,

Have you played the new *Gods of Destruction* yet? I haven't picked it up but I hear that it's good.

-Ani

What if he doesn't like *Gods of Destruction*? I didn't see it at his house and it's still such a stupid thing to write. At least it's conversational, I guess. He's still going to think that I'm a moron. I lick my lips and delete it. God, if I was actually honest he'd never email again. I type:

Tyler,

You don't want to have anything to do with me. Date some cute, nice girl from your school or something. Listen to Mr Anderson and stop emailing me. You'd be better off without getting involved with my terrible, messed-up life. Besides, I've never had a boyfriend before and I would do everything wrong.

I squeeze my lips together as I look at the words. That's what I really should send, isn't it? The truth. But the truth is that I don't want him to stop emailing, not really. I move my fingers over to...

"Miss?" A voice calls from over my shoulder.

I jump. I turn and see a librarian standing over my shoulder. "Yeah?"

"I'm sorry, but your time on this computer is up, we have other people waiting."

That was close. "OK, let me just sign out."

I look back over to the screen. Oh. No.

Blinking on the screen in front of me is a little box:

Your message has been sent!

●●●●

TYLER

Is she here? How would I know? The lobby whirs. Buzzes. Like it's alive. People everywhere. Can't believe a midnight movie is so crowded. Don't these people have jobs that they need to go to in the morning? I shove my hands into the bottom of the pockets of my sweatshirt and wait. I should get some popcorn, maybe. Hungry. Forgot dinner. I forget that a lot. Mom never remembers to ask. We used to sit together, have a regular family meal… I should totally get some popcorn.

My sneakers half-stick to the floor of the lobby. I bump into some guy, mutter sorry and hide my face further in the hood of my sweatshirt. I'm never going to be able to find her here. Too many people. They need to leave. I rush up to the line. Nah, too long. Don't really want popcorn. I want to find SlayerGrrl, Ani.

Such a nice name, Ani. Sounds soft, like her hair, like the skin on the back of her hand.

I head over to my place against the wall, pushing my back in hard until I can feel the cool concrete. Feels good. I watch as the lobby starts to clear. The 11.45pm movie's just started. Gearing up for the 12.15am show. Had to get here early. Make sure she's here, can only pull this once.

Palming the ticket in my hand, I turn my head as a group of girls walk into the lobby. Preppies. Not her.

I wait until another big mass of kids come through the doors, and I scan. Rooting through the crowd like a kid set on a hidden cookie jar. Blond guy, brunette, not her, guy, guy… bingo.

I throw my eyes to the floor. My heart leaps into my throat. Let her not see me let her not see me let her not see me.

It's her. I can feel her, like she has some sort of gravity of her own. My eyes are pulled to her. She's why I'm here. Probably never would have had the balls to try and pull this off if she didn't send me that email this morning. Damn.

She looks so good. She's wearing a short corduroy coat and tight jeans and black shirt. Nothing special. But the way she looks in them. It's like she just stole all my air. Now I'm stuck. Can't even breathe. It's gotta be like three hundred degrees in here.

Go, Ty, go. Go now. There's only one movie left. You know which theater it's gonna be in. She doesn't see me. She's with a guy and a girl. He's sort of a goth-looking guy with a crazy-ass mop of black spiked God-only-knows-what on his head and has chains all over his jacket. The other girl has long brown hair, real frizzy. But she must be good to talk to because SlayerGrrl just can't seem to talk to her enough.

How can she not see me? I bang my back into the wall again. Feeling the collision ride through my muscles, giving me strength. Then I push off. I go.

I hand my ticket over and look back over my shoulder, checking to see where she is. In line for popcorn. Cool. That gives me what, like six minutes? Ten? Maybe I should just wait until I know she's in the theater. I mean, maybe that guy she's here with will talk her into sneaking into a different film and she won't even...

Stay focused. I pull some gum out of my pocket and shove a few pieces into my mouth. Focus.

Why do they hang giant reels of film from the wall, really? Are any movies actually shot on film anymore? I thought they all went digital. That's a stupid way to decorate. *Akira* is showing in theater number six.

Following the arrows down the red carpeted halls, I find theater six. I move past it. Need to find the door that leads to...

EMPLOYEES ONLY. Just like CineNerd23 said. I pull my hood up further around my ears and turn the knob.

ANI

So despite being a complete waste of time, freshman English did at least introduce me to Seth Castigliano and Maura Sweeny. Maura and I are supposed to work together on a paper about freedom as represented in nineteenth-century French literature. Joy. But the good news is that she's really sweet and introduced me to Seth, one of the officers of the anime club. I work on the nights that the club meets, but Seth now makes sure that I get all the info on any fieldtrips. Like tonight's outing to see *Akira*.

Seth and Maura were nice enough to wait until I got off of work to head over to the theater so I wouldn't have to walk alone. They're both really into *Ghost in the Shell*, Maura even named her cat back home Batou, and it's clear that they're both much more into it than I am, but listening to them talk as we go sorts of sets me at ease. It's nice to be out, with people, doing normal college things. The rest of the club came over early and should be holding some seats for us inside. Seth's a nice guy, a little chubby for the super-goth look he prefers, but he's got an honest smile and is clearly crazy about Maura.

They are both great people, though, and it's nice to have something to do on a Saturday night.

I check my email again for like the sixth time this hour. God, I am such an idiot. I can't believe that message went through to Tyler. Now he's never going to email me again. Which is a good thing, I guess. There's a buzzing as I put the phone back in my pocket; I pull it out, look down.

I don't want another girl. I have nothing to talk about with other girls. I want to get to know YOU. –Tyler

Oh my God, I don't think I can breathe. I look at the ticket in my hand, do I go in? Or do I go find a quiet place to return Tyler's email?

TYLER

The staircase is narrow. Climb, just climb. The walls are cold, cold running up through my hands, into my heart. Please don't let me get caught.

I take my hand off the wall. Climb. The door to the projection booth is unlabeled. I lick my lips. Wipe the sweat off the top of my forehead with the back of my sleeve. Why did I wear this sweatshirt? Too hot. Gonna get heatstroke or something. I nudge the door open a sliver with my shoe. Can say I'm lost. If they ask. If they're here, then I'm just lost, is all.

"Hello?" I call through the sliver. Can't see anything. Don't really hear anything, either. Thought I would hear the slapping of film against reel. That's the way it sounds on TV. I guess not anymore. I open the door fully. "Hello?" I say again, a little louder.

Nothing. Just the regular purr of a room full of computers. Great. Perfect. The room is not as big as I thought it would be. No windows. No glass walls looking out over the screens. Just four walls and a bunch of computers. I walk over to the monitor and get to work.

Pulling out my phone, I open the email with CineNerd23's instructions. Hurry, Ty, hurry. They'll be back and you'll be caught and it'll all be over.

I bite my bottom lip and type in the codes as fast as I can. Was that a noise on the stairs?

Numb fingertips racing over the keyboard, I type the message. Clanking on the stairs. Heart in my throat and pulsing up through my ears, I wait. Loading… loading…

Can't this thing go any faster? Pulse so loud I think I'm gonna vomit from all the noise, I leap when the screen I need pops up. Thank you, God. I hit enter and run.

Throwing open the heavy old door, I pound down the stairs, each foot slamming into the concrete so that the impact rides up my legs, so that I feel it.

Then I'm in the hall. Breath quick. Did anyone see?

No. Don't think so. I'm the only one standing outside the EMPLOYEES ONLY door in the long hall with the red carpet and the stupid bags of fake popcorn hanging from the walls. Shit. Well, alright.

Deep breath. Count to ten. I force my feet to move… slowly… across the carpet… slowly… one foot in front of the other… left… right… slowly… calmly… and then I open the door to theater number six.

The ad loop is up. Is she here? Can't see in the dark. Shit. Should have thought of that. How will she know where I am? Will she even want to?

Scanning the crowd. Damn there are a lot of goths here. Them and nerds. Well, I guess that's who comes to the midnight showing of anime flicks. Where is SlayerGrrl, though? Where is Ani?

I can't decide which name I like better. SlayerGrrl makes her sound invincible, like some force of nature that can blow you over and just carry you off. I like that. I like everything about that.

Ani sounds like something sweet, something breakable, something precious. Something you want to hold and protect and whisper things to. Something to take care of and worship all at once. I like that, too.

My foot sticks and I pull it up. Stupid gum. Where is she? My eyes go back to the crowd. Goth, loser, nerd, nerd, fat guy, girl, bad hair.

Bad hair? That's the guy she was with. Next to him is the girl and next to her... SlayerGrrl. She's sitting two rows up from the center divide, talking to the girl with the long frizzy hair.

Steady. Now where do I sit? Behind her, in front? I didn't think about this part. Someplace close to the door, probably. In case I have to make a quick exit.

OK, well, next to the door. Pulling the hood up over my head, I try and hear, try and listen in to her conversation. I get nothing. Nothing at all. I press my back into the chair, hard, trying to feel, digging my feet hard into the cement floor. Shaking. Have to move, have to hear, have to wait.

First there's an ad for some car dealership. A photo of some guy in a nice shirt and pants standing in a parking lot full of nice cars, smiling. With balloons. There are always balloons in those ads. Wonder why that is. Then a picture of a local restaurant, trying to sell me steak. Does look good, though. Damn, I'm hungry, should have eaten something. Should have waited in line for that popcorn, at least.

What the hell is taking so long? Heart nipping at my ears. Shake shake shake, my foot can't go fast enough. I grip the armrests. What if they don't have time before the movie? What if they don't show it? Shake, shake, shake.

Then there it is. A big white screen. Big plain black letters:

SLAYERGRRL: WILL YOU SIT WITHE M? –TY

Shit! Fucking typos are you serious?! I am such a freaking loser. My foot goes ballistic and I stomp it into the floor. This is totally embarrassing. Now she's gonna laugh, gonna leave and I'm gonna get caught on some surveillance camera and have to have Mom bail me out of jail and I couldn't even spell the damn thing right this is such a freaking nightmare.

I can't stay. I grind my boots into the floor and leap out of my chair. I walk. Quickly. Out of the theater. People could be talking, they could be totally silent and I wouldn't know I just have to leave just have to go have to get out of here I never should have come this was a terrible idea.

I don't look at the red carpet, I don't look at the ticket guy pulling the sack of trash out of the can, I don't look at the big annoying bag of fake popcorn glued to the wall; I just look at the sign over the big double doors at the end of the hall that says EXIT. Throwing my shoulder into the door, I push my way through, feeling the cold air hit me like an aluminum bat in the face.

Doubling over, I wait. Wait until my stomach unclenches, until I can breathe again.

"Tyler?"

Great, now I'm hallucinating. The voice is gentle and sweet and edgy and *hers*.

"Tyler," she says again, and I feel pressure on my shoulder, I look up. Up into her sweet heart-like face and those pouty lips curving upward and her eyes, her eyes are like a whole other world. I stand up straighter. I should look at the ground or something, keep my cool, but I can't break myself away from those eyes. "How am I supposed to sit with you if you run out of the theater?"

I open my mouth. Words should come out of it. But they don't. My head races. She left. She's here. With me. Now. There is no re-entry once you leave. And now she's in the alley. The alley that's cold and full of boxes and overflowing dumpsters that smell like trash and old popcorn. What do I do? I should say something, at least. I lick my lips. Brain just not connecting with my mouth. Think, think, think. I shove my hands into the pockets of my sweatshirt, hard. Still, nothing. She's waiting. The curiosity in her eyes dimming... shit... I have to do something...

Her face sinks. She turns, she's gonna walk back into the theater.

"No!" I get out. Somehow. She can't leave. I grab her hand. It's soft and warm and... tiny. Delicate. Hot, hot, hot. Say something smart, Ty, smooth. "I'm hungry."

I *suck* at this.

She just stares. One eyebrow raises slightly, making the eyeshadow she's wearing catch the exit lights and sparkle. She's so pretty. She's standing there, but she's not leaving, which is good. I hope.

"Wanna get something to eat, maybe?" My words have a hell of a time getting out of my pinched throat. Please say yes please say yes ditch your friends and come with me and just eat just talk just sit...

She shrugs her shoulders, her breath frosting in the air, sparkling like glass. She looks like something magical. Like an angel. "OK."

It's after midnight and Books & Brew smells like people and coffee and dust, sounds like electronic jazz and hipsters pulling their cooler-than-thous, and looks like rows and rows of used books in lots of different languages polka-dotted with clusters of small tables and folding chairs. Tons and tons and tons of people. Only late-night café around. Don't freak, Ty. Relax, you can do this. She's here, right? But the noise and the pictures of old writers and musicians and three billion bulletin boards and the noise hit me old-school information-overload style and I look over at her. Her dark brown eyes roll over the three hundred names for caffeine and sugar scrawled in chalk on the board behind the counter. What does she drink? Is she old enough to like coffee?

That's stupid. She's in college. I hope she doesn't see any friends here and ditch me.

My eyes run over the people at the tables. Yalies, a lot of them, I bet. Pulling that cooler and smarter and richer routine on the older after-theater crowd.

I swipe the sweat off the top of my forehead. I don't belong here. I can't freaking pass Math and if she sees somebody she knows and talks to them they are going to know that I'm a–

"So, what do you want?" Her eyes are wide and her brow is raised and this is probably not the first time she's asked me.

My eyes rise to the board. "A large caramel macchiato."

Her brown eyes get even wider, and her sweet cherry of a mouth twists up at the corner. "That's like…"

Oh shit. Girly. It's girly, isn't it? That much sugar, that much milk. Shit. I should have asked for just a black coffee. Black coffee is plain, manly. Tastes like piss. But manly.

"That…" She pauses again and my throat clenches, waiting. "That sounds good, you know? I haven't had a caramel macchiato in a while."

Thank you, God. "Why?"

She looks at her feet, then over at the board again, not at me, not at my eyes, back down at her feet. "Julie… my sister… she's really weight-conscious. We always get iced skim lattes."

"She fat?" I ask. She's so close, next to me in line. She smells sweet and spicy, like not hippie spicy, but something darker, something different.

"No."

"Then why does she care?" My fingers ache. Reaching a little, wanting to hold her hand, to run my fingers up her arm and wrap around the back of her shoulders and hold her.

"I don't know, it's easy to gain weight and…" Her voice drifts off, like she's hearing herself and not liking the sound. "We're from California."

Like that explains everything. Girls are weird. I look down her body, fitted jacket, tight jeans, she's real thin. Not like scary thin, but thin. I say, "You should try one, you'd look good with a few extra pounds."

Her face looks like I stung her. Shit. My face heats up, burns. So many books. Can't one just like fall on my head and put me out of my misery? Please? Her hand is so close, hanging by her side.

"Two large caramel macchiatos, please." Her voice sounds strong. Lifted. Like a rocket. Strong and excited and makes my stomach challenge gravity.

"And a piece of cake," I add. Just for good measure. I grab her hand, and pull her over to the other side of the bar.

She feels great. Soft and small and strong and absolutely perfect.

ANI

Is this good? He's holding my hand and my heart is out of control. This is bad, I mean good. I don't know. It feels good, but Mr Anderson. What if I'm wrong? What if Mr Anderson will care and will turn me in?

But here we are, here I am. With a boy. A real boy who is cute and actually isn't afraid to be seen with me, a boy who *wants* to be here with me. This is crazy. Julie will never, ever believe me when I tell her. My heart jumps just thinking about it. Even though I know that I shouldn't care, should just leave, I can't. He looks at me like I am someone worth being seen. And that's something worth hanging around for, even if Mr Anderson doesn't like it. It deserves a coffee and a chance, anyway.

"Wanna sit?" he asks as he drops my hand to grab the coffees and cake. We weave our way through the crowds to a table sandwiched between the brick wall punctured by pots full of ferns and a floor-to-ceiling wall of glass. The glass picks up Tyler's reflection as we sit, and I accidentally hit the guy behind me when I pull out my chair.

Tyler sits, his muscular legs stretched out beneath the table. He's so hot; long, light brown hair hanging down to the base of his chin, and his features look like he might be part-Cherokee or something. He's certainly built more like a warrior than a gamer. I could just sit here and stare at him. He doesn't even have to talk, really. And wouldn't that be an easy way to avoid running into trouble with Mr Anderson? Just sit here and admire the boy who thinks I'm not fat enough of all things.

His eyes are everywhere at once, like he's scanning for signals, patterns. "So, Ani…" he starts, voice breaking, knee bobbing up and down, making the table shake. "Tell me what it was like to school ILG."

His smile is slight, addictive, heat slides from my head down… lower and my shoulders relax. Well, isn't he just the smartest boy ever? Going right for my sweet spot. How does he do that? See right through the things that no one else can manage to get past. I sigh, take a sip of my drink, enjoying the decadence of it, wondering if this is why Julie was always telling me to date, to take one of those geeks from programming and drag him out to dances, to the prom. I look into his dark eyes and my heart short-circuits. "Great, I guess, the same that it did for you the year after I did it."

"Nah, it's not the same, you were the first to do it solo, and you're a girl."

"What does being a girl have to do with anything?"

"Everything. Guys can be dicks, you know, I know the way they talked to you. You knew the shit the crowd was saying, and you just kept winning, like you didn't even hear."

"I didn't hear." I knew, of course. "My sister would tell me what the crowd would say when I was plugged in, but I had them all tuned out. I just wanted to play, you know?"

"You were amazing." He sips his coffee and stares at me, smile reaching his eyes and lingering there. "Still are, and now you're designing the games. It's unbelievable, I mean, most people will complain when they play games and all, this should be faster or the graphics should be sharper, but most of them have no idea how to make them faster, clearer, much less design *World of Fire*. Now a whole sim program? It's crazy."

"Not so crazy."

"It is, though, it's awesome." He drops his gaze back to the table, which is moving a little bit because his legs are shaking beneath it. "How did you get started designing the games?"

"My Math teacher, Ms Bellerwin." My throat feels heavy as I think of her. "She was the best. She went to MIT, and she ran the computer lab in my middle school. I'd hang out there after school to get my homework done, and after a while she started showing me how to do things. It was great, she was always taking the things apart and rebuilding them, plugging in and typing code. I thought it was the coolest thing ever, you know? Whenever she would put something back together, or spend a few hours working, you could see the improvements right away, she'd have made something new, or something old better. It was like magic. So I started helping her out. When I went over to the high school, I used to go back and help her run the computer club."

"She must be really proud now, with Yale and all." His leg is moving and he leans back in his chair, like he's trying to keep his leg under control by pushing it into the floor for leverage. "Not to mention your parents. They must be telling all their friends about their kid in the Ivy League."

"I guess." It hurts to fill my lungs, but I try. "My mom's not happy with anything I do. She's not really happy with anyone. Dad was deployed, sent to Afghanistan, now he's in jail for assault. He got pulled over for a seatbelt check one night, he" – the words are like lead leaving my tongue, falling into the unknown – "got confused, flashed back or something and he attacked the officers. Mom had thrown him out two nights before, so he was really upset." My eyes sting and before I know it the pools of tears weigh down my lashes. It's not Dad's fault; he's sick, he came back from Afghanistan sick and they don't help him. He spent two years away from his family to serve in the war and nobody cares, they just leave him in jail to rot.

"Hey." He grabs my hand across the table. "It's not his fault, OK? Wherever he is, once he gets better he's gonna be crazy proud of you." His eyes, oh God, his eyes look like they can see straight through me. "He'd be stupid not to be."

"Sorry, I just get…"

"Don't apologize. You've got nothing to be sorry for," he says, his knee making the table wobble like an electric toothbrush. He looks at the edge of the empty cake plate, bites his lower lip, and says, "My brother's in rehab trying to kick heroin. Can't pick your family, right?"

Just like that, as easy as typing in a favorite password, our darkest family secrets are out, sitting between us on the table. Bits of our lives that make us who we are, out, open, acknowledged. "Guess not."

"Are you going to answer that text?"

What? I look down at my purse and my phone is pinging. "Sorry." I mutter and grab the phone out of the bag. I check the message, send a quick OK in response and tuck the thing back into the folds of my bag.

"Do you need to call them back?" He asks, eyes raised and he plays idly with the fork on the table.

"No, it's just Mr. Anderson sending me the route coordinates to program into the game, I swear he never sleeps," I say. Oh no, wait, I told myself that we weren't going to talk about the-

"Waypoints? Like where the sim has the drones flying?" His eyes are up, meeting mine, like he's looking for something.

"Those are the ones." What's the point in stopping the conversation now? He flies the thing, it's not like knowing how it works is really that big of a deal. It's not like I'm giving him any sort of information that would give him an advantage. That would be wrong.

"I thought those were computer-generated?"

"Nope. Mr Anderson sends them to me daily, I put them in."

"If he had you design the program for the simulations, why didn't he have you generate a program that randomly picks coordinates?"

I shrug and take the flimsy plastic top off of my cup of coffee so I can get the pile of foamed milk and cinnamon up from the bottom. "He says that it maintains authenticity or something."

"So you're SKY?"

"Yeah, I guess I am." I shake my head. "Well, not really. Only for the set targets. The road patrols, which I think are like eighty percent of the program, are on a pre-programmed route."

"And it's not your voice that makes the call through the headset," he says, leaning forward over the small round table just a little. His full lips twist up a bit at the corner into a sneaky smile.

"No."

"I wish it was." Something in the way he says it, in the timbre of his voice, makes me shiver. I look at my cup as I put it back on the table with shaking hands. Grabbing the napkin, I twist it around my finger.

His smile grows as he watches me wrap the napkin up and around and down my fingers. Feeling warm, I tilt my head to the side. His face turns, eyes zeroed in on me and way down inside of me, something aches, sort of like a drive to get up and cross the table and...

He cocks his eyebrow up and stares at me as if he's uncertain, then he abruptly pushes back his chair. "I gotta go. Last bus home leaves in like ten minutes. But I really want your number, if you'll give it to me."

Right. Yes. Of course. I stand up and say the numbers without thinking, too lost in watching his thick, beautiful lashes as he programs the info into his phone. Tyler slips his phone back into his pocket and reaches around me, holding open the door as we step outside, the night air turning cold.

We stand there. I have to go across the street and he has to go towards the town green for the bus. But neither of us moves. Neither of us wants to go, I guess, I hope. What do I say now? I am terrible at this. Goodnight? Do I kiss him? Maybe just on the cheek. This isn't really a date, but still. He certainly looks pretty kissable, *really* kissable. I wrap my arms across my chest and look down at my feet.

"Thanks," he says and I look up. His cheeks are red but that could be from the cold. They look so sultry, though, that color... his skin is so olive that the red just makes his whole face look, wild, edible almost. What is wrong with me? I should be kissing him.

He leans over, reaching out his hand to shake. I don't think. I grab his hand and yank him towards me, reach up on my toes, and kiss him square on the mouth. His lips are soft and shaking and taste sweet like caramel and cinnamon. Oh God, am I doing this wrong? Why isn't he responding? He just...

His shoulders unclench and his large hands wind their way around my waist and he pulls me closer. Closer. Fire races to my center. I part my lips and he comes in, closer, heat rushing up in waves. His tongue touches mine. Closer, Tyler, pull me closer. I snake my arm up behind his head and run my fingers through the delicate strands of his hair. Wanting more.

But he pulls away, eyes and lips looking heated, looking blissed out. "So, will you take my calls?"

I nod, not really certain whether or not I would be able to speak even if I wanted to.

TYLER

Holy. Shit. She's kissing me.

It can't be. My throat is tight and my head blows right off the top of my head but I don't feel anything except shaken and blown and oh my God she's so close, so soft and then my head is up in space again and I can't... should I put my hands somewhere... should I open my mouth... oh man, now her tongue and I think I am going to pass the fuck out. Grab her, Ty, just grab her and bring her closer and make sure she doesn't stop and doesn't back away but she is so sweet I want to just stay here forever and not move another inch for the rest of my...

Then it's gone. She's looking up at me with this smile. Oh man that smile that says she wants more and that she's happy but she's not sure if she's gonna give me anymore and that she might make me beg. Which, well, damn, I might just beg if it means we can do that again.

No, Ty! Walk. Away. Bus. Need to catch the bus or you are stuck in the city. Maybe I can crash at her place. The wind whips my hair into my cheeks and I feel kinda cold now that she's not with me, holding me anymore. Play it cool. B would be cool. He would say something perfect and have her dreaming about what he meant for days.

I look down at her. Her eyes are all like half-shadowed and heavy looking, her lips look a little raw, open, just a little like she wants me to... wants me...

Think. I want to say something hot, something memorable, but all that comes out is something totally lame about her taking my calls and missing the bus. I am such a loser.

Can't stay pissed at myself, though. Cause she kissed me. She. Kissed. Me.

As I walk past the homeless guys on the town green I smile. Not at them, really, just at everything. It doesn't matter if the city is dark and that those guys are sleeping in boxes and smell bad and could have knives or whatever. One yells something at me, chases after me waving his hands, and I run. Feet grinding into the pavement, I feel great. It's cold and the city smells rank like old urine and rotting leaves and overripe dumpsters, but I run across the green and pass the old churches that look out of place surrounded by tall, neutered skyscrapers and just for a second I swear I could fly. Can't not feel ecstatic when I finally slow down and drop into one of the frigid-ass benches of my bus stop.

Nope. Can't sit. The bench is too cold and bites at my ass so I stand and pace. Walk over to the map hanging inside the plexiglass beneath the old canopy. I kick at some papers lying at the bottom of the post.

A grunt. Oh shit. Is there a person in those papers? Don't look, Ty, it's rude. But I do. Can't help it. A grubby hand reaches out and readjusts the papers. No. Focus on the bus. The bus will be here soon. Some homeless guy is not my problem. The nervous laughs of a few drunk college kids rise up over the quiet whoosh of cars driving through stoplights turned off hours ago.

I could probably see his face if I looked really hard. He's facing me. This bus stop is a really shitty place to live, stinking of diesel and rot and body odor. I lean forward. Streetlight filters in. In from the street, and if I move I might be able to make out his...

Shit. He's young, man. Real young. Not like a kid or anything but too young to live here. Drugs. Has to be drugs. Why else would this guy be here and not in a hospital or shelter or at a home or something?

Headlights hit him in the face as the bus, my bus, turns the corner and rolls our way.

He doesn't move. Looking back at the bus as the brakes squeal and the metal undercarriage grinds to a halt in front of us, I dig my hand deep in my pockets so

I won't move them. Won't throw him the money that I want to give. Knowing that it won't buy him anything other than the next hit.

The papers around him shift and I run to the bus, trying to erase the memory of him as fast as I can. But I can't. It all comes up like a vomitfest of worry. Whose brother is he? How could a boy let his brother just lie there, in the street? Like I did. When he left. How could a mother? Like she did. But we found him. He is safe and he is not here and this is not him and you can't take him home can't make somebody care who doesn't but what if there is some boy lying awake in bed because he doesn't know where his brother is and if he's alive or dead or here living in a shithole bus station?

I beat them down, the questions that sleep inside me and wait for the right time to wake up and eat me raw. I climb the stairs of the bus and plop down into one of the blue seats near the front that always seem to feel sort of slimy but at least give you enough room to push your legs out and dig your feet in to the round hump of the wheel cover.

My eyes can't help themselves. They go back to the pile of papers. Like my eyes are on autopilot, taking me back to just the thing I want to ignore. What I want to never see. To never see ever again.

I would rather see Brandon dead than like that again.

CHAPTER 13

MONDAY, OCTOBER 8

TYLER

It's too brown. Too many different shades of brown just stretching on for miles and miles and miles. Does that part of the world really look like that or is it just the sim? Damn. They need to plant some serious trees there or something. Well, I guess they do have some trees, but even they are sickly and thin and barren just like the rest of the place. No wonder they blow so much shit up. Sick of staring at acres of sand.

The sim keeps my drones on their routine flight pattern. Bored. Really. Bored. These surveillance missions just seem to last for hours and nothing ever happens. But it's cool that SlayerGrrl programs in the coordinates. Makes me feel like she's close to me. Like she's here, somewhere, in this program, in the calls. Makes me feel OK with the boredom. Getting close to ten hours for the week. And the week just started yesterday. Ten hours of nothing happening is a lot to take, though.

I get up and stretch my legs, it's like what, 3am? Right. Late. I should turn this thing off and get some–

A tiny flash in the far right-hand corner. On the central screen. Change of call. I pick up the headset. "Bravo one, this is whiskey three. Radio check, over."

Huh? The game is evolving, I guess. I say, "Whiskey three, this is bravo one, read you loud and clear, over."

"Requesting immediate CAS, advise, danger close, over." The guy sounds hurried, like a real dude requesting close air support. Their sound programs are getting better. SlayerGrrl's program rocks.

"Whiskey three, request confirmed, gimme an address."

"Bravo one, say again? Over." He sounds pissed. Totally real.

Shit, what was the... right. "Um... Whiskey three, request coordinates, over."

"Bravo one, hostiles at X24F and X45G." His voice is rushed, tight. Shit, how did they program that? Actors? "Friendlies in building at X37G. Pinned down. Taking fire from north and west, RPGs and small arms, over."

His voice is muffled on the other end of the line. I hear screaming and small-arms fire and someone shouting to someone else to get down. A bigger explosive sound must be coming from the rocket-propelled grenade. Fuck, this upgrade is tight.

I check the drones. Three close to the designated targets. "Pulling tail 403 and tail 416 off of designated route G72, wait one." I type in code and program in the new route. "Whiskey three, this is bravo one, request confirmed, strike inbound, ETA six minutes, over."

403's new destination pops up about 120 degrees left. Banking hard, I initiate a gradual descent. Giving altitude, gaining airspeed. Max throttle, approaching 130 mph. From seventeen thousand feet, the wide-view displays little more than mountains and half-assed scrub trees. But I remember there's a village just over the horizon…

Toggle over to 416. Set the course, max throttle. Inbound three minutes.

None of the other missions were anything like this.

"Bravo one, be advised, big purple on our roof, over," he says. My heartbeat amps up as he speaks. He's putting purple smoke on their building so I can pinpoint their location. "Hostiles to our north and west. Requesting visual confirmation of goofy grape, over."

He wants to make sure I don't drop a Hellfire on his roof.

I log into the data collection system. Try to find the nearest satellite to attempt to get a real-time view of their location so I can set my targets. There's one, satellite 7T5NUSA. Punching in my memorized access code, I pull up a live view of the village with X37G centered. A purple cloud is billowing eastward off of the roof of Whiskey's exact location.

"Whiskey three, this is bravo one, I have eyes on big purple, over," I say.

"Bravo one, you are cleared hot. Repeat, you are cleared hot, engage hostiles, over."

Small black figure on the top of adjacent building. Code in and zoom, I target set the loser and call him target one. Paint him red. Done. Find target two.

403 and 416 approaching fast. I type target one's hit code into drone 416 and then go back to the sim's real-time satellite view. Type in the building locations where the grenades seem to have come from – looks like a shed. Cool. Toggle back to drone view, initiate targeting sequence for drone 403 and paint it red, set target two.

Heart racing. I get a visual on fire between our guys and a building with a big domelike oven out behind it a little further down the block. It's tall, like three stories high, that same ugly brown concrete and looks like it's half torn apart already. Small fence, probably wood, in front and approximately five hundred feet from the smaller building spewing a purple cloud.

Coding in the laser target, I hit the timing mechanism so that the Hellfires will hit at approximately the same time, give or take a differential of... look at the timer screen... eight seconds. That's too long. Two minutes inbound. I re-program the codes, trying to get a hit at a tighter... yes! Differential lowered to four seconds.

Pulling the safety off the firing mechanisms, I make the calls into the machine for the Hellfires. Waiting for the exact "go" moment to get the time differential that I need. Fingers hovering over the keys, waiting, shaking. Ninety seconds. Pause, inhale, exhale.

Waiting's hard. I think of the time Rick took me to the firing range. Shot his 9mm Glock. The way it felt in my hand. How Rick had me pause and control my breathing. Feel the lethal weight of the gun. Target only when perfectly calm. Perfectly focused. The grip of the gun. The feel of the controller. Breathe.

"Whiskey three, this is bravo one, strike package inbound. ETA thirty seconds, over."

Laser set, laser ready, lasing. My heart pounds, thrumming in my ears. Damn I feel so alive. Weapon set, weapon ready, firing.

Wait… wait… wait… The drone view is a thing of beauty, with only a four-second lag on the satellite view. The building blows. Gray-brown smoke rising, then the sniper, he stays right where he is, a blurb of bland browns and khakis and now there's a cloud and he's gone, the building is gone. Soldiers, our soldiers, leave their location and take care of the man that jumped from the windows of the building as it blew and the one running from the shed.

The rush rises up from my heart and makes my fingers shake and my breath all wild like a laugh.

Whiskey three comes back on, over the headset, which is unusual, but then this whole mission was unusual. Must be changing, upgrading.

"Bravo one, thanks, you just saved our asses, out." His voice is high and full of something that I never thought was possible to program into a computer… relief.

Is she going to answer? I hope she gave me the right number. B said to wait a few days before I called her. It's been like a day and a half. That's like a few, right? Or should it have only been the full two? What if I should have called yesterday?

She gave me the wrong number. It's been like five rings already. I mean, she kissed me and all, you'd think she'd give me the right number, or was that before the kiss? What if the kiss sucked so bad that she changed her number?

"Hello?"

Her voice. Shit, now what do I say? "Hey."

Silence. Fuck, this is hard. Ideas, ideas, quick I need ideas. I look at the poster hanging on my wall, Miss January. Well, that's not going to help. "Have you been making changes to the game? I had this pretty tight mission and thought I'd let you know."

"We're always making upgrades, we do it daily."

Quick, think of something else, something smart, thoughtful, Yale-like. "Um, I went to Pepe's for pizza last night. You been?"

I sound like a fucking moron. Moron! You'd think there'd be a book, like dating for dumbasses or something.

"No, I hear it's good, though."

Well, alright. She hasn't hung up yet, at least, that's good. "It is. It's like a New Haven landmark and all. Didn't they take you on any tours of the town or something for college orientation?"

"They did, just not of pizza places."

"That sucks." I lay back on my bed, looking up at the ceiling. How come ceilings always look like they have sand mixed in with the paint like that? Wait. I stand up and grab my wallet off the desk. I look at the clock. It's 4.30pm. "Are you done with classes today?"

"Yeah, why?"

"Text me your address, I'll be there in half an hour," I say.

●●●●

"You have to be kidding me," Ani says as I place the order. "We're really going to eat three small pizzas? Just the two of us?"

"Hell yeah. This is one of the best pizza places on the planet. You have to try the margherita, the sausage and the clam."

"Why three separate pizzas, though? Why not just get one with the three different toppings?"

"Because then the flavors mix together. Mess everything up. Has to be three different pies." Damn, it smells good in here.

"How much pizza do you expect me to eat, exactly?"

"At least one slice of each pie here, then we go to Sally's." I take a sip of my root beer. Love root beer with pizza. "Think of it as like a pizza taste-test."

"I don't know if I'm going to make it. That's a lot of food." She's wearing this pink sweater that makes her skin look too soft to even be real, and her brown hair is pulled back in a braid, the bleached strand left out and tucked behind her ear.

"Oh, you will. And then we'll go out for cannolis." The brick and candles and gleaming wood floors mix with the smell of pizza and garlic and the noise from tables full with college kids and business executives and families as they set the day behind them and sit down for dinner. I have to lean in close across the table to hear her when she speaks. It's kind of nice.

"I think that there has to be some rule against carb-loading like this, it's unnatural."

"You're only saying that because you haven't tried it yet." My knees hit the leg of the table, I shift them around and the waitress shoots me a dirty look for blocking the tiny path between the tables. "Tonight is going to change the way you see pizza for the rest of your life."

"We'll see." She shakes her head and her ears flush pink. I like her ears. Not too big. Pretty.

"You have nice ears." Oh shit. I didn't just say that out loud, did I?

"Um, thanks?"

"Can't believe I just said that. It's just they have this shape. Nice shape. Pink." Crap. I suck at this. Shoving the straw from the root beer into my mouth, I look at the table. Not at her. God, she's gonna get up and leave. I'm such an idiot. Change the subject. Change it quick. "So, why do you call Rick Mr Anderson?"

She raises an eyebrow. She answers, "Because he's my boss."

"It's weird." Great. Now I just said something she did was weird. This so isn't going like I wanted it to. "And where did you get the phrase 'goofy grape' for the sim? I had to Google that – it's like Vietnam-era or whatever. You might want to update that term before the sim goes into use."

"What are you talking about?"

"In the sim… never mind." Great. Now I've broken two rules. One, never insult a girl you want to impress, and two, talking about the program. Why is taking a girl out for pizza so freaking hard? Talk about her. Bring it back to her. "Your dad was in Afghanistan?"

"Yeah, with the Army."

"Why'd he join? Was he like career or something?"

"No, he was laid off and couldn't find another job. The Army would pay him, pay for more school when he came home, so he joined." She pushes her glass around with her fingers. Her eyes on her napkin. Not on me. OK. Change the subject.

"So, you miss LA?" I ask.

"I miss the weather, definitely. And my sister, she's at UCLA."

"What's she studying?"

"I don't know if she's studying anything, really. I think Julie sees college as a way to kill time before some big producer finds her and decides to make her a star."

I laugh and she smiles and my heart sort of jumps. "So what's next for *World of Fire*? You're gonna make more, right?"

"I want to, but the storyline is kind of getting away from me. I don't really know where I want it to go."

"Tell me," I say.

"Well, I have Janra rescue Philus at the end. So what's next? I mean, she extinguished the fire, right?"

"Well, yeah, so have her have to battle her way through a world of ice or something."

She coughs on her soda. "You think it would be that easy?"

"Why not? It's your world." By the time the small pizza is placed on the table in front of us, we've kind of outlined a rough plot for the next three *World of Fire* games. I actually *like* talking to her. My mouth waters. Ani's face wrinkles as she eyeballs the globs of mashed potatoes on the pizza. But she slides a slice of pizza off of the pan and onto her plate. She cuts off a bite-sized piece. Gives me a wary look. She's so cute. "I don't know about this," she says.

"Trust me."

She puts the piece of pizza in her mouth, eyes slowly closing as she chews. Her face softens, glows, even, with surprise, and when she opens her eyes again, she's beaming. "Oh my God, that pizza is unbelievable."

She stuffs another piece in her mouth and I grab a slice. "And we're just getting started."

ANI

How did we get from eating all that pizza to running around in Wooster Square? I feel the touch of his hand as he tags me and bolts over a bench. "C'mon," he calls to me.

Oh, right, the espresso he insisted that we have with the cannolis at that last café. What does that make it, then, four restaurants, total? My stomach might just pop. I run to chase after him, he's just a flash of movement beneath the lights of the park, but my side cramps up. "Ouch. Tyler, we have to stop. I think I'm going to throw up." That would be so like me, though. Vomit on my first real date? Julie would never let me live it down.

"Not a chance. Well, maybe a small chance." Another flash and he's got his arms wrapped around me from behind. I stiffen, then let myself relax, let the lingering scents of wood smoke and pizza soften my shoulders, let him hug me. We stand in the middle of the square, the sound of cars and the people walking home from evening mass at the church washing away as we stand beneath the moonlight. His lips brush the side of my forehead. "So, which was your favorite? Sally's or Pepe's?"

"I can't decide."

"What do you mean you can't decide? Everyone in the area has to have an opinion. Stamp it on your driver's license and everything." He smiles and it's as if he's lit from within.

"I mean I can't decide. We might need a do-over."

He pulls me closer. "Guess we'll have to do it over, then. Maybe tomorrow?"

"Guess so." I rest the back of my head against his shoulder. He wants to see me again. Tomorrow. My heart races. "It's late, where did we leave the car?"

"Forget the car. I don't want to go back yet," he says.

Leaves falling from the cherry trees of the park catch in our hair and I turn, reaching my hands up around his neck. I stand on the tip of my toes and I kiss him, honeyed sparks shooting straight through to the tips of my fingers, lost completely to everything else in the world.

CHAPTER 14

WEDNESDAY, OCTOBER 10

TYLER

"Mom would freak out if she knew I went to class without any makeup," Ani says. I love hearing her voice. Love it. It's even better when she's actually next to me. When I can feel her breath on my skin. Look her in the eyes.

But I'll videochat if I have to.

"Your mom sounds like she has issues. What the hell do you need makeup for?" I put the laptop on the kitchen island as I grab the milk out of the fridge. So hungry. Need some cereal or something. "What time is your class again?"

"I should head over to class now, actually. Talk to you later, OK?"

"Yeah, bye." I close the fridge and end the connection. Is that Mom's car? I walk over to the window. Mom's talking with Rick. On the driveway.

I open the door, balancing a bowl of cereal in one hand. "Hey, guys."

It takes a fraction of a second for Rick's smile to take over his face. He wasn't expecting me to be home. Mom's trunk is open and she places a bag in Rick's arms. She says, "Tyler. I thought you'd be out with that girl."

Oh no. Don't say Ani, please don't remember, I only mentioned it once. Rick will be pissed if I broke his rule. Might take away the sim. Can't take away the sim. I need it. Please forget.

Mom stares over at the neighbor's lawn. They're running their sprinklers. In October. Not sure why they'd do that. I can feel the weight of Rick's gaze on my face. Physically feel it as Mom says, "What was her name again, honey? Samantha?"

Samantha was the name of a girl Brandon dated like four years ago. "Yeah," I say. "Samantha." Relief so strong it almost hurts. But, "What are you doing home, Mom, it's only like 4 o'clock."

And what is Rick doing here with her? Did he know I'd be home? Rick's arms are full of grocery bags, and he brushes past me into the house. If he was secretly into my mom, he would at least blush or some shit, right? He can't be into her. They were on the driveway. Must have just run into each other. My hands clench.

"Samantha, Tyler? That's great," he says with a grin.

Mom rustles around in the trunk with the bags.

I say, "Forget Samantha, what are you doing here?"

"Your mom called me" – he walks into the kitchen and puts the bags down on the counter – "she's worried about you dropping out. She asked me to meet her for coffee so we could talk about your options going forward."

Are his cheeks red? Are they fucking red? "Coffee?"

He lowers his voice. "I've been your mentor for two years, Tyler, I've been telling her for just about as long that I'm here for her, too. She's concerned about your future. Thinks she's failing you as a mother. It's a good thing that she's starting to reach out, starting to talk to someone about what's eating at her."

I look into the bag Rick carried in. It's full. Full of boxes of citrus fruit snacks. Brandon's favorite. I hate them. She hates them. We have a cabinet full of them already. Waiting for him to get better. Waiting for him to come home.

"This is the first time she's called you?" I ask as Mom walks through the door. She looks tired. She drops the bags in the front hall and goes back out to the car to grab some more.

"Yes, but I hope it's not the last. Does she have any friends, Ty, anyone she talks to?" I shake my head no. "She's frightened and depressed and feels like she's all alone. I'm glad she's finally reaching out."

"Yeah" – I hear the hope in his voice. If Mom could get better, if she could smile, like really smile again – "me, too."

We walk outside together, to help Mom carry in the rest of the bags.

CHAPTER 15

FRIDAY, OCTOBER 12

ANI

I shouldn't be doing this, should I? Still, my homework is done and that paper for Spanish isn't due until Monday so I can stop by... right? No. Probably looks too desperate. We've been talking every day but he has the sim to fly and homework to do so maybe I should just get off the bus here and turn around and go back to campus.

He doesn't strike me as particularly studious, though. Watching as the gray bus wheels along route ten, my heart jumps up just a little as I pull the string.

The bus stop isn't far from his house, and the walk down the tree-lined street is pleasant. Smells of burning leaves and the noise from an army of leaf blowers greet me as I go. The air is slightly damp, like it's threatening rain, and I find his house, walk up the broken concrete path to the door. This is fine, I'm almost certain that Mr Anderson can check my email, and it's not like I've been hiding my communication with Tyler. I didn't set up a Hushmail account or anything.

If he hasn't said anything about it yet, then it must be OK. I haven't been feeding Tyler any code, haven't been helping with the sim. I'm not really brave enough to *talk* to Mr Anderson about it or anything, but maybe as long as I don't help Tyler with the sim then our relationship falls into a sort of Haranco *don't ask, don't tell* policy. Maybe. Probably.

I take a deep breath and tell myself that everything will be fine. I can't come all the way out here and not ring the doorbell. I ring the bell and wait.

There's no answer. OK, this is bad, is this bad? My fingers move over the button again, feeling its chalky texture and pausing, waiting.

He opens the door and his face with those high cheekbones and bronzed skin registers shock. Oh, no, what does that mean? But then the look of surprise fades into the shy smile that I can't seem to stop thinking about. "Ani." His smile widens as he checks out my outfit. I hope he likes it: I borrowed Christy's really tight jeans and went to Victoria's this afternoon to get one of those push-ups that dig into your shoulders so that they can lift your boobs into the stratosphere. His smile gets even wider as his eyes return to meet mine. "Wanna come in?"

"Yeah, thanks." He moves aside and makes room for me as I go. My foot hits an old boot lying on the ground and I fall right into him. Grabbing at him to keep myself steady, he winces in pain before I'm caught by his arms. My God, those biceps. I tremble as he steadies me.

"You OK?" he asks. My heart jumps. He's so big and so cute and I can't believe that I just fell and he must think I'm a total idiot. I nod, eyes staying steady on his full, soft lips.

"Why me, Tyler? I mean, out of all the girls that you've met, why me?" I ask before I even know what I'm saying.

He looks down at my shoulder, eyes lingering there, like he's trying to find an answer hiding somewhere in the strands of my hair. "My world, Ani, it's so... dark, sometimes." He looks me in the eyes. "And whenever you're around, you light everything up. You make everything seem less... hopeless."

I grab him, digging my hands into the flesh of his muscled back, and kiss him.

He shuts the door.

TYLER

The machine. Something, a woman's voice is saying something on the answering machine. Voice turned all tinny echoing through the empty house. Don't want to hear. Don't want to know. Want to stay right here.

Ani pulls back, looks up at me with those heavy lids and that look that just screams totally sexy. "Are you gonna answer that?" she asks. Voice low, slick, hot.

Kiss her, kiss her again and again and again. Heart flying, head spinning and hands trembling, I shake my head no.

She still has her shirt on but the sleeve is halfway down her shoulder. Nice shoulder, round and tanned and firm. My head moves towards it and I kiss her shoulder, her neck, my hands roam over her body and I tug at her shirt to move it up, move it off.

She arches her back and I kiss lower, moving my hands over her tits. Damn. How do I get this bra off, anyway?

I kiss them right through the shirt and she moans and I think I might literally die.

The phone rings again. This time it's my cell and it's in my pocket and sort of hurts when it rings. Ani backs away from me. Gives me a lame smile. Shit. Now I'm gonna look like a moron if I don't take the call.

Sighing, I pull the phone out. "Yeah, what is it?"

My shirt is lying next to Ani on the bed and she looks at my chest and I am so freaking hot right now this better be good.

It's Knesha from the Rehab Center. Sounds like she's talking from underneath the ocean. Can't make out a freaking word she is saying. Nothing. Just static and dribble and words that come out in a collection of sounds that don't work when they're pieced together. Shit. Check for the payment must be late. Knesha always gives me a heads up. "Knesha, I can't hear you. Call me back when you have better reception, OK?"

I shut the phone and look at Ani, SlayerGrrl, on my bed… waiting… She smiles as her eyes leave my abs and come back to my eyes… I am so going to…

The phone rings again. This time the one in the kitchen. I want to rip it right out of the damn wall and send it flying. Ani smiles. "Must be important."

The shrill sound of the ring reverberates through the house, like a bird pecking out my brain, and each time it rings feels like a punch to teeth.

Ani hands me my shirt. "Get it, Ty. I should get going anyway."

Shit. Not what I wanted to hear. "But you just got here." I take my shirt, wanting to rip it to shreds but pulling it down over my shoulders instead and stomp out of the room. The kitchen isn't far down the hall but the ring sounds different in here, like it floats up into the air of the high ceilings a little more and I want to just calm down because I don't want to snap at Knesha. She has no idea that she's calling at a bad time and wouldn't call if it wasn't important shit, but is it important? I pick up the phone. "Yeah, Knesha, what's up?"

"Tyler." Her voice is lost, floating away from me and just like that I'm not mad anymore. "I'm callin' with some bad news."

My heart seizes, balls up in a painful clench, waiting, just waiting, for a blow that I know is coming. I can't say it. Don't want to say it. My throat closes up, spit going salty and my legs feel weak, sea-weak. Don't say it. I don't want to know. But I do. "Brandon?"

My voice. Can't believe that I could say it. It was only one word but it sounded so small, so unsteady, so painful that it is hard to believe that she heard me. But I know she did. Now the word hangs in the air between us. One word. Five heartbeats. One little boy who will just curl up and die if she says...

"He left."

Her words hit me like a sledgehammer. Right in the stomach. She doesn't stop, either.

"He failed a drugs test this morning and just walked out." Her words fall together like beads on a string, each one hitting the other as they go, each one hitting hard. So nice, Knesha, always smiles at me when I go to the center. She shouldn't be calling, even. A doctor usually does, calls all cold and not like Knesha, not sweet, not caring. "We don't know how he got any drugs in here, but I'm sure he'll be callin' you soon, so don't go worrying. Let me know if there is anything I can do for you, shug, OK? Even if you just need to talk."

Numb. Just for one second I can't feel. Can't think but to say "thanks" and I hang up the phone. Hang it up and stare at it. Stare at the phone like it has some sort of code that will make any of this make sense. Any of it.

Three thousand thoughts hammer me all at once and my lungs keep catching and my heart dissolves and bubbles up and fills my whole ribcage with pain and I want to just scream and I can't. Can't do anything.

"Tyler." Her hands touch my shoulder, softly, like an angel. "You OK? What's going on?"

I look into her dark eyes. Beautiful eyes in the delicate face and her sweet cherry lips. So beautiful. Tell her. Tell her that he's gone and you can't find him. Tell her that he's as good as dead. Tell her that he lied again and again and again and you thought that it couldn't hurt you anymore.

My legs shake. I kick them into the base of the cabinets, making the dishes next to the sink clink. Can't she tell? Can't she see? Could she help?

"Tyler?" she asks again. She takes a step closer to me.

Backing away, I take a deep breath. Put my eyes on the tile floor. Words get stuck in my throat. Too many words. Too much pain. Pain moving too fast inside my skull to be able to catch and put into words and get out through my mouth. Too hard. He lied he lied he lied.

Throat tight, breath short, I say, "I have to go."

She doesn't leave. Why doesn't she leave? Isn't she scared? Should be scared. Instead, she takes a step closer and I feel her arms wrapping themselves around me and pulling me to her. Don't want to go. Can't. I break away.

Color leaves her face in a quick rush. Like I hurt her. I did hurt her, I guess. Shit, now I'm an asshole, too. "Do you want to talk about it?" she offers. But her face is hard now, like she already knows the answer.

I want to, I do. But I can't. "Later. I have to... can't... it's too hard..."

The hardness to her face softens a little. Her shoulders relax. "OK, well, I'm going to go, then. Call me when you can, alright?"

I nod. Look at the floor, not at her, at the floor. She comes right up to me. Wipes the tears out of my eyes with the back of her sleeve. Kisses me, slowly. For like one second I feel a little better, then she grabs her bag and walks out of the front door, closing it behind her with a gentle click.

Running, I hit the garage. Put on the gloves. Beating the punching bag hanging from the ceiling. Hitting. Hitting until my knuckles are sore and my hands ache. Hitting the weights hard with a gazillion sets of everything. Have to keep moving, have to keep hitting that bag and the weights and then the burn comes. The pain, the good pain, the burn that helps to slow down the thoughts until they make sense. The burn that echoes through me until everything comes together, everything fits in my head.

Once it comes, once things are ordered, I curl into a ball on the weight bench. Curl into a ball and wish myself dead.

CHAPTER 16

TUESDAY, OCTOBER 16

TYLER

The pain doesn't leave. Doesn't go anywhere. Stays right up inside like it lives here. Like it's always just been part of me. Like I wouldn't be me anymore if it left.

I throw the empty bottle of Mountain Dew on the floor. I look back at the screen. Flying more, flying along more highways, more culverts. Desert stretches out as far as the three screens can show and they take me there, too. Just for a second as I'm flying over the desert, taking out bad guys, keeping the good guys safe, my life has meaning, I'm doing something important. And then I remember that it's all just a lie. One big fucking lie. I'm not doing anything for anyone. My whole life is a sham. Flying here in a fake pilot's chair watching over a fake desert and guarding fake troops. What a joke.

Hitting the volume up on the sound dock, I blast some Minor Threat. They were Dad's favorite. I close my eyes. Bite back the pain, tuck it back inside and clamp down on my racing heartbeat. Grinding my arms into the chair I try really hard to focus, to lose myself in the endless bleakness of the desert, to be somebody. The call comes for a single target. Hooking up the MTS autotrack, I quickly send over one of the Predators. A moving target. Cool. They're harder to hit. In a big city, well, big for the sim. It's a gray truck moving through a crowded street. People. Lots of people. Other cars and mud buildings built in tight around the narrow roads. Can't hit them. Not now. It's dark in the sim so I know the Predator overhead is just about impossible for anyone on the ground to see.

I open my eyes and concentrate. Pretend it's all real. Pretend that there are real people in those buildings and that the target in the truck is a terrorist who wants to kill them. A terrorist who wants to beat up on women and shoot little boys in public squares for listening to the wrong kind of music. I feel a little better. I force myself to forget the broken phones on the floor. Forget that I smashed Mom's houseline after the fifth shelter said that B wasn't there. Forget that everyone on B's Facebook list said that they didn't know where he was and that the Twittersphere was clueless. Forget that he's probably dead. Alone.

The swell of bile rises up and I want to choke and spit and smash the phones all over again. But I don't. I slam my body into the chair. Feel the stiff leather against my back, feel it hurt.

Follow the truck. Follow the bad guy. Stop him. Help those good people on the ground just trying to get their lives back together. Where the hell is he going, anyway? I keep tracking the truck, waiting for it to take a turn onto one of the wider boulevards where I can probably hit it without a lot of damage to any buildings. Someplace clear of people. There aren't a lot of paved roads over there, though, so it would suck if I had to wreck one just to kill some loser. Let's see.

I pull a satellite image map up in real time on the second screen, keeping the drone tracking every millimeter the loser takes down the road. Driving slowly down the main drag of the town like he's casing it, which he probably is. Shit. Have to stop him. All the main roads look like they go back to dirt once you leave the city. If I were a terrorist, what would I want to strike? One, a big building in the middle of town, is probably like their town hall or something. Doubt anyone would hit that at night. Wouldn't be like a terrorist to hit an empty building. OK. Scratch that. Too bad, that parking lot would have been a great place to take him out with minimum damage to infrastructure.

Keep looking. What's that? Big, looks like a two- maybe three-story building and a couple of smaller shacks inside a high wall with a guard tower. Barbed wire. Jail. Has to be either a jail or one of our bases. But it doesn't really look like the other bases, which usually have more buildings and an airstrip. Bet that's where he is going.

I check the truck. Slowing down. Stopping. Shit. That's a big building, too. I check the map. Shit. Shit! That's a school. Some other guy gets in the truck. Gets in the bed of the pickup. Along with a big bag. Relax, Ty. It's the middle of the night, there won't be any kids in there now. But the thought makes me burn. Those terrorists have to go. Wish I was killing them for real. The truck starts up again.

Where else could I hit them? The boulevard is the widest street but I don't want to damage it if I don't have to, and unless they roll into a parking lot the other streets are just too narrow. Shit. I wait. Hate waiting. Hate it. I grab the sandwich off the end table and bite it. Chew. The truck is rolling through town. Passes the big building in the center, turns onto another narrow-ass little street. But this narrow street leads out of town. Leads towards the building that looks like a jail.

I lase them. Type in the code for permission to hit. The second they get out of town. Green light blinking. SKY. Permission granted. Awesome. Sixty-eight thousand dollars' worth of hurt is about to rain down on their asses the second they get away from those houses. Get away from the good people. Get away from the kids. Weapons armed. Less than half a mile before they reach the jail. I wait. Wait until they are far enough away from the center of town.

I fire. Wait. Three. Two. One.

The truck disappears in a cloud as the missile hits. Yes! I wish I could hear it. Everything on the screen is so quiet. No noise. I feel good, man. Proud.

Then I remember. Remember that it's just a game and that B is missing. Remember that everything in my life is a sham.

Turning the music up even louder, I shout along with the lyrics and just fly. Fly around and see a fake truck blown to bits on the side of a dirt road. Fly over a fake desert with fake people with a fake sense of purpose.

CHAPTER 17

WEDNESDAY, OCTOBER 17

TYLER

Mom's watching the news. She's in the kitchen, reading a paper on her tablet and sitting in front of the news on the TV as she ignores the phone smashed to pieces all over the floor. "Hey, Mom." I kiss her on the forehead. It's nice. Boys should kiss their moms.

She does her usual, and doesn't look me in the eyes as she says, "Any luck finding your brother?"

I grab the dustpan from the closet and stare at the ticker on the screen. Dow is up, apparently. That's good news for somebody, I'm sure. I sweep up the plastic remnants of phone. "No."

"We shouldn't have let him go back into rehab. We should have known that it does no good. A lot of money for nothing." She takes a sip of her coffee. Eyes on the tablet. Hate tablets. Their gaming platform sucks.

"We had to give him another chance," I say.

"He doesn't need another chance. He doesn't use

them. Do you know how much rehab costs? Money for nothing, Tyler. For nothing."

I'm too tired for this. "Mom, of course I know how much it costs."

"It's money I should have used to help you," she says, her voice trembling.

Shit. "Mom, I'm fine, OK?"

"No. No, I should have seen you sliding, baby. Should have gotten tutors or counseling or something to help *you*. I know you and Rick think it's OK but I don't. I'm your mother, I should have been doing more for you." Her lips press together. Press so hard they turn white. "We can't make Brandon get better if he doesn't want to get better. He's selfish. And he's a liar. We shouldn't trust him, shouldn't believe him, shouldn't believe that he cares…"

I throw the broom into the cabinets, chest tight. "Jesus, Mom, he's your son!"

She puts down her coffee, hard, liquid splashing on her shaking hands. "No, not really, not anymore." Her shoulders tremble and her lips can't keep steady and she cries. Cries in her power suit. Doesn't look so strong when she's crying.

"Mom." She does this. I forget. Forget how easy it is to break her. Especially now that B's gone again. I should have known. I grab her, wrap her up in my arms, let her cry. She's so delicate, like a kitten. Even when she looks normal, even when she looks tough, she's not right. Her mascara runs onto my shirt and she wipes her eyes and she sobs. Big, earth-moving sobs from such a small woman. "Sorry, I wasn't thinking, OK? You have me,

Mom. You'll always have me." I kiss the top of her head and hold her until she steadies. But I still hold her after she stops. Hold her tight so that she knows that I love her. That I'm not Brandon.

Some guy is talking on the news. Financial stuff is over. Now there's a breaking story. Hate the morning news. Hate that they act like some nine year-old playing the violin is real news. This sounds like real news, though. At least to me. "Good news in the War on Terror. The Pentagon announced the morning the death of Bashir Hamad, a former ISI officer and a known Al-Qaeda sympathizer. Anonymous Pentagon sources have stated that Bashir Hamad was known to have operational links to insurgent forces in the region. It is also believed that he had ties to some of the individuals who funded the 9/11 attacks. Bashir Hamad and his accomplices were killed overnight en route to a planned attack on the Al-Quaddari prison in the Helmand province of Afghanistan."

My heartbeat picks up, one beat at a time, like kernels of popcorn starting to go. They show a picture of some guy in a turban, in-set eyes and long, bushy beard. "Hamad has been wanted by coalition forces for some time. He is believed to be responsible for leading a 2006 attack on Marines in Marjah that led to the death of three US servicemen."

I'm happy he's dead.

Mom slips out of my arms. Grabs her coffee and walks it over to the sink, shuffling her feet along the floor. She kisses me, quietly, quickly, on the cheek. And waits. Waits for me to say something, to look at her. Anything. But I can't move. I can't. Freaking. Move.

It's the truck. The image on the news. It's my truck. Gray truck blown to bits on the side of the road. It's my truck. My jail. My heart beats so loud that it rings in my ears.

Rick's got one hell of a sim if it can simulate a mission that took place, hours, minutes, before.

Fuck. Or did I just kill Bashir Hamad?

CHAPTER 18

THURSDAY, OCTOBER 18

TYLER

The phone. Stupid phone, ringing again. Don't want to get it. Want to get to Yale. I pedal faster, hoping to burn. Needing to feel the burn. I should get the phone. Don't stop pedaling. The wind snaps my cheeks. Tip of my nose and ears burning in the cold. Get the phone. Don't stop pedaling. Fingers and nose and ears will be numb in a second, just keep going. Have to get to Ani. To New Haven. Almost there. Stupid phone.

I yank the handlebars off to the right and veer off the bicycle path. I grab the phone out of my pocket, heart racing.

"Yeah," I say. Breath bouncing off the device and hitting my frozen cheek, making it hot, making it burn then freeze all over again.

"Mr MacCandless?" A voice, unsteady, nervous.

Shit, it's a telemarketer. "Take me off your list, OK?" Balancing the still bike beneath me, I kick at the gravel.

"No! No, it's not like that. I'm a friend of your brother's," the voice adds quickly, like he's trying to rush it all in before I hang up, like he didn't just stop my heart.

I feel cold. Cold all over, even inside me, and my legs holding the bike don't feel so steady. I want to sit down, I want to scream, I want to ask a million questions. They rattle around between my ears, hurting. Where is he is he safe did he call you why isn't this him?

"Mr MacCandless... um... Tyler? You still there? Don't leave me hangin'," the guy says and I let the bike fall to the ground with the sickening clang of metal on stones, metal on pavement, metal slicing through the fog in my head.

I stomp. Pace. Walk fast. Real fast so I can say, "Yeah. Have you... Where is he?" Six days. B's been gone for six days. I need to know. Need to find him.

"Oh, well, I don't know where he is, but..."

"If you don't know where he is then why are you calling?" My head. My freaking head. I push my free hand into my head, grinding into my scalp, pulling at my hair.

"We knew each other when he had his show. Man that was a great vlog, great show, great guy, your brother. Shame about... Listen, maybe we got off on the wrong foot here. My name is Todd Sevier and I'm a reporter for the *Montreal Standard*. I'm sure your brother told you about me, I even came down to meet him once, when Ralph Nader was giving a talk in Hartford. Man, what a weekend that was."

Montreal? What, like, in Canada? My chest expands and fills with ugliness and pain and worry and I can't seem to keep it all from flowing over, from gushing right out of my mouth. I grunt.

"Yeah, well, he called me this morning, said he had a story for me. Also mentioned that he couldn't believe that I actually landed a job as a journalist, but hey. Anyway, he said that you're involved in a program with Tidewater and that I might be able to help you out, maybe fill in some blanks, give you some info."

Keep him talking, keep him talking, don't let him stop talking. Did B not tell him why he doesn't have his show anymore? Does he know that B has less chance of becoming a serious journalist now than I have of being an actual pilot? I find a tree. Tall, big thing with crackled bark and punch my fist into the wood. Punch it, hard. Again. Bleeding. Stinging. Feel the impact travel up through my arm, feel it cover the fact that Brandon called him and not me.

"Yeah," I manage. A hoarse whisper. Thank God there's no one else down this far on the trail today. No one really likes the parts of the path behind the abandoned shopping centers.

"So what's this about some guy from Haranco contracting you to test flight simulation programs for him? Sounds cool."

Shit. This is bad. His words roll through me. I shouldn't be talking about it. Rick told me to keep the fact that I had the sim quiet. I shouldn't talk about it. At all. Especially not with a reporter.

I shouldn't have told Brandon.

I say nothing. Can't even bring myself to punch the tree. Just stand there like a moron, letting the cold eat me.

"He said that the program even comes with specialized equipment, and that they put it in your house? Is it like a huge Xbox or something?" His voice is steady now, beneath the banter, primed, on the hunt.

"Yeah," I whisper. Probably can't even hear me.

"So, is it like a videogame or what?"

"No, it's not, it's..." I stop. Look up at the clouds, shifting. Ani. If anything happens to Rick, to his program, then Ani gets in trouble, too. "Look, I shouldn't be talking about this."

"No worries, man, I just wondered if you could maybe send me a picture or something. I'd love to check it out."

"No, I can't."

"OK, then. I don't want to put you on the spot. I just wonder why they'd need someone who worked at Althea to help you set up the system."

"What?" Shit. Stupid Brandon running his mouth to some reporter starting trouble. Why am I worried? This is Rick's program. Rick's a good guy, right? "She's the programmer."

"Really?" His voice is light, but underneath I can hear metal. "Did you ever ask yourself why an employee of the United States' largest defense contractor came to the house of a seventeen year-old boy to give him a videogame system with multiple high-definition surround screens?"

How does he know what it looks like? Has to be from Brandon, I told him all about the system last visit we had before he disappeared. I'm gonna *kill* B if he messes up my chances for this flight school. My heart turns to stone and falls down to meet up with the rest of the gravel. "What exactly are you trying to say?"

"All I know is that drone attacks kill a lot of people, Tyler. A United States senator stated last week that drones have killed forty-seven hundred people. I imagine that at least half of them were civilians. We're talking women, children. Your government even redefined the meaning of militant to include any military-aged male, whether or not they were known to have any ties to actual insurgents. Kind of serious stuff."

Turn this around, turn this around, un-hear what he said right now, dammit. Anger and pain and worry force the feeling from my belly and all I can feel is pressure in my head and heart and bowels and I am going to explode if I don't get off the phone right now. Can't even think about talking to a reporter about this until I talk to Ani. Until I talk to Rick.

"None of that has anything to do with me," I say.

"Look, Tyler, I don't know what your brother's told you about me, but I spent a lot of time researching Tidewater, I've published a book about them, even. I want to make sure that you know exactly what it is you're getting into."

"What, Todd? What is it that you up there in Canada and my brother, wherever the hell he is, think is going on?"

"Well, that's what I'm trying to figure out."

"Yeah, well, until you do, why don't you tell me where my brother is?" I ask. Save it, save the conversation, turn it around.

"He didn't say where he was calling from. I'm sorry."

"I need to go."

"No, wait, let me leave you my information… how you can reach me…"

"Text it to me." Have to go. Now. I slam my fist into the tree. Bark tearing through the skin on the back of my knuckles.

I hang up. I feel the buzz of the text coming through. I am so screwed. Brandon thinks I'm flying them. How did Brandon know? Just because Haranco gave me the system? Brandon's always been into conspiracies and shit. But am I flying them? Did I really kill that guy? I don't know. But it can't be good if a reporter is calling me. Can't be good for Rick or Ani or me or Brandon.

Rick wouldn't do that. He would have told me if it wasn't just a game. I slam my fist into the tree. Again and again and again.

Doesn't make me feel better, though.

The water of the fountain flows in quick, choppy little waves. I stare into it, each little crest of water rising up to taunt me. He's alive. B's alive and able to use a phone. To call some guy in Canada. Cause he's worried about me. But he can't call me. Can't call his mom who doesn't sleep anymore.

Angry, sharp little waves. Wish I could jump in. Wish it was deep. Even though it's cold. My face is wet. Stinging.

Hurting in the chill wind. I wipe my eyes with the back of my sleeve. Don't care. Don't care if people notice. Who are they to judge?

I turn my head to the Beinecke rare book library. Odd gray and white cube. She's in there, Ani. I'll wait. Class should be almost over. Weird place to have class. Who designs a building shaped like that, anyway? I can't decide if I like it or not. Doesn't matter, though, one way or the other.

I hear her. Soft voice, like rain. Talking. About homework or something. I get up, walk over. She nods goodbye to the girl she's talking to and I say, "I just got a call. Some guy in Canada."

"Canada?" Her eyes narrow and she readjusts her backpack on her shoulder. "What are you talking about?" She looks down at my knuckles, bleeding, sore. "What happened to your hand?"

"Nothing's wrong with my hand, it's fine. Listen, a reporter. B called some reporter in Canada. The *Montreal Standard*, I think."

"Why would he call some reporter?"

"He's an old friend of B's or something, an investigative journalist, wrote a book about Tidewater. You know, Haranco's parent company?"

Her mouth opens slightly. "Oh no."

"Yeah." Some guys at the edge of the fountain are looking at us. Why are they looking at us? Totally creepy. I motion to Ani, start to walk. Walking helps me think.

"What did he want?"

"Information."

"About?"

"About Rick, the UCS sim." Those guys. Staring. Are they looking at her ass? I'll kill them if they are. "He thinks there's something weird going on."

Her eyes follow the trail of a bus. Watching as it takes a corner. Then she looks up at me. Brown eyes open wide. "What about you, what do you think?"

"I don't know. Sometimes I think they might be right." What if I killed Bashir Hamad? "There's been some nights, some missions that just seem too real, you know?"

"But the simulator—"

"It's built to be a model of the real remote-access terminal for the UAVs, right? So would it be that hard for Rick to have linked it up with actual drones?"

"No. It would be easy, actually."

"Right." I have to ask, have to know. "You didn't link them, though. You didn't do that."

"No."

"Even if it paid the cash for Yale that the scholarship didn't cover?" I have to see her face when she talks. To know.

"Never." The word is solemn, face pinched. "How could you even think that?"

"I'm not thinking anything. I'm just trying to make sense of this. I mean, we're both a part of whatever's going on."

Her hands start to shake and her mouth sets tight. "Mr Anderson wouldn't do this, though, would he?"

"I don't know." I grab her hand. Hold it in mine as we cross the street.

••••

We're sitting in the Bulldog Noodle Barn, a crazy little joint with cheap, ginormous servings of greasy food, sharing three dishes and swilling dark, punchy black tea at a grimy little table pushed back against the far wall, near the steaming entrance to the kitchen. It's loud and dirty and the spoon is wide and flat and plastic and hard to eat with, but I don't care. I'm too hungry, too pissed-off to care.

Ani's ranting. "How could he? How is this possible?" Anger at Rick dripping from each and every vowel. The banging in the kitchen and the radio of the cook and the people talking in Chinese and the action between the packed little tables of people eating and talking helps me focus on what Ani's saying. Doesn't give me any answers, though.

I watch her lips as they move. I watch her shoulders rise and fall as she speaks, as she eats, firm shoulders. And her eyes. Unyielding. Intelligent. "So what do we do?"

"Nothing," I say. "We don't even know for sure…"

"Nothing's not an option. What if Mr Anderson lied? Lied to us, lied to me. Aren't you going to talk to him? I mean, I think it warrants at least a conversation."

I take a swig of the black tea. The thin cup burns my hands, but the tea is good: hot and strong.

"You have to talk to him. He *likes* you. I knew I shouldn't have done this, taken his job, this was a huge mistake."

"Relax. We don't know that he's done anything wrong yet, right? If, and it's a pretty big if when you think about it, he did link the sim up to actual drones overseas, then he had to have a reason. A really good reason." I let the steam from the tea hit my face. "He wouldn't just do it to mess with us. There had to be some emergency. What if the military got hacked? Lost the ability to use the consoles to fly the drones or something and knew that Rick had his sim game that could be hooked up to the real thing? What if whoever it is that hacked the system did it so Bashir Hamad could do his planned strike on the prison? But Rick hooked me in, and I got him. Yeah. Yeah, Rick's gonna mention it next time I see him, I'm sure. I mean, it's not like he could call us before to tell us what's going on. Like for security reasons or whatever. But if he had to link the sim to the real thing, he'll tell us. Soon."

"I think that's a stretch. Drones don't just go offline. They're really hard to hack."

"Some kids in Texas did it."

"Not the ones with the weapons. Besides, you know how many people they have piloting those things now? There's no way that no one in the entire country except for you was able to make that hit on Hamad."

"If I made the hit on Hamad." I shrug. "Rick has to have had some reason, Ani. If he did it. If he even knows."

"*If* there was some change made to his project, he would know. If there's some connection between the sim and actual drones, trust me, he knows about it." Ani looks away from her tea, fingers pushing the cup around the table.

It can't be real, well, it could, but then Rick lied. And Rick wouldn't lie to me. He couldn't. Unless. Unless he had to. Unless there was something so important that he couldn't tell me the truth. Something to do with national security, maybe. Still. Still my stomach twists. It's like there's so much going on, so many things to be pissed-off about that I don't even know how to pick just one to pluck out and confront. Brandon. Rick. The possibility that I'm killing people.

No. No. If Rick lied and the sim is real, then I'm killing terrorists. Then I killed Bashir Hamad. And that's something to be proud of. He wasn't just a man, he was a threat, and getting rid of him is good. Is making everyone in America that much safer.

If. *If* I did it.

But if I did it, then Rick lied. To me. Fuck. My head hurts. Hurts like I just bashed it into a tree. And Mom? Is he lying to Mom, too?

She says, "You have to talk to him. People could be dying. Are dying. Tell me that you'll talk to him."

"I'll talk to him about it, sure." But Rick and I have talked about drones before. I told him that someday, if I couldn't pilot a real plane, that I'd love to fly drones. Fly anything. It would suck if he lied. But keeping America safe, keep people in Afghanistan and around the world safe from terrorists, doing something in my life that *meant* something, well, that would be great. "But Ani, what if the people that we're killing represent a genuine threat to America?"

"Oh, so it's 'we' now? There's no way I'm OK with this."

"But you're already OK with this!" The thoughts whir in my head, shaking themselves into a cocktail of pain and hurt and pride and confusion. "What the fuck were you doing at Althea over the summer? You were designing a Universal Control System for them. For people in the Army or the Air Force or whatever to fly drones. Drones kill people, Ani, it's what they do. What they have to do to keep us safe from–"

"That was different! I only wanted the internship with Althea because it's like the top internship in the country. It's like a ticket of admission into the Ivy League."

"You took the job with Rick–"

"To pay for Yale! I didn't get the full scholarship I was hoping for, I don't play sports and I didn't do a lot of clubs and I needed a way to pay for the rest of the tuition. I didn't sign up for" – she waves her hand around – "all this. I didn't. I just wanted to go to school, maybe get some job experience so I could put it on my resume after college."

"But you designed a system that pilots drones, if you're not OK with the–"

"I designed a game! A simulator! It wasn't supposed to be used to fly the things for real, to kill people!"

"What's the difference? The people who trained on the simulator are going to be flying the real things eventually! You designed something that trains people to kill terrorists, Ani" – I reach my hand out across the table to hers. She pulls hers away like I have acid on my fingertips – "it's not like it's a bad thing. Drones are like the next big revolution in warfare. Like the nuclear bomb. Rick says the number of pilots needed to control them is going to boom, and right now he might have just put us, both of us, out in the front of the industry. We're the good guys, here, Ani. If your machine is actually killing people, then it's killing the right people."

Tears run down her cheeks and she shakes her head. "No. No, I don't think it's like you think, Tyler. And what if this is real, are you, am I now complicit in some sort of crime? If Mr Anderson connected the system to actual drones used in combat operations, I'm pretty sure that's got to be some sort of crime."

I don't know. Rick wouldn't do anything illegal. But until just a few hours ago I didn't think he'd ever lie to me, hide something like this from me, either. "Ani, look, I can't lose this, OK? If I piss Rick off and I lose this chance, then I lose everything."

She tilts her head to the side, takes a deep breath. "You'd have what everyone else has, a senior year, a chance to bring your grades up and get into–"

"I dropped out" – she lets go of my hand. I wince – "I meant to tell you but it didn't seem like a big deal at the time."

She throws her hands up and then back down, shaking her head. "Perfect. Just perfect. Good for you. You know what? I have class in half an hour."

"Wait." I stand up. Hit the table. My tea tips over and gets all over the table. "Are we... OK?"

She wipes her eye with the back of her hand. "I have to go." She walks out of the restaurant.

Heart racing. She has to understand. Terrorists. There's nothing wrong with killing terrorists. Why can't she see that? Even if Rick lied, which would suck, then it's still OK because America is that much safer with each terrorist that goes down. I stick the spoon in the noodles. What is that? Bok choy? How am I going to get that huge hunk of green onto this tiny spoon? I shove the spoon into my mouth and chew. How can I make her see that? Shit, wait, did she just break up with me? How can you tell? Facebook status? Man, dating's complicated.

My phone rings in my pocket.

Shit. I drop the spoon. Reach around to the pocket of my coat where it's hanging behind the chair. I bang the low-lying table with my knee by accident as I turn to dig through the pocket, practically tripping a waiter as he walks by in the tiny aisle.

I hit talk and: "Hello?"

Silence on the other end of the line.

Shit. Probably can't get good reception in here. "Hello?" I try again.

"Tyler?" The voice is distant, shaky, nervous. My throat tightens and the shouting from the kitchen and the clattering of the plates and the swoosh of the swinging door beside me all cluster up and hang around me until it's just a muffled ball of nothingness. A tunnel of light and sound and the world shrinks in around me, making me desperate for some air so I can breathe enough to say, "Brandon?"

"Hey, bro. Thought I'd just–"

"Where are you?" The words fly from my lips, hot, loud and shaking.

"Don't get all tough-guy on me, Ty, I'm just calling to tell you that I'm OK, alright?"

"No, it's not fucking alright, B. You left rehab six days ago and you can't even…"

He's not there. I hear the click and he's gone. Just gone. Leaving me holding a phone. All at once the restaurant that seemed so overwhelming and chaotic goes. Disappears. Staring at the black phone in my hand. Staring. Like the phone has the answers. Like it can make things better. I should be pissed. Upset. Whatever. Too many times. Too drained. Too tired to be pissed.

The waiter. He's talking to me. Sliding a bill in front of me. "Need anything else? You alright?"

I don't know if I'm alright. If anything is alright. I pull a twenty out of my wallet and slap it on the table with a nod.

Why did B call that reporter before he called me?

CHAPTER 19

SUNDAY, OCTOBER 21

TYLER

Three days since the phone call from B. He called me from a pay phone. A *pay phone*. I don't know where he even found one. He hasn't called again. But if he showed up dead in some morgue I guess we'd hear about it. Every time a cop car goes by I hold my breath, hoping that they'll just keep driving. They do.

Rick's here. It's been a while. I can't find the words. The right words to ask what's creeping around in my head.

"So, your mom said that you took the GED?"

"Yeah," I say. "I think I did pretty good. It'll work out, get me a job or whatever."

I turn my head back to the sim screen, watching as it goes back to the start screen and I hit the key to shut it down. Rick just watches me. Watches me fly. Says it's for his recommendation for the flight school.

He leans back in his chair, pressed pants and sweater doing nothing to hide the fact that he's watching. His eyes. They're hard, solid, unyielding. He's no desk jockey. Don't think he ever could be. He's built for action.

"I like that about you." He reads my face for some hidden signal to continue. "Fortitude. Men like you and me, we display fortitude in the face of adversity, in the face of pain." He leans forward. "A strong man learns to accept the mistakes and move on. Like me, like you."

I think of the mission the simulator just flew. Bombed a house. Got target twenty-three. Target twenty-three was sitting on a roof. Drinking tea or whatever. With other people. Lots of other people. Six other people. I dropped a Hellfire on the house. Flew back around. Nothing but rubble. And a dog. Limping. Covered in blood. Can't shoot it. Can't use the ammo. Can't drop a Hellfire on a dog to put it out of its misery. On a building that is nothing but rubble. Rubble and bits of bones and fabric and stuff that used to be seven people. My stomach hurts. Sick. I can barely keep it all inside. Terrorists. They were all terrorists. I did the right thing, probably saved lots of American lives. I swallow. "Fortitude. Sure."

He pulls a flask from his pocket and takes a sip. It's a small, silver thing, etched from wear, not decoration. I look at him, his brows pinched like he's angry.

Voice small, I say, "It's cool, you know."

His eyebrows lift up and he leans forward in his chair towards me just a little.

"I know that some of these missions are real." I don't know, not for sure, but as I see the mix of worry and fear and the hint of a smile curl up the tip of his lips I become more certain. "I know that I'm actually flying the drones. It's cool, Rick. I want to help. It's all I've ever wanted. To help."

His face freezes in an odd expression for a moment. Light seems to rise up and radiate through his skin, his lips squeezing tight then opening up into a full smile. He leans over quickly and slaps me on the leg with a great booming laugh. "See that. That right there, Tyler. I saw that in you from the first. Intelligence, integrity. Some scraggly little kid who wanted to fly a plane, sure, but there was something more. There's always been something more."

I look down, eyeing my feet, my boots. "Sure. Why didn't you just tell me?"

"Telling you wasn't an option. Part of the rationale behind the program was to keep stress levels of pilots down. Too many have been breaking down. We've seen some adverse psychological effects on some operators who go home to their wives and kids every night. Having our test pilots not know that they were actually flying was our way of seeing if it would help with their anxiety."

"Has it?"

"Well, so far. You see, the government is having problems with the software that it uses to control the drones. The Air Force and the CIA buy these remote-access units from Althea, and it would take two, sometimes three men to fly a single drone. Three control units, three men, to fly one drone. They say they need one to pilot, one as a sensor operator, and then an intel officer to OK the missions before either one of the other two is allowed to do shit. Not to mention the fact that they still haven't figured out how to launch the things without men on the ground. They see the future, I see inefficiency." He takes out his flask. Takes a swig. "So I got the best minds in the business together and came up with a way to automate take-offs and landings. Then we put multiple drones on one control unit, but the problem was that none of the pilots trained were able to run the damn thing. The pilots were too old, not used to the way things are now, not capable of the manual dexterity of the young."

"How do you get your intel?"

"We have intelligence operatives on the ground who relay mission objectives and target in real time to SKY."

"But is it good intel? I mean, like, we're not hitting civilians, are we?"

He takes another swig from the flask. "Our people on the ground are the very best. They have years of training and experience in the region. Everybody's human; some mistakes are unavoidable. But, Tyler, those operators love you, you saved their asses the other day."

"Really?" The men on the ground, asking for close air support.

"Really. They needed help immediately, didn't have time to go through SKY, so they chose you, and you came through in a major way."

"So what does all this make me, then?"

"You, Tyler, you are the next generation of soldier. You're the next generation of hero. You can not only use the machine, but can control multiple drones at one time.

You're exactly what we need. That and hundreds of men just like you. We can revolutionize the face of modern warfare. Streamline the system. Save our government money by providing a more efficient way to make war."

"The government would really hire a private contractor to fight its wars?"

"Sure, it saves a lot of money." He points to the screen with the map. "One hundred percent of your missions, both simulated and live, take place here, in and around the border of Pakistan and the Helmand province of Afghanistan. This is basically the center of gravity for the Taliban insurgency, and we still have something like eight thousand coalition troops in bases throughout the region. These forces require massive amounts of ammo, fuel and food. Now, the Jihadis won't go toe-to-toe with conventional NATO forces because they know that they'd lose. Instead, their primary goal is to attack our supply routes and make the occupation unsustainable. Road security becomes essential to our success."

"So that's what I'm doing? Protecting the roads?"

"Basically. Haranco can't achieve the same results as a battalion of infantry and the accompanying helicopters and such, but a squadron of our UAVs can handle eighty percent of their objectives at only five percent of the cost."

"Cool." So I'm doing what the military does. Keeping people safe, saving money and saving lives.

"Currently, most of your live routes have been flying cover for a Pakistani company that has hired us to assure that the supplies it carries to NATO forces arrive safely."

"Great. What do we do now? I mean, did I like throw off your whole program because I figured out what was going on?"

"Not at all. And now I can pay you what you've been earning, Tyler."

"Pay me?"

"It was in the fine print of the papers you signed, not that you were really flying the mission, but that you agreed to be an employee of Haranco and that you would accept payment in full at the end of your term of service." He clasps me on the shoulder. "Since you're no longer in the dark, we can just go ahead and pay you as a beta tester."

"How much?"

"You're gaining a highly specialized skill-set, son."

"How much?"

He holds the flask out to me. "A lot."

Rick's sitting at my kitchen table. Should have cleaned it a little more. Sitting next to an envelope full of two thousand dollars in cash and in front of his laptop. Two grand. Cash. On my table. For me. To pay me to fight terrorism. Never seen so much cash before. Kind of strange that it can all fit in one little manila envelope. Weird to think Rick just walks around with that crap in his car.

"Like I said, part of the reason for keeping you in the dark was to keep your stress level as low as possible. Now that you know, I don't want you flying more than twenty hours a week to start."

"But that's barely flying," I say. Leg shaking as I try and sit. Sit at the table. Legs too long. They hit the bottom of the table. Knocking the old newspapers and pile of bills that I shoved out of the way to make room for Rick.

"Twenty hours. Just to see, Tyler. Then we can increase it again, I'm sure. Not to worry. We're hoping to set up a type of virtual band of brothers. Men in the field deal with stress through camaraderie, through having people who go through hell with them. Drone pilots have to try and pull themselves together in time to pick up Junior at soccer practice by 5.30pm. Part of Haranco's plan is to use the clan system that you kids use in your gaming networks. Set up sort of a 'clan of brothers,' if you will, a way for our new generation of pilots to bond. Our problem right now is that you're the only one who figured out that some of your missions are real, so we don't have a clan in place for you yet. So we need to watch you carefully."

"You gonna tell whoever else has the sim?"

"Later." He pulls out three tickets to tonight's Patriots game. "But first we've got some celebrating to do. Let's go get your mother, we don't want to miss kickoff."

CHAPTER 20

MONDAY, OCTOBER 22

ANI

What do I do with him? I thought that having a few days to clear my head would help, but I still don't know what to do. I don't want any part of this, but it's not like I can walk away, either. Maura skips up to the table and sets her tablet down around my limp half-sandwich and mostly soggy carrots. She says, "So, why the face? Did you finish *The Awakening*? You did, didn't you? It was sad. But at least I know what I'm going to write about for the essay: marriage as repression. Good, huh?"

"Yeah, but everyone's going to be writing something pretty similar." I grab a soggy carrot, and drop it back down again. How do raw carrots get soggy like that? It just doesn't seem like they should. I hope it's not some sort of mold.

"It's that guy from the theater, isn't it?" She takes a huge bite of her sandwich, grilled eggplant drooping just below the bottom of the bun. She chews and I wait, resenting her sandwich. Maybe I could go back and get something else, like a bag of chips. "The one that keeps sending you those songs?"

"That's him." Tyler's been sending me different mp3s every hour to my phone, choosing the song by title. Every one is some variation of either "I'm sorry" or "Don't be mad" neither of which make that much sense. If I'm being honest, I'm not really mad at him. Well, I am, which is why I haven't texted him back, but I'm more upset with Mr Anderson, with myself for getting into this situation in the first place. Tyler's a patriotic guy, he's never once tried to pretend to be anything else. He wanted to be a pilot in the Air Force and there's nothing wrong with that. I mean, Dad was in the Army. And I love my dad. But I sort of hate the Army for taking him away from me for so long. I hate them for not seeing he needed help before he ended up in jail. And I want to be proud, I want to be proud of everything Dad ever did, it feels jealous and wrong of me to resent the armed forces. To blame them for what happened. But there it is.

"You guys get into your first fight? If the song choices are any indication, it's pretty clear he messed up." Maura chews with her mouth open. She really is nice and I like eating with her, but I can't watch her eat when she does it. I push the remnants of my lunch away.

"I don't *know* if he messed up, that's sort of the problem." I don't think I can remember feeling this confused in my entire life.

"Look" – I look up and regret it instantly when I catch a view of a mouth full of eggplant, I look back down at the table as she says – "everybody fights. Unless he like slept with your roommate or something, it's probably salvageable."

Grabbing my phone, I feel its weight in my palm.

"Besides" – Maura reaches for her fries and I cringe – "we're in college, if things get too complicated just dump him. There are plenty of guys on campus, Ani, plenty of guys."

I think of Jim from freshman Lit who, in all seriousness, offered to teach me the meditative power of the positions found in the *Kama Sutra*, and of Christy's new boyfriend, who lectures anyone who will listen about Jungian philosophy.

Standing up from the table, I text Tyler.

How do I handle this without wrecking everything? He's on the sidewalk, pacing by his mom's car. I say, "Hey."

Tyler turns, wearing crisp jeans and a sweater that he may or not realize clings to every muscle in his arms. "Got these for you." He holds out the bag of salt and vinegar chips and a bottle of designer perfume. "You said that you liked them that time at the house so I thought that you might want some."

Potato chips? Perfume? His face looks almost childlike in its eagerness and fear. I take the chips, thankful that my bag is big enough to hide them. "Thanks. Why do you think I need perfume?"

"The lady at the store said that girls like perfume."

"Well I don't." No one has ever given me perfume before. Why would they? I'm not exactly a perfume sort of girl. "I don't smell or anything, do I?"

"No, I just thought it would be nice." His face falls a bit.

I gesture with the gift box. "Are those new clothes?"

"Yeah, and shoes." He looks down at his shiny boots. "They're Doc Martens. I've always wanted a pair, but they're sort of giving me blisters."

"Why all the new stuff?"

He shrugs, smiles. "I wanted to put money down on a car, actually, but they said I had to be eighteen."

I swallow back my worry. "Where did you get the money?"

His face is stern, like a man about to explain the birds and bees to a child. "Look, I talked to Rick, and I think we might've been overreacting. He has this plan, this *system*."

"I wasn't overreacting." I lift my chin and look him in the eyes. God, how can I fall for someone who's so blind? "So it's true, then? He used something I created to trick minors into committing murder? Tell me again how I'm overreacting?"

I want to reach over and shake him, scream until he wakes up and realizes the implications of what he's agreed to do. The street teems with people, good, honest people going to jobs in suits and ties. Buses full of them hide the bushes on the town green from view, and I wish that I could take one, ride away from here, from all of this.

"The fact that gamers are able to use the technology is the whole point, Ani. It's genius. Eliminating stress levels and making sure that supplies get where they're needed and that our troops over there stay safe."

"What about the civilians? When you bomb a building, the machine only counts the people who are out in the open, who are visible to the drone's heat sensors. But there could be other people in the buildings, Tyler. People who have nothing to do with Al-Qaeda or the Taliban – real people, children, even." Why can't he see that this is wrong?

"Rick says that there are intelligence officers on the ground who set the targets and that they are careful to avoid any civilian–"

"Rick says?" I push him in the chest, sending him stumbling backward into a street vendor's cart. "Why should you believe anything that he says to you? He lied to you, to me, to all those other kids still playing what they think is a game."

"I know, I see what you're saying, but Rick says that this was a test, he had to keep us in the dark to make sure that the program works the way he wants it to, that's all. If he says that he has good intelligence on the ground locating the targets, I believe him." He walks closer, but doesn't try to reach out for me. "Besides, I don't see any reason to doubt that everyone that I killed was a terrorist. Hell, one was even on the news, I stopped him before he could carry out an attack on a prison."

"Just because somebody's wearing a turban doesn't mean he's the enemy, Tyler."

He moves his head up into the sky as if he's looking for patience, like it will rain down from heaven and give him some kind of answer. Hands in his pocket, legs straight, when he speaks his voice is tense. "I'm killing terrorists,

OK? I'm doing something good here, something right. It's different from what you think."

"It's not different. They're still people." My voice is sharp and bitter.

"They have intelligence, Ani. Military intelligence doesn't make mistakes like that. If they say that these people are terrorists then they're terrorists. Period."

"Military intelligence? Really?"

"Says the girl who worked for Althea."

"What the hell does that have to do with anything?"

"Everything. How can you doubt the intelligence of an organization when Althea is the company designing all of their software?"

"It's not the software that I'm doubting, it's the grunts that are using it."

"What are you saying? Oh, wait, I get it. I'm just some grunt, then, to you?"

My mouth feels dry as I say, "Well, what if you are? You're more than happy to be Mr Anderson's little pawn."

"No." His eyes are wide, wild, desperate, and his words are jagged. "I think that this conversation is over. Oh, and here, I got this for you."

He puts something in my hand, and when I open it I see a gold chain with a little heart. How did this conversation go so wrong? I have to say something, to try and turn this around somehow. "Tyler…"

"Keep it. I'd feel stupid returning it." His eyes look down at my hand and he walks away.

I stand, wiping my eyes with the back of my sleeve. Oh, God, please don't let it end like this.

CHAPTER 21

THURSDAY, OCTOBER 25

TYLER

The days move. Like move fast. Ignoring Rick's suggestion of only clocking twenty hours a week, I fly all day, knowing that I'm changing the world. Making it better, safer. The kill count at the top of my screen keeps going up: for every terrorist down, that's another American life saved. That I saved. *Me*. Sending another dad home to his kids.

I don't think too much about the fact that I'm killing real people. Except at night. Late in the middle of the night when no one is watching and it's just me and my conscience and that voice that tells me that someone is dead because of me. It's wild. Wild and lonely and maybe just a little bit wrong because how do I know for sure that the people I am blowing up are terrorists? I have to trust the intel that tells me so but sometimes, I wonder who that intel guy is and pray that he's as good at his job as I am at mine. He better be right or I'm... well, I can't think about what that makes me.

I throw the sheets back, T-shirt sopping wet and clinging to my chest in a damp world of badness. I rip it off and throw it into the floor with the others. Have to do laundry. Wish Ani were here. A whole three days since we talked. Sucks. Bet 3am wouldn't feel so bad if she were lying next to me. I could just roll over and wrap my arms around her waist and listen at her back, listen to her heart, listen to her breathing, and then I could sleep. But not tonight. She's not here.

Shit. I hit call and dial up Peanut and Alpha, see if they're on. Alpha's not picking up but Peanut's light blinks and then the video box opens up and I see him rub his eyes, red curls flying all over like he's some kind of punked-out clown. "Tyrade, man, what's up?"

"Nothing."

"Better be something or I just blew my shot at getting through this level of *RAGE* before the hour's out for nothing." He smiles. Wide, lazy, stoned.

"Nothing. Just, fought with this girl."

"Girl? Wait, not SlayerGrrl? Like that *girl*, girl?"

"Yeah."

He stares into the webcam, leaning in. "Let me see your face, man, move in closer."

Peanut's a little off. Thinks he can read auras and shit. He's cool, though, if you overlook all that hippie stuff. Good gamer. I lean in, squinting a little from the light on the screen. "What?"

"Ah, shit. Man, you're hittin' that, right?"

"What are you talking about?"

"SlayerGrrl, man. You guys hooked up, I can see it."

Maybe he can read auras. Like that guy on TV. Or does he just talk to the dead or something? Are ghosts like auras? Can't keep track. "No. Well, kinda. She's pissed at me, though."

"What'd you do?"

"I have this... job that she doesn't like." I think that ghosts are different from auras. Think auras have something to do with crystals.

"What? You get a job as a bouncer in a strip club or something? If so, I totally need in on that." His smile gets even bigger.

Hitler. Hitler was into crystals. I saw a show about it on the History Channel once. "Yeah, no, well, something like that, I guess."

"Can you quit the job? Girls can get hung up over stuff like that."

"No."

"Well, hell, you say you're sorry?"

"Sorta." No. Maybe. "I'm not sorry, though, I mean, I need this job."

"Alright, well, there's your answer, man."

"What, where?"

"Tell her you'll do it just until you get enough money or whatever to stop, and that you'll quit as soon as you can."

"Think that'll work?"

"Hell, yeah."

"She's like, really smart, though."

"Well, shit." His eyebrows come together a little bit. "That is a problem."

••••

She did look totally hot when she was mad. Just have to keep that image in my head when I call. Sure, she may be mad, but it'll be hot mad, and that's gotta be good, right? I mean, if she was really angry she wouldn't have looked all cute, she would've looked, I don't know, bad or something.

I sit up, grabbing the days-old bottle of Mountain Dew from the nightstand and taking a swig. Gross. Flat and nasty and it tastes like I feel. Digging my hands into the bones in my face, I stand up and move over to the old monitors, over to where I have the PS3. Right, call Ani, don't play. Gotta apologize or something. Deep breath. Here we go. I dial. Wait. "Ani?"

"What… Tyler?"

"Hey." Apologize, dammit. "I'm sorry."

"Sorry? Tyler, it's like 3 o'clock in the morning."

What? Shit. Should've checked the time. "Are you sleeping?"

"Not *now*." Her voice is slow.

"Look, I'm sorry about the Rick thing, OK? It's just that I don't have anything else. I'll just do it until I get into flight school, promise."

Silence.

"Ani, please, don't make me lose you, too," I say into the darkness.

I close my eyes and I see it.

The bright sky. The pier. The excitement to get to see Dad in action. The day was different. Still bright and virtually cloudless. I held Mom's hand. Back when it was strong. Back when it was tender. When her face held feeling. Brandon ran ahead. He was thirteen. It wasn't cool to stay with me. To stay with Mom.

I feel hot as the memory pulls me under. Pulls me down like it does sometimes at night. Dad smiling.

We were at a Memorial Day celebration at the soccer fields. My game had ended hours ago but we had to wait for Brandon's game to be over. His team lost but Dad bought us all ice cream anyway. Flags and bands and hot dogs lined the picnic stations on the field. Dad in uniform. Dad telling me that one day I was going to be the fastest thing on the field, telling Mom to relax when I climbed on top of picnic tables and jumped off again and again.

Music. Flags and smiling people all around. Everybody cheers when the floats with the old guys in uniforms and the trucks with lots of colorful flags pass by the park. Some man I didn't know bent over to ask me if I knew my dad was a hero. His face was wide and red and smelled like beer. I hid my head in my mother's sundress. It was soft and pink and everything she's not now.

I ran. My feet beat against the gravel of the picnic area. Stomping out my own little rhythm as I ran up and down. Taking my toy chopper, my toy Black Hawk, and ran up the length of the playground and up on top of unguarded boxes and crates and jumped as my mother ate her hot dogs and hamburgers and salad. As Dad kicked the ball back and forth with Brandon. Brandon was slower than me, couldn't move like me, but Dad liked to help him out. Told me I had to be patient with my brother. No big brother liked to be shown up by his little brother. Dad said that it was up to him and me to help Brandon out.

I climbed the jungle gym. The grit and yielding rust and taste of iron as I climbed. I tucked the chopper up under my chin. Both hands pulled. Tugged, moving my body upward. I looked at Mom. Gave her a triumphant smile. I was too high. Wait till she noticed. I jumped. Landing hard. Grinding my little feet into the gravel. Liking the sound. Liking the feel of the landing. Mom shrugged when people watched me. When the clucking old ladies would chide me and made like they cared if I hurt myself. Mom looked sick when she watched but she knew. Knew that I had to do it. Knew that it made me feel better.

Dad caught me in his arms mid-jump. Plucking me out of the air and tickling me till I cried out for him to stop. "Brandon and I are going to go, OK? We'll meet you and Mom at home, OK?"

"I wanna go, too. B always gets to go, it's not fair," I said, wanting to ride with Dad, who always drove fast and listened to music. Not like Mom, who went slow and listened to people talk about cooking on the radio.

"Listen to me, buddy. You have to stay with your mom. I can't leave her here all alone, you have to watch out for her. Promise?" He looked serious.

I nodded. "Good, see you at home."

Brandon waves and they head out towards the parking lot. Their outlines fading into the sun as they went.

It was the last time I saw my dad.

We got home and they weren't there and they didn't return Mom's calls.

A policeman at the door.

Mom. She said, "Hello." And then he said something, I couldn't hear from where I was on the couch so I snuck closer. He looked at me and shut his eyes. Turned his head away.

Mom's face shattered. Shattered and then she fell and she was screaming. It was at that second, that second that my world of rainbows and tadpoles and bedtime stories became a world of black. A world of gray.

They pulled Brandon from the wreckage. He was alive but barely. We rushed to the hospital. The police said that Dad saw the drunk driver heading towards them. Saw that there was no way to avoid the crash. They said he turned the car, changed the angle at the last second before they hit so that they wouldn't hit face-first but rather so that Dad's side would be the first to make impact, the first to hit. So that Dad would die and give B a chance to survive.

I wonder if Dad would have done that if he knew what surviving would do to B. Mom knew. Mom and I both knew that world of color and light and happiness was over and would never come back. But B couldn't deal. Couldn't ignore the thud thud thud of the test choppers flying over our house day after day after day. Couldn't stop reading about collisions and angles of impact. Couldn't help but to smash the oxy they gave him for the pain.

Couldn't give up on the fucking rainbows.

CHAPTER 22

FRIDAY, OCTOBER 26

ANI

Why does my phone always ring when I'm running late for class? I shuffle to the side of the stairwell and pull it out of my pocket. "Hello?" I huff as someone bolting down the stairs knocks me in the shoulder.

"Miss Bagdorian."

My feet freeze into the stairs. Mr Anderson. What do I say? Does he know that I'm aware that the kids are live? If I tell him that I know, then that would unlock a world of badness. He's been very clear about his position about my contacting the test pilots directly, and if I talked to him about it, then he'd know that I've been talking to Tyler. I say, "Hi."

"Listen, pilot three has been reporting that the images on monitor B are grainier than the others. Doesn't matter which camera he directs over to the monitor, that screen is just always grainy. Is there anything you can do for that?"

So he doesn't know. Well, doesn't know that I know. "Yeah, I guess I can get into his unit remotely and dig around, see if I can figure out what's going on." I have to try it and see. "But it would really be easiest if I could speak to him or her directly. You know, troubleshoot while I have them on the phone."

Silence. The stairwell around me teems with students coming to or from class, voices echoing around me, but all I hear is the silence on the other end of the line. "I know. Speaking to the test pilots directly would make things simpler on your end. I completely understand. But your having any contact with the test pilots could compromise the success of the program. I've explained this before."

"Sorry," I say, voice sounding small in the cavernous space. "It just seems more *efficient*."

"Well, I agree. It would be. However, our focus is the integrity of the feedback that the pilots give us." His voice softens somewhat. "Besides, I can't have them lying to show off because there's a girl who's smarter than they are on the other end of the line. One who knows her way around a motherboard better than just about anyone else on the planet. Men aren't used to that sort of thing. So we just have to make do with a less-than-ideal manner of providing tech support."

"Sure, well, which pilot, number three?" I'll fix it the second I get to my laptop. "Got it, I'll see what I can do."

"Let me know when it's fixed, and check the other units for any similar errors."

"Will do," I say, leaning against the wall, allowing the chill of the concrete to seep in through my sleeve, hoping that it cools the still-rapid pace of my heart.

Oh my God. Is that Tyler outside of my dorm? Sunlight trickles down through the orange and yellow leaves giving his brown hair reddish undertones. A group of girls in front of me smile as they pass him, and I feel sort of, I don't know, happy that someone so cute is here for me. Damn, do they even make guys hotter than him?

He swipes his hair back and out of his face as I walk up to him. "Hey. You eat yet?"

"A little."

"You hungry? Cause there's this falafel place around the corner that's really good."

"I have class in like five minutes. You should have called."

"Which class?"

"Chem."

"You failing?"

"No, I'm not failing."

"So skip it." He looks me in the eyes and for a second I forget to breathe.

"I can't skip class." He reaches out, but I don't take his hand.

"Look, Tyler. It was rude to hang up on you the other night, but I'm not so sure if–"

"Stop. Listen to me. I need to talk. Need to tell you. I don't care if you forgive me. I don't care if you think that I'm wrong and that I shouldn't be OK with what's going on. I don't care if you hang up on me or even if you don't talk to me. You don't ever have to talk to me again, ever, if you don't want." He leans closer to me, so close that I can catch the scent of the shampoo lingering in his hair. My throat tightens. "But please just be here with me. I'll take whatever it is you can give me, however you want to give it, I just need you to be next to me. Need to know that there's one person in this world I haven't lost."

My fingertips stretch out, tracing the delicate skin on the back of his hand. "Tyler–"

"Skip class. Don't. That's fine. Just don't leave me." He leans down and kisses me. His lips are soft and his breath is ragged and he licks my bottom lip with a flick of his tongue and I'm alive. It's as if electric currents hum through my veins. My bag hits the ground as his arms snake their way around my waist and he pulls me in closer. "Please."

I run my fingers up through his hair and take his lips again. He did say "please."

CHAPTER 23

SATURDAY, OCTOBER 27

TYLER

Bristol Street is off of Dixwell Avenue, only minutes away from Yale's campus, but in socio-economic terms it could be measured by light years. Yale has architecture and fountains and courtyards with trees and Bristol Street, well, doesn't. It has clapboard three-story houses and abandoned warehouses surrounded by chain-link fence and all sorts of little side streets that function as drug drive-throughs. Those one-lane, one-way side streets where the dealer stands off to the side and a car slows down so he can come to the window. Scary, but it is what it is.

The three-story house that matches the address B gave me looks like it's coming undone. Like Lego stacked by a two year-old. Wires running to defunct antennas and satellite dishes that pre-date the Clinton era stick out from the sides and top of the place like birthday candles gone wrong.

Mom's car is so in trouble. It's the only car I had access to, though, and there's no way I was walking. Hell of a way to spend a Saturday night.

B wants to see me. Tonight, the text said. In person. I didn't want Ani to come, just in case, well, in case things were ugly and B was hurt or things with his friends were... bad. I didn't want to leave her room. I shiver, remembering the way she moved. She got hungry, after all, and wanted to order in some Indian food. So now I'm late since I can't say no to her like ever. It's only been what, a month since I've met her? Little more? Crazy how fast things can change. Maybe I can go back to the dorm and see her after I talk to B.

The door to the building does that click thing that signals that I can go in and I pull it open. Walking down the tiny, wood-paneled hall that smells like day-old frying oil and sandalwood incense, I feel a little sick. My brother lives here and he doesn't have to. He could be in a nice home or at a nice school or whatever.

The sound of *Jeopardy* and a chorus of people shouting answers in English at the TV and Spanish at each other flows through a door just in front of the staircase leading up. Damn, if I were that family, I wouldn't want Brandon and his crew living here.

Did I really just think that about my own brother? My heartbeat ticks up. God, I am an asshole. Assclown. Jackass. Brandon is *sick*. Druggies are not bad people, they are *sick* people and he just needs to get better. That's all. God, I am such an insensitive dick sometimes.

Upstairs. I can do this.

The industrial metal door creaks as it opens and I climb the stairs. The corners of the stairwell are full of crap. Condom wrappers, empty Doritos bags and broken, well, everything. No needles. Don't look for the needles.

Upstairs. Gotta get upstairs. My heartbeat's practically pulling me along, now, as I keep climbing, turning around the bend and everything seems to be a blur of blue and gray and squalor.

This hallway is worse. Even smaller, tighter than the first. The junk lines the baseboard of the hall. Dust and water bottles and old shoes lie kicked to the side, doors clustered and thin. The smells aren't as nice up here. Hot. A sticky hot that climbs up underneath my jacket and rises up to sit around my neck. My hand is shaking, pushing a button in front of a thin white door at the far end of the hall.

"Ty!" B's grin takes up his whole face, and he pulls me into him. He smells like shampoo and body wash and that cologne he's always liked.

"B, man, how've you been?" I choke on the words, eyeing him as he pulls me inside. His color is awful. Skin like old chalk. His eyes hollow. He's wearing a sweater and it's like eighty degrees in this apartment but he's still shivering. "You sick?"

"No, fine, just tired."

Cut him a break. He called, finally. He invited me over. He needs something.

I wish I could stop being such an asshole. It's an invite to check out the new digs, that's all. Relax.

His eyes widen as he sees me alone. "You didn't bring your girl?"

"Nah, she has to work tonight."

We walk into B's small living room and he shuts the door behind us, being sure to latch the deadbolt. The place is actually sort of neat. Like he cleans it sometimes, which is good. The couch is small and the fabric is tearing. A bicycle leans up against one wall, next to a bookcase full of papers and books and magazines. Just on the other side of the couch is a small table with three unmatched folding chairs, leading into a pretty crappy, pretty cluttered kitchen. B doesn't cook, so if it's being used, it's not by him.

"Can I get you anything to drink? Ty, you need a beer? Pabst was all they had but it'll do if you really need one. Might have some Coke…"

I kick at the floor with the front toe of my boot. "So, B, whose place is this?"

"Kelly's." His smile gets even wider. "She's at work now but she'll be back in a minute, if you want to meet her."

"Sure," I say, though the word sounds weak even to me. I don't want to meet Kelly. Kelly, the reason he's here. The reason he's not getting better.

I take my coat off, throw it over the back of the ratty couch. He walks around the couch, staring at me.

What? Why is he staring? I look down, did I spill something on myself? Typical. No, I don't think so, what the hell is he looking at?

"You're huge," B says, voice soft, sad.

The long-sleeved tee does fit a little tighter around my arms, but wow, that's not really what I was expecting. I look at my brother. He looks small, old, even. So damn thin that he might just float away. Cheeks look too white beneath his long sandy hair. His sweater is high against his neck, sleeves long. Looks like it was a nice sweater once, like Abercrombie or something, but it's like him, worn. His jeans don't have any holes in the knees, and he looks way too preppy for his craptastic surroundings.

Does he expect me to say something to that? Like what? Yeah, I'm the freaking Hulk and you're back to being a junkie, holding your left side like it hurts to breathe. I shrug. Can't say that. Can't think that. "Why did you leave the center, B?"

He ignores me. Just walks past me and into the side bedroom, taking my coat from the couch to the bed and coming back. He needs time to think up an answer? Didn't he have all that time when he wasn't calling? When we didn't know where he was or if he was still alive? Couldn't he have thought of something then? He sighs. Looks at his feet, then meets my eye, smiling. Lame smile. Half-smile, not real, not true, not him. Shit.

"I don't need all their steps. They didn't show any respect for me as an intellectual, you know? Talked to me like I was some kind of idiot. I'm not unintelligent, I'm an addict. It's different." He coughs. "That and I'm worried about you."

Lying son of a bitch. He expects me to believe that line of bull? Like Rick is the one who's doing me wrong?

Heart pounding, hurting my ears, my voice is low. "So you left rehab because you're worried about me? Really, B?"

His face, that half-smile, falters, shakes. I've never in my life questioned him before. Not really. He knows it. Knows he's gone too far. "Yeah."

"Because, I mean, if you were really that worried, you'd think that maybe you would've called, I don't know, sooner?" I can't stop it. Can't keep my voice steady. I want to fucking kill him. Hands balling into fists, I want to throw him to the ground and hurt him, hurt him for this, hurt him for Mom, for me, for Dad.

"Tyler, man, you don't understand, it's complicated, we just got a phone and–"

"Bullshit," I say. Voice tight. Vowels clipped. Heart breaking. Broken. Smashed.

Brandon goes. I can see it. It's like he falls into himself just a little, just a bit, and then I can see the dark around his eyes and how thin he is and the pain written into his face. Just a junkie, getting older. "You don't get it, Ty, you can't trust that guy. Haranco is a division of Tidewater. They do contract work for JSOC and they *use* people. I had to get out, find out what he's really up to–"

"Rick isn't my problem." My cheeks are burning. "Rick's hooked me up with a job, with a future. What have you done for me, Brandon? What have you ever done that hasn't brought me anything but pain?" I can't breathe. Need air. I force in a deep breath. "You know what? Just tell me what you need. Money? Tell me how much."

"No, Ty, I don't need money." The hurt in his eyes is real, but distant. "Maybe a little. I'm having a tough time finding work in the field."

"Did you even call Mom? You know, let her know you're not, I don't know, dead?" He hurt Mom, he hurt me, he hurt Mom, she cries, oh God she cries at night when she thinks I can't hear and he probably hasn't even called. My eyes sting and my cheeks are wet and my heart is screaming. He looks like I slapped him. Fuck him. "Can I see your phone?"

"What?" His eyes get all hollow-looking and his posture sort of slumps over.

I do a quick, angry pantomime of a phone. "Can. I. See. Your. Phone."

He pulls out his phone and gives it a quick glance before handing it over. "Here."

Good. Let him feel like an ass. I scroll through the call log. Nice phone, not the latest model or anything, but decent, probably a pre-pay. Calls, so many calls. Swallowing the bile that mushroom clouds up through my vision, I ask, "God, how many people did you call before me, B?"

He doesn't answer, he looks at the floor. My stomach feels empty and like lead all at the same time. He never called Mom. Leaving me to tell her that he's alive, leaving me to do the hard stuff for him, to shield him from seeing. Seeing how he's destroyed his mother, how he's wrecked her life, how she doesn't trust herself to love anyone ever again because of what he's done. I shut the phone. Squeeze it in my right hand. Squeeze it. Feel the smooth shell and the weight and squeeze, wrapping my palm and fingers around it, squeeze, not wanting to know who ranked first on that call list, not wanting to know why they got the first call.

Eyes wandering the room, he talks to the air, to the world, to everything but me. "It's hard to find any kind of job in journalism, you know. They all want transcripts from college and my work history. No one wants to give anyone a break anymore, and you need to be in school to be an intern, so it's just been rough going, you know?"

Should have thought of that before sticking that needle in your arm. "You can get a job flipping burgers or something to pay the bills, B. You know, like the rest of the world." I feel my head wind up tight. "Why'd you call that reporter from Canada? Planning to move?"

"No. He called you?"

"Yeah. Why?"

"Because Rick's using you, Tyler."

I laugh. Not a happy sound. "That's funny coming from you, B."

He stops. Stares. Does he not see? All the lies he's told and the money he's bummed and the…

"It's different. Rick's company–"

"Haranco."

"Yeah, Haranco, they're mercenaries. That flight school he keeps talking about, I don't think that it's going to be the type of flight school that you've been counting on."

"I know what I'm doing, B."

"No, I don't think that you do."

"Brandon. You're not listening. I. Know." I look at him. Dead in the eyes. "I know exactly what I'm doing."

"Oh shit." B's voice is like a whisper. Light, breathless, shocked. "You're actually piloting the drones."

The truth just hangs. Hangs in the air in between us. And he looks small. I can't remember him ever looking so small before. He's thin and has tiny lines around his eyes because his face is too skinny and even his hands look sort of hollow. But it's his eyes. They're still Brandon's eyes. Always Brandon's eyes. Eyes that can look at three billion pieces of shattered vase on the floor and figure out how to make them fit back together. Put everything back together but his own life. "It's a good thing, B."

"It's not good." He backs away. Physically takes a step away from me. From *me*. "It's not good, Tyler. You're a hired gun. You kill people for *money*."

Bodies torn apart lying by the road, dog limping covered in blood against a desert. "No." I swallow. "I kill people for America. For my country. It's just like being in the Air Force."

"Except you're not in the Air Force." He thrusts his arms up in the air like he wants to shake me, punch me. "Haranco may take contracts from the government but they'll kill for the highest bidder."

The dog, covered in blood, limping. "Maybe you should take a good look at yourself, B, before you go around shitting on other people. I mean, you only asked me over here so I could give you money, right?"

"No, it's not like that." Brandon's face is pale, painted with disbelief, horror, disappointment. I don't care. I just want to get out of here.

"Right, well." I reach into my pocket, pulling out a wad of bills. I put them down on the back of the couch in front of me. "Here's two hundred bucks. Hope that helps. I gotta go."

"Wait."

I grab my coat and unlock the deadbolt on the door. Need to go. Need to go now before I hurt him. Need to leave and run a mile. Or hit something. Hard. Now.

"Tyler," he says, voice soft, muted, "tell Mom I said hey."

That's it? I'm going to kill him. Grab him and tear at him and scream. I throw the door back wide, feeling it pull at the muscles in my arm, ripping up through my shoulder, pulling at my neck.

"Tell her yourself," I shout and let the door slam behind me.

"Are you serious? What do you mean you didn't get it yet?" Peanut's voice. High. Happy. Incredulous. I look up at his face on the screen, popping the last of the chips in my mouth. Don't need this. Seeing B really messed me up. Ran for an hour outside in the rain and it didn't help. Didn't kill the pain.

"I mean I didn't get it yet, OK?" I answer. So calm. So calm. Three months ago I would have rather chewed off my own leg rather than miss the release of *Zombie Ninja Dojo 2*, but now, well, I don't care.

"You OK over there man, cause I thought you just said that you haven't gotten *ZND2* yet." Alpha's face laughs at me from monitor two.

"Got other things going on," I say, taking a swig of Red Bull and sitting down. The stuff tastes like ass, but it works alright. "Playing the flight sim game a lot."

"Aw c'mon, that's boring as shit," Peanut says, red curls looking lank, unwashed, even through the lens of the screen.

"Nah man, not if you do it right," I say, pushing back into the chair.

"Oh yeah? I tried that free online version the other day. What's your kill count at, man?" Peanut asks. "Mine's at like one. Slowest. Game. Ever. How can their upgrade be any better? That game sucks."

"Um, ninety-six." I try and remember the number every night before I turn off the game. Knowing each digit is a dead terrorist. Or at least a few of them are. Wish I knew for sure how many were real. To know exactly how many terrorists won't kill anybody else because I stopped them. I have to figure out what those convoys are doing, though. Sometimes their stops don't make any sense. Like when they deliver their goods and bring the empty trucks someplace else to fill up. What the hell are they filling up with in Afghanistan? Do they recycle the crates or something?

"Ninety-six! Ugh. How many hours that take you? I hate it. Moves too slow, and all the math. It's like a learning game and shit."

"C'mon, the calculations are easy. It's like third-grade stuff." I pop a few chips in my mouth. Thank God Mom remembered to go to the store. "Oh, wait, I'm sorry, didn't you fail third grade?"

"Ouch, man. You're hit, P." Alpha laughs.

"Whatever, look, I gotta go. Go play a real game." Peanut's face is like his hair, bright red. "Alpha, man, check the cheat codes and get back to me, alright?"

"Yeah, man, later." Alpha smiles at me from the inset pic on the monitor. "Me too. Tyrade, get your ass to the store tomorrow and check in later, OK?"

"Yeah, maybe," I say. I hit end.

Leaning back, way back in my chair I stretch, feel everything get long, get ready, get loose. Flipping on the switch, I bite back the nagging in my head and start to fly.

ANI

Why does everything we read for freshman Lit have to be so depressing? I throw *Madame Bovary* to the side and get up to grab my water bottle out of the mini-fridge. Picking up the book again, I read one line and throw it back into the pillows. I wonder what Tyler's doing right now, and I push the back of my head into the bed as I imagine him flying the sim. I'm just not OK with this, but I have no idea what to do about it that wouldn't end up hurting one or the both of us.

Just the thought makes my stomach turn. I don't know how I'm going to be able to eat anything for lunch. Dad killed people, and look what happened to him. Everything was different for him when he came home. Dad used to be so open, so much fun. Now he's not even allowed to cut his own steak because he might try and kill himself with a plastic butter knife. Tyler doesn't understand and I don't know how to warn him, how to explain what this might do to him. What war did to my father.

My throat's killing me and my nose won't stop running. I run my hands up the side of my face and push in at the temples, anything to make the thoughts of Dad alone in a cell disappear. God, I can't let that happen to Tyler, too.

Sitting up, I plug in. Mr Anderson has to have another programmer. I don't think that he could link the system that I made to the drones overseas by himself. And it sounds like not all of the missions that the kids fly are real, most of them are just a sim. But I now know for a fact that a couple of Tyler's were linked up to the UAVs, I just have to figure out which ones.

Pulling up my Haranco files on my laptop, I scan through the different lines of codes. If I can figure out which code links the sim machines to the actual drones I can tag each time someone flies on those codes and record it. Back it all up.

I start a new file, call it Jericho. I have to figure out how to bring Haranco down.

If only there was a way that Tyler wouldn't go down with Mr Anderson. I take a sip of water, and wonder what the price of saving him from a future like my father's will be.

CHAPTER 24

SUNDAY, OCTOBER 28

TYLER

"Tyler?" Ani's voice is all nose when she opens the door to her dorm room. Wow. She even looks sick. Eyes all red, nose all red, hair all matted and wild. Kind of cute, in a way.

"Hey." I hold out the bag. "I suck at cooking, but I bought you a big thing of chicken noodle soup from the deli down the block." I walk inside, shoving papers out of the way to make room on her desk to put down the bag. Hope they aren't important. I can put them back later, maybe, but I have to put the bag down. It's one of those thin white paper bags that's leaking and burning my arm. "Oh, and some ramen noodles for later, in case you need some. And Gatorade powder. You need to stay hydrated. Some vitamin C chew tabs, which Mom used to make me take whenever I got sick, and here" – I hold out the little boxes. Covered with my terrible wrapping job. Please let her like it please let her like it – "Got you these, to cheer you up."

Her mouth is open. Gaping. Can't tell if it's because she's surprised or if it's because she can't breathe through her nose. Her robe hangs open wide. She looks so good in that little tank under there. Short shorts. Right. She's sick. Not in the mood to make out. I probably should have gotten tissues for her. The college probably only has those thin, rough ones. Hate those. Make your nose feel all raw and chapped. Should have gotten her the soft ones.

"What are these?" She takes the packages. I put my arm around her waist. Lead her over to her bed. Should I fluff her pillows? Does that actually do anything? Don't think I've ever had my pillows fluffed. I pile them up against the wall. Help her sit down. She runs her slender fingers underneath the packaging. Shit. It's the small one. My throat gets a little tight. What if she hates it? What if it's awful?

"I thought of you when I saw it," I say.

She pulls it out of the box, holding up the ax on the thin gold chain. Dangles it in the air over the box. Her eyes go all distant and soft and she presses her lips together. What does that mean? Don't know. She must hate it. "It's beautiful. You really shouldn't have."

"Wait, you like it?"

"Yes." She sits up a little straighter, leaning in as she unhooks the clasp.

My heartbeat picks up. I did it. She likes it. "Let me help you put it on," I say and grab the thing. Wow, is it small. I move her hair off of the back of her neck. The lines of her neck are so perfect. Like a painting. I want to kiss her. Kiss the back of her neck. See what her skin feels like against my lips. I don't. I fasten the clasp. Put her hair back where it belongs.

"How does it look?" She turns to face me, beaming.

I want to kiss her. Throw her down on the mattress and pull her arms up over her head and just kiss her forever. But she obviously wants an answer with words. And she's sick. Right. "Looks great." I bite my lower lip. She smiles. Bite my lip harder so I won't kiss her. "Here, open this one."

She takes the second box and carefully undoes the wrapping. "*Zombie Ninja Dojo 2*." She turns it over, studying the back cover. "I've been hearing a lot about this."

Is that good? I walk over to the desk. Get her a Styrofoam bowl of soup and a spoon from the bag. Smells good. Salty and warm and like... chicken soup. "Here. Eat. Then we play."

"Tyler MacCandless," she says as she puts the game aside and grabs the bowl full of soup, "I swear you're the best boyfriend ever."

My face gets hot. Like real hot, and I look down at her comforter. A mess of pinks and purples. Then I look up at her face, her eyes shining. At me. My breath gets quick and my heart sort of does this little leap. Happy. Think I'm happy. No. I know that I'm happy. I kiss her. On her forehead, which is sweet and salty all at once. I say, "Eat."

ANI

How can I hurt him? He's asleep, arms wrapped around my waist, their weight wonderful and frightening all at the same time. Sleep washes away all the fear and the worry from his face, and he looks beautiful. Maybe I shouldn't think of him as beautiful, but that's how he looks: innocent, delicate, sweet as he dreams.

Sitting up, I shuffle out of bed and down the hall to use the bathroom. The threadbare carpet scratches the bottom of my feet and I swear that I'm sneezing loud enough to wake the whole dorm. I splash some water on my face as I wash my hands after I'm done, and as I walk back out of the bathroom I hear someone call my name. Christy's sitting at the far end of the hall, chatting with one of the other girls on our floor. She waves me over and I wrap my robe tight around my shoulders against the cold as I make my way down there.

Christy and her friend are crouched around newspapers placed flat on the floor and a few different bottles of nail polish and emery boards. "Hey Ani, come sit." Christy pats a space on the floor next to her, careful not to mess up the new polish. "Saw the guy. He's totally cute."

Oh. "Yeah, sorry about that, I guess I should have–"

"Not a problem, Monica's roommate is off visiting her boyfriend in Boston this weekend so I'm crashing with her." Christy pushes the bottles towards me. "Pick your poison. I think the blue for you."

I nod at Monica and she gives me the briefest of smiles before she goes back to holding her tongue steady between her lips as she paints color on her nails.

"I don't think I could paint my nails right now without sneezing and messing everything up," I say.

"Here" – Christy grabs my hand in hers – "I'll do it for you, then."

"But–"

"Your guy is sleeping, right?"

"Yeah."

"So what else do you have to do?" She smiles as she reaches for the bottle of blue, knowing that she's already won the argument. It *is* a pretty color, dark with a nice sheen. If I were a character in a videogame, I would want that color hair.

I let her paint my nails, and she tells me all about her latest boyfriend, who she thinks she is going to dump for this other guy in her biology lab. But she feels bad, of course, because the first guy really is sweet. I don't really have anything to add, so I just smile and try not to sneeze.

Monica, once she finishes painting her own nails black with neon-pink tips, says, "I left my boyfriend back home, but I'm probably going to run into him at this year's NARAM."

Christy and I look at each other. "Can you put that in English, please?" Christy asks.

"Oh, the National Association of Rocketry's Annual Meet." Monica blows on her nails. "We're both into building model rockets, it's how we met."

"Is this something that's going to happen soon, or do we have some time to find you someone new?" Christy asks, her eyes not leaving my fingertips.

"I don't know if I want someone else, really." Monica launches into her history with both the boyfriend and model rockets, and my mind wanders in and out, wanting to get my nails good and painted so I can go back to sleep, but then Monica says, "So we had to try and get into the base to get our rocket back."

"Wait, I'm sorry, what? You flew a rocket over some kind of base?" I ask, heart fluttering as I remember Mr Anderson sitting at my table, telling me that flying my little SkyPet over a military base was a federal offense.

"Yeah, Wright-Patterson Air Force Base, it's right near where we lived in Dayton. You should have seen him, he offered to climb the fence to get it back for me. I told him not to be stupid and we walked around front and begged the guys at the entrance to let us in. No big deal."

"Should have just cut your losses and left. It was just a model, wasn't it?" Christy asks.

"Wait, but isn't it restricted airspace? Flying anything over a base is a federal offense, right? Did you get in trouble?"

Christy and Monica both stare at me, their eyes wide and round. Christy backs away a bit from my nails. She says, "Ani, it was clearly an accident. And they were in high school. No one's going to slap a federal charge on some kids whose toy went off-course."

Blood sears through my veins, skin stretching tight over my skull. I'm an idiot: a complete, total and utter moron. Christy and Monica move along with the conversation, like they're sailing along downriver without me, leaving me stuck in the mud by the shore. "Monica," I say as I stand. "Did the model rocket you flew over the base have a camera?" Is that it? Is that the difference, is there any way that Mr Anderson wasn't–

"Yeah, all of our models have cameras. We even had a channel on YouTube, if you want to check it out," she says and holds her nails up in front of her face.

Mr Anderson lied. He was lying to me in the sales pitch for this job. Played on the fact that I was young and would be terrified of being sent to jail like my dad. I reach out and touch the wall to hold myself steady. "Goodnight, guys. I have to go."

Every word Mr Anderson said to me that day, every word he said to Mom, selling us this job like it was the best, most noble thing in the world, plays over and over again in my head, until my mouth sours and ears ache with the memory.

Careful not to wake up Tyler as he sleeps, I grab the tissue box and crawl onto the far side of the bed. I tuck the laptop close into my body, looking for a solution that I know is there, waiting for me to find it. I type, writing the first lines of a virus.

CHAPTER 25

MONDAY, OCTOBER 29

TYLER

The call comes at dawn. I'm in bed, arms draped around Ani. Can't mess around when she's feeling sick, but I held her. Held her all night. Just stayed there and slept. Slept well, even though she snored.

I've been expecting the call. So when my phone rings in the morning and I hear the sterile voice on the other end of the line I'm not surprised. I don't feel anything. I whisper to Ani that I have to leave, kiss her on the top of her head, and go.

As I walk over I send Mom a quick text to let her know what's up and make my way to Yale-New Haven hospital. Wonder if I should text Rick, too. Not sure what I think about him and Mom becoming friends. But if he could help me convince her to come down to the hospital, it would be great. I send him a quick message.

The hall is long and dark and warm and reeks of Lysol and cardboard-like hospital food. I don't know how I manage to speak, feels like a tennis ball lodged itself in my throat. The nurse guides me back, pushing apart the swinging doors. Metal on the bottom. Metal on the faces of the people who work here. Doctors and nurses and orderlies immune to the people like me. To the people in the beds. The nurse points me to the door.

His door.

Visions of B at Little League and soccer. Staying up in each other's beds at night. Playing Hot Wheels. My stomach and heart leap up and tangle together and the heavy air hits me. Can't take this feeling of everything rising and then freefalling back down into the base of my throat.

I walk past the other rooms. The hall seems really long, other people, people like me, not-sick people stand around, grief and disbelief and pain shocking all humanity right out of them. Standing, like me, in a hall, looking like a zombie. Like a boy who used to be Tyler MacCandless.

Please God, let it not be now. Let it not be now. Give him another chance please God let it not be now he's only twenty-three he can't die now please not now.

I don't think I'm man enough to go in. I stand at the door. Frozen. Adrenaline icing my veins and terror weighing a ton in my belly and my throat and burning up to my eyes and maybe if I just stand here it won't be true. He won't be dying. If I don't see it then it can't be real.

Fuck. I can't. If he's dying then he's not doing it alone. He'll do it with me. I just have to take two steps more and he's not alone.

My eyes are burning. Like on fire. But I open the door. I feel like somebody took a baseball bat and pounded me straight in the gut. I can't. Can't see him like this again he's so far gone I'll never get him back. Not ever. So thin.

B's stick-thin, a speck of color in an ocean of white sheets and blue tubing and God knows what else. Slowly, like a trek through to another universe, I walk to the side of his bed. The heart-rate monitor is steady, his blood oxygen level is OK because if it wasn't the little thing would be beeping, but he does have a mask, so that's probably why. I take his chart off the side of the bed. And there it is. Naloxone. The drug for an OD. It's what they gave him last time. And the time before that. A tickling, slimy thread of grief squeezes me tighter. How does he do this? Every time I hope. Every time it only gets worse.

It hits me, comes up to the top of my head. The thought that now goes off like a revolver in my brain. He's not getting better. No matter how much I want him to, no matter how much I love him it's just not enough. Will never be enough. I look over the list of the billions of drugs it seems like they gave him. He's got a fever, I guess. Lots of vancomycin.

I push the chart back into the slot on the bed, dragging a chair next to B and sit. The sounds of the hospital seem strange, distant all at the same time. He's sleeping. But not even sleep can wash the life he's lived off his face. Every inch of him looks hollow, stained. Doesn't look real, even, anymore, with all these tubes and gadgets he looks like something else and not like the boy who used to be my brother. Everybody used to say that we looked so much alike, and now, like this, he barely looks human.

Running my hands over my scalp, I rub, try to erase this, erase everything from my head but I can't. Just can't. A voice, tired, stretched thin, says, "Are you the next of kin?"

"Yeah, Tyler MacCandless. Brandon's brother." My head clears. Have to get sharp. Stay together.

"Hi, I'm Dr Feinburg. I'm the one who called." Dr Feinburg's white coat falls over crumpled khakis, and that together with his balding head and thin wire glasses gives him the look of a guy who works really hard. I hope he has a nice life to go home to. This job's gotta suck.

I nod. Then look down at the bed.

He waits. I know he wants to ask about Mom, but I can't go there right now so he's just gonna have to talk to me. He says, "Your brother's very sick."

"No shit." Leaves my mouth before I want it to and I cringe. Great. Pissing the doctor off really isn't what I want to do. "Sorry. I–"

"It's OK." He moves to the side of the bed, so he can talk to me across Brandon and still check the machines. "Are you aware of your brother's drug abuse?"

The laugh rockets out of my mouth. Short and bitter. "You could say that. He overdosed again, right?"

"He's done this before."

"Yeah, but last time the ambulance brought him to St Raphe's." I shrug. "They might have his records there if you call."

"His information is in our system. He had you listed as his next of kin." Me. Always me. Mom should be here, should be hearing this, not me, not alone, not again. The doctor's eyes come together slightly as they look at me. Not in a mean way, more like he feels bad but doesn't want to look like he feels bad. Probably a good guy, Dr Feinburg. He holds my gaze, voice steady and says, "Your brother, aside from his drug abuse, is suffering from a very serious heart condition called endocarditis."

My heart balls up, hard like stone, rises up into my neck then crashes, washing away everything.

"Endocarditis is an infection of the heart lining and valves. It's not uncommon in people with a history of drug use. We're treating it now intravenously, but he will have to continue the treatments when he leaves or it will be fatal."

I nod. Fatal. Everything is fatal. Driving a car or walking down the street or playing ball: all roads lead to the end, eventually. But this, this disease, looks like it's hurried up and stamped an expiration date on B's forehead. Does he even know? Does he know what he's doing or that his card is up? Every time he gives me this talk about how life is worth fighting for and he wants to live so he's going to rehab and blah freaking blah blah blah but now it's up. Does he want this? He has to if he keeps coming back here. If he beats this, it'll just be something else. That chick he's banging will give him AIDS or that guy's needle he borrowed will give him Hep C and it will never end it will only get worse if he keeps this up but I don't see him stopping. Not now. Not after he tried and couldn't... again.

"Drug addiction is a disease. He can get better." He reaches his hand out, touches my shoulder.

Again, that laugh. That short sound that I don't even recognize as being mine leaves my mouth and words singe my tongue as I say, "I don't buy that line anymore, doc. But thanks."

The doctor pauses, like he wants to say something else, then takes his hand back, and moves over to the other side of the curtained room to check on the other patient. I look down at B, all fucked-up. All skinny and weak with a bad heart. And I know, deep in some pit inside me, that he's not going to get better. Not ever. And I'm too chickenshit to even kick him awake. To talk to him now while there's still time.

Have to walk, have to get out of here. I stand, pushing my feet hard into the tile of the floor, and stomp down the hall, down the stairs. Pace the food court. Pace and wait until the doctor's words enter my head and can stay there without hurting so much.

The cafeteria's closed, but I walk over to the vending machine, buy some crackers and a Powerade, the noise from the machine echoing in the darkened room. I grab the food and pull out my cell.

"Mom?" I say as she picks up.

"Tyler? Where are you? Aren't you home?"

Can't she fucking function? I need her, dammit. Swallow it, swallow it, Ty. You love your mom. "No, Mom. I'm at the hospital. With Brandon. He OD'd again."

A cleaning cart making its way down the hall outside the cafeteria is the only sound I can hear. "What can you do about it? You should come home."

"He's sick, Mom. Has some heart condition, disease, I don't know. They say he's…" Can't say it can't think it saying it makes it real. "He's dying."

The cart clanks and then a boom and then a vacuum starts up, sucking up grime. "Come home, baby."

Fuck. I end the call. Fine. What did I expect? I sit at an empty table, head heavy, aching. So tired. If I just close my eyes maybe all this bullshit will go away.

I wake up with a jump as some lady kicks the back of my chair.

"Sorry," she mumbles and wipes her eyes with the sleeve on her sweater. Damn, did I fall asleep? How long have I been down here? Got to get back to his room, I can sleep up there. Those chairs at least are padded.

Grinding my hands into my head, I get up. I pound my way up the stairs, hitting each step hard. Maybe by now it'll just be the nurses on duty and I can spend the rest of the day without having anyone else come in the room and talk to me about B. I want the quiet.

Making my way down his hall as I open the jar of Powerade, I swing into his room.

But it's empty.

CHAPTER 26

WEDNESDAY, OCTOBER 31

TYLER

The car outside is honking. What time is it? I roll over. Hate it when people honk at dawn. It's rude. Sore eyes looking over to the clock. 8am. Great. That gives me what, like, three hours of sleep last night? Honk again.

Dammit. Throwing my legs over the side of the bed, I rub my hands over my face. Hard. Get up, walk down the hall. "Mom," I call. Suitcases lying around her feet, cup of coffee in her hand. She yanks a bungee around her two carry-ons. She's leaving. My head tries to keep up with my eyes. "Where are you going?"

She looks up. "Oh, Tyler. On that business trip to Los Angeles, remember?"

"You didn't tell me you were going on a trip."

"I thought I mentioned it."

"You didn't." I grit my teeth. "You can go to California on business, but you can't bother to call B. He's really sick and-"

"I have to go. The car is outside." She locks the cord around her suitcase and opens the door for the driver, lips pressed tight together, eyes down. Why do I even ask? Just pisses me off. Should know better. Should stop being pissed that she's too burned to care.

"You have to help me. We have to get Brandon back into the hospital, he's says he's taking the antibiotics as pills but Dr Feinburg said that he needs to get them intravenously and–"

"I have to go, Tyler." She kisses me on the cheek. Light kiss. Like she didn't even hear what I just said. Maybe she didn't. Maybe every time I say B's name she goes someplace else. Someplace where he can't hurt her anymore. My hands ache to reach out and shake her, wake her up, make her help me, make her fight for B, but I don't. I can't.

At least she's telling me she's leaving. Last time I only found out she was away on business when I called her office at like eleven at night to find out why she wasn't home. "How long?"

"A week."

"Can you text me the name of your hotel?" Sounds reasonable. Like something family is supposed to ask.

"Sure." I walk up to her, kiss her on the forehead and she wipes her blond hair back behind her ear as she looks up at me. "My car keys are on the counter, OK? Love you."

"Love you too, Mom." I watch the guy load the bags in the car. Hope he drives slow. Hate those drivers that go too fast. Scares me thinking about Mom being driven around by some guy I don't really know. Deep breath, Ty, she'll be fine.

I wait until the car drives out of sight, then I walk back into the kitchen. How soon can I get to Ani's? The keys are on the counter, just like Mom said. Her car is nice. Rides real nice. But I have a lot of time. Sucks. Maybe I'll drive it over to the bagel shop and eat some breakfast.

It's mid-afternoon. Ani's at class, Mom's gone and I'm flying. Following a bunch of trucks. Mostly I'm a traffic cop, really. Flying over a gazillion miles of road. Really dull. At least today there are trucks on the road. The ones for that Pakistani company Rick says brings in supplies for a few NATO bases in Helmand province, I guess. For the past two days it's been nothing but roads. Roads and the damn trucks. Rick says it will get better soon. After the "big reveal" or whatever so he can put me in charge of a drone clan. Says it will give me someone to talk to. About what, though? I mean, should I tell them about the missions or the fact that my brother was in a hospital dying and my mother wouldn't even call him? They're gonna talk to me once and run away screaming.

The trucks roll over the border, which is only marked on my screen with a big, yellow, superimposed line like the first down line in a TV broadcast of the NFL. They take forever to get through the damn checkpoint. I put the primary drone on a circle pattern over them and stand up. Have to stretch. I reach out behind me and go over to the iPod dock for a second. Getting bored with the same old songs. Need something new. Need something fast and hard that will keep me awake for a few more hours so I can see these trucks through the rest of their run. Hate to leave something not finished. Perfect. They're through the checkpoint and moving again. I set the tail.

Want Rick to get his money's worth. They're paying me so much. In cash. It's weird. Cool as shit. But weird.

I yank the cuff off my arm for a minute and roll down the hall to the kitchen. Grab a Pizza Pocket. Go back. Great. They're on the road. I hook up the cuff again, sit down in the leather chair I swear is molded to my ass permanently, and watch.

The delivery goes as it usually does. Takes a few hours. The trucks roll into the city and pull up to the building which I guess is like a hospital or distribution center or something. Maybe a NATO base: all buildings look pretty much like big concrete rectangles from the sky. Guys all wearing the same kind of uniform come out and meet the drivers. They sit and have tea or whatever after unloading all the trucks. The first time I watched I sort of freaked because the drivers just got out of the trucks and disappeared for a while.

So boring. Seriously. Watching a bunch of empty trucks idling is about as exciting as watching rocks. Whatever. SKY comes through. Another drone needed for cover on a different road. Great, now I get two screens of nothing.

I put the second drone on the surveillance route and give it screen two. Drivers on screen one are getting back into their trucks. They roll out, driving slowly through town. Back towards the border. Surveillance mission on second drone is clear. No activity, just empty highway.

But the trucks. The trucks, once outside of the city, pull off the road, take a detour. Pull up in front of some building. The drivers get out. Greet the people on the ground. Then they all start loading up the trucks. Filling three trucks with crates. Crates that they're going to drive back over the border into Pakistan.

My throat itches and I take a swig of Dew. Doesn't help. My stomach tightens. This is the fifth time I've seen them do this. I look at the latitude and longitude of the building. Just outside of Baram Cha.

It's not right. I'm supposed to make sure that supplies get into Helmand province. Bring soldiers food and medicine and good things. But what the hell are the trucks taking out?

The drivers shut the back doors of the trucks and before long they are rolling through the border. Border guys just wave them on through. Do they see me? Up in the air, flying over trucks that are supposed to be empty? Hell of a thing, to have protection like these trucks have.

It's cool. It has to be cool. Rick would never be involved in something that wasn't cool.

Unless he doesn't know. I pick up the phone, dial. "Ani?"

"Hey, Tyler. I can't talk, I'm walking into class." Her voice sounds so good. Need to hear it. Need her.

"Can I come by later? I need to talk to you about something," I ask, leaning forward. I run my hands over my scalp, not wanting to watch the trucks anymore.

"Not today, I have a test first thing in the morning. I can see you when it's over, though. How about tomorrow night?"

Sucks. "Yeah, fine. See you then."

"Perfect. Talk soon, OK?"

"OK, bye." I hang up. Stare at the phone in my hand. Look up at the screens. The trucks are rolling past the border, rolling through Pakistani territory. What the fuck are they doing?

CHAPTER 27

THURSDAY, NOVEMBER 1

TYLER

Think I just got overrun by a bus full of zombies. Doesn't matter.

"What do you know about the missions, about the routes?" I ask. Holding my voice steady. Level. Calm.

Ani looks down at her controller, puts it at her feet. She looks better, feels better, but her voice is still a little nasal. "I help program the targets."

"Right, but do you program in the patrol routes? The ones Rick said were for a contract Haranco has with some Pakistani security firm?" I don't watch the screen.

"No."

"You know where I fly them, though."

"Everybody flies those routes."

"Ani, I…" I take the controller out of her hand. Put it down, look over my shoulder, making sure the door to her room is closed. "I need to know what's in those trucks."

She looks distant, like her eyes go someplace else. "Why don't you ask your buddy Mr Anderson?"

Right. "He says that the trucks move supplies into Afghanistan."

Her face is hard, eyes set, looking at the game screen. "Well, then what's your problem?"

"They're delivering the supplies like he said, but then they're stopping. Stopping before they get back to Pakistan, picking up truckloads of... something. Then driving it back over the border to Pakistan. I need to know what that something is."

Silence. I'm looking into her face, angled away from me. Like she's counting the specks on the tile of the floor. After what feels like forever she says, "How many times have you seen this happen?"

"I don't know, at least four or five times." I don't want to say it, but I do. "Twice yesterday, few times over the past couple of weeks. They can't be moving the same type of supplies back out of Afghanistan."

She opens her mouth but doesn't speak. Not right away, still looking at the damn floor. "I wouldn't think so. This is in Helmand province, right?"

"Yeah, just outside of Baram Cha." I take my eyes off of her, lines of her face telling me nothing. I run my hands through my hair. "What's in those trucks?"

"Are you going to make me say it?" Her voice soft.

"What?"

"I mean, there's only one obvious answer here, Tyler, and I think you know what it is." Her words come fast now. "And if what you're saying is true then I'm walking away. I know it's all you've got and I know it means I'll have to leave Yale but I can't anymore. I can't be a part of this."

"What are you talking about? I don't know, that's why I'm here talking to you."

"Come on. You're not stupid." She stands up, eyebrows coming together. "You wouldn't be here talking with me about this if you didn't know the answer to your own question. He's been lying to me from the start, but this? I can't believe Mr Anderson would do this! I can't believe that he would use my program to do this."

"Do what?"

"Drugs, Tyler." She pushes at my chest, throwing me back against the base of the platform bed. "Helmand province. The only cash crop they have over there is opium poppies. Opium, heroin, morphine – call it whatever you want but I can almost guarantee you that that's what is in those trucks."

"There's no way. Rick would never agree to fly cover for them if they were running drugs." Rick will kill them when he finds out. Have to tell him. Tell him what's going on so he can stop it.

"He knows about the drugs." She stands up, wrapping her arms around her own waist. "It's his business to know everything about Haranco and their contracts."

"No way. Those guys are shits. I mean, like, they just load up the trucks, out in the open, people just drive on by and they don't even care. If it was drugs people would stop them, say something to the police."

"In Afghanistan? In Helmand? It's one of the largest opium-producing regions in the world. Don't be stupid here, Tyler. It's drugs. It has to be drugs."

No. Can't be drugs. Rick can't take a job from a bunch of drug runners. He would never do that. He hates drugs. Believes in his country. Believes in honor. Believes in the war on drugs. He would never have me fly missions for some drug lords. Not ever. "Rick doesn't know that they're running drugs."

"Are you kidding me? He knows everything!" She stands right in front of me, taking my face in her hands. "I'm sorry he's not the man you thought he was, but trust me, he knows what's in those trucks. And he's paying you to make sure they get to where they need to go."

I feel the touch of her hands on my cheeks. I hear her words. Hear the sound of her voice. But I can't put them all together and make things fit the way I need them to go.

"No." I hold her hands in mine. Take them off of my face, gently. "No, he doesn't know." Because if he knows, then I'm a drug runner. And a murderer. And that just can't be. That's not who I am. Not who I want to be. "It can't be true." I kiss her. Kiss her on the top of her head. "I'll talk to him about it. Tell him. He'll cut them off. Take care of it. But trust me, he would never agree to work for those people. Not ever."

"Why do you keep defending him? It makes no sense. He knows everything about this program, he controls everything!"

"You don't know him."

"This is insane. Insane! I can't, can't do this anymore, Tyler. I just can't." Her whole body's shaking as she backs away from me.

"What?"

Her eyes shine so hard they look like they're on fire. "It's him or me. Your choice."

Fuck. This. I turn around and walk out the door, slamming it behind me.

Don't have to wait for long. Rick's in my driveway when I get back. I creep Mom's car in behind him and turn off the car. Deep breath. He doesn't know about the drugs. He can't know.

The day is warm for October, afternoon sun hanging low, painting the sky orange. Rick's wearing a fleece pullover and jeans. Deep breath, Ty. I fidget with my phone, tucking it into my pocket. He waves his hand in greeting. "Hey, Ty, got your text." He looks at me as I get out of the car. Then the smile leaves his eyes. Grabbing the envelope. My next envelope, he hands it out to me.

I take it. Don't want it, but I take it. Maybe I'll mail it to a rehab center. Give it to somebody good. Somebody who helps people. Slip it in my back pocket. I shrug. Honest, Tyler, just be honest. This is Rick. You've known Rick for years. "Hey, yeah, come on in, I need to talk to you about something."

He follows me to the front door. Big guy, standing right behind me, smelling like a mix of aftershave and whatever the stuff is he has in that flask that he carries. Damn, I wish he'd stop drinking so much. I unlock the door and we go in. Go over to the fridge, open it. Take out my phone, fiddle with it, put it back in my pocket then grab a bottle of Gatorade. I offer one to him and he accepts. We move over to the dining room. I don't want to sit in front of the sim. And the dining room has this great long window that lets in the light. Help me to read his face.

"What's your worry?" he asks, tone light.

"Rick, I need to talk to you about the missions. The ones where I fly cover for the convoys."

His face becomes stone. Just like that. Shit. This is bad. "What about the missions with the trucks? I haven't noticed you reporting anything having gone wrong. Do you have a question?"

"No, well." His face oh shit, his face. No. He can't know. Tell him. Hear him when he gives a reasonable explanation. "It's just that after the trucks deliver their cargo, they stop on the way out, before the border, near Baram Cha and load up again. They don't go home empty."

"That doesn't sound like a question." His voice is cold, cast in steel.

Now. Chest wound tight. Ask now, just say it. "Drugs, Rick. I think they're running drugs. I know that this is probably shocking and all that but I think you need to know what the Pakistani company hiring us to fly cover for them is doing."

He takes a sip from the flask. Then another. Swallowing long, deliberately, like he's weighing his options. Shit. Shit. If he was innocent he would be mad. Outraged.

And he's not. He's drinking. Thinking of the best way to spin his lies. Are you fucking kidding me? Rick? Rick's lying to me using me all this time the only person who's been there for me tricked me into running drugs for him this has to be a lie has to be not true but he's quiet too quiet. "Dammit, Rick. Are you paying me to fly cover for a company that runs drugs out of Helmand and into Pakistan?"

He stares. Please say no, please. He looks me over, face unreadable. He stands up, moves over to the china cabinet, grabs two tumblers. Bringing them over to the table, he takes out his flask and fills the glasses, pushes one over to me. "I've known you for, what? Two years, three now? I'm asking you now, as a man, have a drink with me."

He takes the tumbler in his hands and brings it to his lips in a sharp motion made fluid by muscle memory, throwing the brown liquid to the back of his throat, banging the empty tumbler on the table. I feel acid leaching down into my heart, my lungs. I grab the tumbler, try my best to mimic his movements and feel the booze burn its way down my throat, hoping it can stop the rising tide of anguish. But all it does is make my throat blaze and my eyes water, leaving me gasping for breath.

"Have I told you about the Ghouls?" He grins and refills the glasses, his eyes lost in the circling surface patterns of the liquid.

"What?"

"Ghouls are the HCNs that the intel team uses for BDAs." Words leaving a bitter taste in the air.

I cough. "Can you put that in English, please?"

"After you hit that house we sent subcontractors, Host Country Nationals, local Afghan operators in to do a Bomb Damage Assessment. They always have some bullshit cover: aid workers, government officials, press credentials, but really they're in the body count business. They go and make sure that we got who we wanted to get."

"You said I hit the target that day, you were standing right there."

"You did. Our terrorist target, Said Al-Jafar, was good and dead. He was on the roof, remember? You also got one of his associates as well, all known Taliban fighters. But the same strike also killed two of their wives, along with three children. Azar, twelve, Amir, six and Faheema, who was only three years old."

My throat's dry. Nerves frozen. Sick. Children. I killed children oh my God I can't have killed children there's no way.

"That three year-old girl, Tyler, was she an enemy of freedom? A Taliban sympathizer? I doubt it. These actions, on some level, are completely counter-productive to the mission objectives. The counter-insurgency doctrine of 'clear, hold and build' becomes 'bomb, kill and make more enemies.'" He moves the glass up towards his lips and I blink back the wet in my eyes. "We just gave Faheema's cousins and any other able-bodied man from that village a reason to join the insurgency. Now I don't know how you may feel about all this but I can tell you that I don't enjoy this aspect of the job. A shit pizza is what it is."

Hand and head tipped back, the empty glass taps back onto the table. His eyes resemble the glass wrapped in his hand.

"But you're the math guy, right? Consider this for me: that missile you fired killed seven innocent people, women and children, who might've helped recruit another dozen or so insurgents. So what I need you to focus on is: how many lives did you save?" He fills his glass again. "As it turns out, you cut off the head of the snake. Without leadership, insurgent activity in that sector has almost completely evaporated. It's been a week now and we've had zero IEDs, zero ambushes, zero mortar attacks on our forward bases."

"But how do you calculate something so…"

"Abstract? I don't know. Dead children are an unfortunate consequence of the business that we're in. Some Pentagon press aide jerk-off comes up with some cute little phrase like 'collateral damage' and that's bullshit. It's bullshit, you and I know it's bullshit because those kids had names, dammit. Azar, Amir, Faheema."

"And Brandon?" The words are heavy, loaded.

Wrist, head, glass tapping down on the table. "Look, those little kids had the grave misfortune of being within the blast radius of a coalition airstrike. They were innocent because they were in the wrong place at the wrong time. I know that you care about your brother, but he made a choice. It's a choice he would've made whether it's the Taliban supplying it or our Pakistani partners."

"No." I throw back the contents of my glass, wanting the burn.

The expression on his face isn't malicious, it's soft, sad, like it hurts him, too. "Sometimes the real cost of freedom is allowing people the privilege to make bad choices, self-destructive choices. That's the horrible reality of the world, Tyler, and I need you to come to terms with that. You think it's wrong, but that's the part that you're not seeing. If we don't profit from it, the terrorists will."

I want to let his words wash away the wrongness of it all, replacing my doubts and fears and horror with relief. Want it more than anything. Gripping the tumbler, I close my eyes and wait to feel better. Wait to get some sense, any sense, that this could be anything other than wrong.

The image of Brandon unconscious in the hospital bed thunders through my brain, tearing everything I am in half. "It *is* wrong, though, what we're doing. I want to think that it's not, but it is."

"I understand if you're uncertain because of your brother's situation. I'll give you some more time."

"I don't need more time." My chest is so tight. Like he just took everything inside me apart and all I have left is these scrunched-up lungs and anger. "We're fucking running drugs! Killing babies! Nothing you can say can make this right. Nothing."

"Think before you speak here, Tyler. I know you're upset." Warning, dark, low, forbidding, rides in his voice.

"No." Whirling, screaming, agony inside.

"I would hate to see you throw away your future like this."

Somehow, through the chaos, I find the words and shoot them across the room. "Get out of my house, Rick."

His eyes go black. Like two pieces of coal going molten. "Don't go against me. You'll regret it." But he turns, and he leaves.

Can't breathe. Can't think. But I wait till he's gone. Pull the cell out of my pocket. Find the voice recorder app. I hit *stop*. I have to call Ani.

I knock. Knock, knock, knock, knock. Is she home? Why isn't she answering her phone? Does she know? Did Rick call her? Is she too scared to talk to me? Rick better not have scared her off. We weren't supposed to be doing this. Weren't supposed to see each other. Would he hurt her?

Hand meeting the hard wood of the door. Each knock rattling up my arm. I feel it in my wrists, my elbows, my shoulders. No answer to her buzzer. She has to be there. Somebody has to let me in. It's not too late, is it? 11pm. No. Kids at Yale should be up. It's a Thursday, they should be around. Someone should be here. Where is she? I pound both fists into the door. Loud, angry, pain now, aches rolling up both arms. Should have called first, but I tried to text from the car. My fingers just couldn't stop shaking and my legs wouldn't stop moving and the music on my iPod just wasn't loud enough to calm the thoughts whirring around in my head and I just want to scream. "Hello?" a voice says over the buzzer. Not Ani. Her roommate. What's her name? Becky? Clary? Christy? It's Christy.

"Christy, it's Tyler. Ani there?"

"No, she's having a snack I think. Check the Buttery."

Damn! The Buttery. "Thanks." I run around the side of the building, please let there be some kids coming out or going in through the side door to... Yes!

"Hold the door!" I call. A little girl. She looks young but who knows? I can't tell who would be too young to be here or not. She smiles and holds it open, swiping a strand of black hair up underneath her hat. "Thanks."

I brush past her. She smells like incense. Do they smoke pot at Yale? Guess so. The halls at Yale are like any other halls. Lifeless except for bad smells of spilled food and vomit and the chemical used to clean them. The smells from the Buttery hit me as I jog down the way. French fries and burgers and pizza. I nod at the guy working the register and scan the hall.

She's sitting under an old window with her ereader in one hand and a sandwich in the other. I think I am just going to break. Break from not knowing where to start or whether I should hold her or be pissed that she can look so normal when everything is so fucked-up.

Walking up to the table I say, "You were right. About everything."

Her back straightens, she looks up. Her brown eyes are wide, glassy, and the color leaves her face in a stunned rush.

Silence. I can't say anything else. Want to explode want to yell but I see the tension in her shoulders and I see that look on her face and I know that she's processing... that I have to be patient but I can't.

I say, "I told him I couldn't do it, told him I can't... can't do that."

"Does he know about Brandon?" Her arms, her posture, her lips quiver.

"Yeah. He was the only person I could really talk to for a long time, you know? But he thought I would take the money, keep taking the money, I guess most kids would still take the money but I don't want to do *this*. I want to fly, I want to so bad, but drugs?" Words flake off of me, hitting the floor at my feet. Inert. Useless.

"That guy, Ty, that guy on the phone who was a friend of Brandon's… from Canada… do you think that this was what he was expecting?"

"I don't know."

"Do you remember exactly what he asked? You don't think that he tried to talk to Mr Anderson, do you?"

"No. I don't think he'd be that dumb. That and Mr Ander… uh, Rick wouldn't talk to him, anyway. Do you think he knows about us?"

Ani, her eyes, oh God, the look in those eyes. She's frightened. Really, truly, utterly frightened. My arms ache to touch her, to hold her, to lie to her with my body, to tell her that she's safe and that everything that she has here at this school, at this job, everything she's ever worked for can't come down in a big pile of shit. But I can't do it. Can't lie. Not to her. Not ever. My hands clench into fists, and I push them down deep into my pockets.

"No, I don't think he knows about us," I say. "We have to keep it that way."

"Yeah," she agrees, voice wispy.

"You almost done? Can we go upstairs?" We have to dig into this shit. Find a way out. Find a way to make sure she's not dicked over because of me.

She packs up the rest of her sandwich and stands. "Let's go."

"What?" I ask, confused.

Ani's leaning into the screen of her desktop, pulling up mountains of records that I never knew she was keeping. "There is going to be a thread of code within that channel that links it to the drones overseas. We just have to isolate that code and then search the code on all the other missions, compress them into a file, and then send them to Althea. Tell them what's going on."

"We can't tell the people at Althea," I say.

"Why? I know the people at Althea have no idea, I just need to find out which codes are tracked overseas and Mr Anderson is busted. I've been backing up all of the missions from all of the test pilots over there anyway, in case my files here crap out."

"How'd you do that?"

"I uploaded a virus into the sim, to give me undetected access."

"Althea's not good enough, though. If their name is linked with this then they're screwed. Wouldn't they want to hide it? Brandon's always talking about how companies do what's best for their bottom line, and scandal is never good." I shrug. "They'll destroy the link to the sim. Maybe have already."

"They haven't." She punches more keys, pulling up lines and lines and lines of code. "They don't know that I'm in their system and using it for backup."

"Rick's not going to take no for an answer," I say, softly.

She stares at the screen. Eyes distant.

I fall back into her bed, kicking my shoes off and laying back so that I'm staring at the grim popcorn ceiling. "I think I pissed him off pretty good."

She dicks around with the computer.

I run a hand through my hair, pulling, feeling it tug up tight against my aching skull. "I have this." I hold up the recording from my phone. Love the app. Now I have Rick. Our conversation from the dining room. "We can back this up, right?"

"Yeah, but, Tyler…" Her eyes look up at mine. Fear clouding them over a bit. "I wonder if it matters whether or not we have all this backed up, I mean, can't he just kill us and take the hard drives? Destroy everything? It would be easy for him, I think."

A sinking. Like an elevator moving just too fast jolts through my system. Would Rick go that far? This is bad. He's going to hurt her. Eventually. Maybe. Will he? Please God let her be too valuable.

"Can he deny this? I mean, how would that even be possible?"

"I don't think a lot of people know about this program," she says, voice strong again as she pounds the keys of her laptop. "Aside from you, me and Rick, there are only four other pilots, and all of them are still in the dark. Didn't you say that your friend Peanut tried the program? Is he one of the pilots?"

"No, he only tried out the free version. Nobody I know actually got the upgrade. What about other people at Haranco? How many people are there, do you know?"

"Just me and Mr Anderson here in New Haven. I tried to get into the system the other day and all of the access codes that he gave me don't work on the company at large. There are a couple of other offices, but the whole company might only be ten people, we don't know."

"Does he pay you?" I ask.

"Yes." She looks up at me. "The paychecks come from Haranco's payroll department. From an office someplace else. I'd bet neither Haranco nor Tidewater OK'd Rick's program. They may fund it, but I'm sure that they're in the dark as to the details."

"How can he hide something like that?"

"He runs the entire drone surveillance department for Haranco. This is only a very small subset of the program at large. And I bet that the retired Air Force guys flying the missions for Rick at Haranco's base don't fly over those trucks." She shrugs. "They would have known the score."

Unlike me. I'm an idiot. "So it's easy for him to hide us within his larger program."

"Exactly."

"Haranco will deny everything if he destroys what we have." The thought of Rick standing over us with a gun feels and tastes and sits like iron in my chest. "So will Tidewater. They'll deny everything, it's self-preservation."

"He wouldn't really kill us, would he?" she says, voice disjointed.

That iron spike in my chest grows, heavy and bringing everything down, but it can't erase the truth. Rick likes me, sure, but what if I was always just an asset to him? An asset that should've known better than to question him. To have a conscience. But he likes me. Loves me, even, maybe. My heart pounds. He wouldn't hurt me. My throat gets dry. Couldn't. "He doesn't know that we're together, you should be safe."

Her face softens, just for a second, then comes back together again, "We have to figure a way out of this."

"No doubt," I say, and we both sit down to think. She searches for inspiration on her computer, copying more and more data onto portable hard drives, and I open up my phone. Can't email because he can probably track that. God, I can't believe this. This is just crazy. I log on to the gaming network. Need to get through to Peanut and Alpha, give them instructions in case, well, in case I don't make it. Hate goodbyes. I suck at them. Should be glad I get a chance to say them, but I'm not, really.

Do I have to say goodbye? Rick couldn't kill me, he wouldn't. I sure as hell couldn't kill him, but he might kill Ani, though. I can't let that happen. Can't let him hurt her. Only how exactly do I stop him?

CHAPTER 28

FRIDAY, NOVEMBER 2

TYLER

The phone's ringing. Man, what time is it? I reach around across Ani. She's crashed out sideways on the bed, can't remember what time we crashed. It was late, though. Phone, phone, phone, where did I put my phone?

The desk next to the bed. I grab it. 4am? Check caller ID. And just like that I feel like I just drank three Red Bulls all at once and I'm awake, alert, alarmed.

"Tyler, son. I was hoping you'd calmed down. You seemed upset after our talk earlier, and I just wanted to make sure that you're OK."

"I know a line of bullshit when I hear one. I'm not OK. You're not OK."

"Think about what you are saying, Tyler. I see you've spent the night in young Miss Bagdorian's dormitory. While I'm willing to forgive your outburst earlier, I will not do so again." Oh shit, how does he know he can't know now he'll kill her for sure and it's all my fault.

Fuck, Tyler, keep it together you have to focus here focus or she's dead. Focus or we're both dead.

I know that I should lie. That I should play along. Play along if not for my own safety, but for Ani's, too.

My fingers are numb. This is it. Everything that I ever hoped to be in life is about to just disappear right freaking now. Hell, my life itself is probably hanging on what I say. But I can't fly cover for a bunch of drug runners. I just can't. Even if I could, I would lose Ani. She would never forgive me if I went back, if I stick with the program. And I either take a stand now or not take a stand.

"I'm saying that I want no part of you, no part of this." My throat squeezes just a little and heat flashes up quick in my eyes, and I think about flying with him and talking to him and him always being there for me. And Ani. I think about Ani and how much it would hurt to lose her how much it would hurt to keep running drugs and dropping bombs on babies. "I'm sorry, man. I just can't do what you want me to do."

Ani stirs, rubbing the sleep from her eyes as she listens, hair tangling around her as she pulls herself to sitting.

"I'm sorry, too," he says, then his voice lowers. "Women, Tyler, are the cancer that eats at men's souls."

I look at Ani. Looking so sweet and smart and perfect and oh shit what if he hurts her and all I feel is rage, burning, aching, screaming up through my system and I try to keep my voice even, steady, calm. "What are you going to do?"

"Nothing I want to do. But you aren't leaving me with a lot of options here."

He's going to hurt me. Rick. Rick, who I always trusted even after I knew that I shouldn't. Now he's going to ruin my life, ruin everything. "You're not going to hurt her, I won't let you."

"I don't see how you can stop me."

"You *will* see. Count on it." My words are solid, fury making them stick, but still not able to hide the pain. I hang up the phone. Staring at it in my hand. I bang it down into the end table. "We have to leave, Ani. I'm sorry."

"What happened, what did he say?"

"I can't believe I brought my phone here, I'm such an idiot."

Right. Well, that's the look I should expect when I say something like that. Her eyes are wide and she pulls her knees into her chest. "What?"

"Cell phones. He tracked my phone, found out I'm here." I hold up my phone. "I'm so, so sorry. You really have to pack."

I grab her face in my hands and hold her so that my lips are so close that she can feel every breath that I take. "We'll take my mom's car, we'll drive someplace and call a paper, like you said, they'll run the story and the reporter will know how to protect their sources and it will be fine."

"You can't take your mom's car, Tyler. He's seen it. And we can't leave the dorm together, he'll be looking for us to leave together."

"OK, well, we'll ditch our phones. Meet up at Brandon's in like half an hour, OK?" I scribble his address down for her on a piece of paper.

"I think I know where we can get a car. Before you ditch the phone can you call the *Times*? There's some reporter there who wrote an exposé on Tidewater, Donovan Jones, I think. And check to see if that guy from Montreal, Brandon's friend, called you back."

"Be careful," I say. Want to say more. But can't. Don't have that kind of time. I kiss her. Quick. On the lips, then I hit the door.

ANI

Is this going to be enough? The virus is in and I use it. It takes all of thirteen minutes to send Tyler's missions off to the cloud and onto a mountain of flash drives and the two backup hard drives I was able to scrounge up, not to mention the server that I tagged the last time I was at Althea. I stare at the address Ty wrote down on a scrap of paper, it's not too far away. Can I breathe now?

My hands are shaking. I can't get them to stop. Drugs? Do I believe it, even? I mean, I see it, and I must have recorded hours of tape that proves it. To go through all the footage is going to take time. But I can't be part of this. I can't be part of a corporation that's running heroin. I just can't.

Still. There's no doubt of the imminent threat. Rick was trained to kill, he'll have no problem killing us, or sending someone else to do it. The trembling rises up through my legs and into my chest, making it constrict with fear and something else – fury. As I throw an extra pair of socks into the bag, I can't help myself, I pick up the phone, and I dial.

"Miss Bagdorian, I hope that you're well this morning."

"You jerk! You lied to me to get me to sign up for this job, then you lied to me about what I was really being hired to do. I get that you get off on lying to people, but I'm calling to tell you now that if you make a move to hurt either me or Tyler-"

"Yes? What will you do? Hack into my bank account? Mess with my identity? I'm terrified. The firewalls of my little program at Haranco were all rewritten as you and Mr MacCandless slept the night away. You're not getting our money's worth at Yale if you didn't expect that."

"Listen, *Rick*." I take a deep, steadying breath, restraining the urge to scream. "You make one move to hurt me, my family or my boyfriend and I swear to you that I will make your program the headliner on the evening news."

"You know why people love the story about David and Goliath, Miss Bagdorian?" He waits. I say nothing. "People love it because the little guy wins. But that's just a dream of the weak, Miss Bagdorian. The little guy never wins. It's all just a lie."

I shove my toothpaste into my bag. "I will bring you *and* your company down. Just you watch."

"I don't think you'll have enough time to try."

TYLER

Fuck. Where do I go? Need to think. Need to stop the spinning that won't stop and the pounding in my head that won't let me breathe. I need coffee. Need to think.

I walk into the coffee shop. Grab an extra-large, willing myself to be comforted by all the soft colors and the smooth jazz, but it doesn't work. I take out the phone, Google the number for the news desk at the *Times* and call. Have to wait through a menu like light-years long. I enter the first few letters of Jones. Crap, there's like six of them. Looking around the shop, I enter the first few letters of Donovan. I look out through the window, out onto the street. The image of the guy, strands of gray dusting his high and tight, the guy with the too-crisp turtleneck and khakis, in the sunglasses, with no hat and only a sleek-looking blazer, cuts at me right through the glass.

It's hard to swallow. It's just a guy going to work. Going to get a coffee, maybe, or something. But he's watching. Watching like he's not meaning to be watching. I look down, letting my hair fall in front of my face and I tug my hood up so far that I feel it tug at my back.

Voicemail, shit. Now what do I say? "Hey, Donovan, My name's Tyler MacCandless and I've been flying drones for Haranco and they're using them to run heroin. Email me back at tylermaccandless@gmail.com, since I have to ditch the phone. Later." I sound like a freak, but hey, it is what it is.

Paying for my coffee, I look outside. The guy is gone. Perfect. Maybe after I have my coffee my imagination will calm down.

I head towards where I locked up the bike yesterday. It's cold, but I know I have to walk to Brandon's. I rode my bike over yesterday, and Rick's seen my bike, knows what it looks like, would tell his guy to look for it. Sideswiping the side of a building, the stone feeling good and solid just for a second, I stop, absorb the impact, let it ride through me. Shit. I push my back into the building. Think. How the hell do I get to Brandon's from here on foot?

Pushing off the column, I keep moving, checking my periphery for anything suspicious. Brandon's. Is it really a good idea to meet Ani at Brandon's? Rick doesn't know Brandon personally, doesn't know where he lives. It's fine. B's safe for now. Have to make sure they don't follow me there, though. Don't hurt B.

I look behind me, all around. Nothing weird, nothing strange, so I turn and take the footpath through the old campus. Scooting inside the bank lobby, I can feel my shoulders relax a little in the nice blast of warm air kicking out from the heaters as I roll on up to the ATM. I'm totally just being paranoid. I hit the max machine withdrawal of four hundred bucks. The worst thing that's gonna happen is that I get mugged with all this cash. Rick *likes* me, dammit. He wouldn't...

Reflected in the window is the figure of the man from the coffee shop.

All feeling gets sucked right out of my limbs. He's on the other side of the street. I leave the building and walk south.

He follows. Still on the opposite side of the street, across four lanes of morning traffic, he's there. I feel him. Heart beating like crazy, cars and buses and trucks roaring by, I put some iron into my stride, thinking through my mental maps of New Haven's streets. If I go up towards the green I could maybe lose him in the alleys of the arts district, or, he could know the alleys and corner me. A red car veers too close, blowing my hair up around my ears.

Shit. Have to think. I turn left, trying to get over to York Street, but way back at the edge of High, I see him stop. He gets into a white car.

Great, see? Totally overreacting. I force myself to take in a long, shaky breath. Just some guy meeting his ride. Not true. Get out of here. I brush past a group of Yalies going to class, then turn, sprint back the way I came. Just in case. If he thinks that I'm headed over to York, then I'll go back, go the other way, just cause.

After about three minutes, the adrenaline slowly leaves my legs and I walk like normal again. Start to feel really, really cold. The cars and noise and exhaust of Grove Street hit me like a wall. Just reaches out and smacks me in the face, but I keep my head down, waiting till I hear the buzzer for the blind people, and step out into the street.

Tires, squealing, up to my right, the white car, *the* white car swerves around the car in front of it and races towards the intersection, tires shrieking. Coming for me. Standing in the middle of the road.

I can't feel anything, can't think, for a second I can't move, all I see is a rusted iron grill and a wide white car speeding towards me. Heartbeat wild, my legs unlock and I sprint, flying the rest of the way across the intersection. The car clips the side of the curb trying to get me, but

I'm faster, running. Legs pounding into the cement, I run the sidewalk, keeping as close to the wall of Grove Street Cemetery as possible. The car keeps up with me, and my one brief glimpse into the window of the car sees a flash of something black. Something deadly. Something pointed right at me. I stop. Just pull a full stop. There is no way they can bang a U in all this traffic. No freaking way. I turn and I run back the other way up the street, along the wall.

I hear tires wail as they try to stop, but I send my feet grinding into the cement, grinding and not feeling anything but the breath beating its way into my lungs as I take the corner, part of the wall is broken, crumbling, perfect. I run right at it, wrap my arm up tight around the top, and pull myself over, landing in a flash of pain and panic and just straight up euphoria in the land of the dead.

The cemetery stretches on forever. Acres of crooked tombs, dying trees surrounded by huge stone walls.

Walking quickly, I stomp over odd lumps of grass and make my way around the tombs to the back wall. Brown stalks of grass whip at my knees through my jeans as I go, trying to not think, trying to not do anything but get to the back wall. Only one entrance in, blocked to cars, at the front. They'll be covering that. Shit. But they're tracking me. They'll know I'm here.

I stop. My phone. Have to lose the phone. Damn. There's the big stone wall to my right, I trudge over, climb up a tree, and make my way up on top of the wall. Brown leaves sticking in my hair, I wait, staring at the traffic about five feet away. I throw my phone onto the top of a Greyhound as it passes. I liked that phone. I'm going to miss it. But hey, *that* they are tracking for sure. So it goes. Or I'm dead.

The thought hollows out the others in my head. Sits in the middle, then I let the other gazillion things rolling around in my head smother it up, push it down. Rick will kill me. Have me killed. I need to focus.

Climbing back down, the grass nips at my ankles as I make my way through the cemetery. Should have worn socks. I jog. Looking around, no one else here, no one else lurking around the dead trees. The yard seems so still, so quiet compared to the madness of the city outside. Running through the street maps in my head, as I jog, breath freezing and splashing little chunks of ice onto my cheeks with each footfall, I make it to the back wall. Tall, stone. No trees.

Check back, anyone back there? Yes. Someone's moving. Behind me. On foot. I duck down behind the nearest tomb, cold stone freezing my back. Shit. Have to move. Guy on foot. Walking. I peek. Can't see much. He's behind a tree, about five hundred yards away. How do I get over this wall? Right. Wall. Most of the tombs are too far to climb for a jump. I look right, rubbing my shoulders to keep warm. Shit, I'm going to die in a cemetery. It'd be funny if it didn't involve me dying. Wait. About two hundred yards down to my left there's a break in the wall, just some rubble off the top that piled up at the base in a mass of broken cement.

The guy behind me is moving. The gravel of the footpath crunching beneath his feet. I don't stop to look to see who the hell he is or which direction he's going, I just freaking bolt. Fly over to the wall, feet meeting jagged shards of rubble, cutting, biting, tearing my legs just over the tops of my shoes as I climb up, hands scraping as I climb, but then I'm up, and then I'm over. And then I don't look, I just run. Don't hear the car tires screeching as I cut out in front of traffic, don't listen to the low growl echoing up through my throat as I run, don't care that my hands are cut and torn and bleeding. I just run across the street and plow between the dividers that mark the beginning to the Farmington canal path. The bicycle path that's going to take me to my brother, if I can only make it...

Warm water coursing over my body feels so good, so alien. Like at first I just feel the drops of water hitting my skin like the surface of an umbrella, bending it, but not feeling the impact, not really. Eventually, my skin yields, adrenaline dissipating into the steam. Safe for a minute, here at Brandon's. I can shower and think and breathe. Scrub my hands through my hair, work through the burn that comes with the start of sensation. Think. I run through my list.

The list. The list, the maps, the possible options that I have for surviving Rick. None of it is good. None of it. I know it was real. I know what they were doing. So I have to go. Easy as that. Brought Ani into it, now it's my fault she's a target.

Turning off the shower after what seems like forever, I dry off and throw on the clean clothes that B left lying on top of the counter. Still smell like him. Like home. God, Mom, should I call Mom again? I used B's phone. Did she get my message? She's where, California? Should brush my teeth, though, Ani will be here soon. Running my hand through the stuff left on the counter, razors and shaving creams, I find a tube of toothpaste and throw some on my fingers. Better than nothing, I guess.

Looking down as I rinse, what's that? A bag? Pharmacy bag. From the hospital pharmacy. Still stapled shut.

Unopened.

Untouched.

He left the hospital five days ago.

Ripping open the bag, I see the big orange bottle of antibiotics. Three times a day. Three times a day or he's dead, right? Endocarditis? He told the visiting nurse to leave. Said he'd take the pills and the shots and take care of it but he left the hospital early. The doctor's words tear through my head like steel.

It's too much. Just too much. Everything, Rick, everything, the hit man, everything, B in the hospital. The room moves in violent, sharp waves around me.

I grab the bottle of pills and slam them into the wall. Everything, everything I've done for him, everything I've given up and he doesn't care. Throws his fucking life away like it's some kind of joke. He's going to kill Mom, kill me. *Slam*.

Palm slapping the bottle against the wall, it cracks. *Slam*. Bitter orange plastic slices the skin of my hand. *Slam*. I pound it against the wall again. *Slam*. Shoving the plastics further into my hand, pills raining down on the floor.

Why doesn't he care why doesn't he just know I need him why can't he see and now I'm going to fucking die and no one will be here to save him to care when he dies to cry when they put him in the ground and all I ever wanted to do in my life was see him get better and now we're both hit.

The door to the bathroom opens with a bang. I think somebody says my name, but I can't hear, can't think over my heart and liver and lungs unhitching as I beat the stupid bottle.

Brandon, Ani right behind him, standing in the doorway. My face is hot, wet, nose running and mouth flopping.

Brandon's eyes pop. Pop up and then skydive when they see what's on the floor, what's happening. Yeah. Yeah, asshole.

He looks at me, and even though I know that his color is totally off and that he's too thin and that his face is starting to look older than it should, all I see is the kid who taught me to ride my bike, the kid who would sneak in my room and read me *Captain Underpants* at night after lights out.

That look that I'm having to grow so used to, like he's there, inside, trapped in a body he can't control, can't get out of, like he wants to see me, really see me, but he can't. Like his life, like this world, are entirely out of his control. He says nothing.

I meet his eyes. I see. He wants it. Wants to die.

All I am right now is pain.

And Brandon just stands at the door. Fighting to stay awake. Watching.

••••

Don't stare. Don't stare. The needle marks on the back of his hand. Still open and bleeding. It's been, what? Half an hour since I got out of the shower? He looks almost like himself again, eyes clear, voice steady. He cut his hair. Cut it like mine. Can't ask why. Junkies do crazy shit all the time. Maybe it was annoying him being so long. Don't know, don't care, cause it'll never be long enough to cover the marks on his arm.

Punch him. Just punch him right in the face. I squeeze my fingers together so tightly in the palm of my hand that I think I'm going to draw blood, to bleed all over. But I can't do this right now. I need to think. I need to be focused or I'm dead. Simple as that.

Ani's dead, too, if I mess this up. I can't let them hurt her and I need to think but all I see are those little bleeding dots on the back of his hand and I...

"Tell me what's going on, Ty," B says, voice steady, sincere, like he means it, which, somewhere inside, I'm sure that he does.

Ani looks to me, wiping the streak of hair that's bleached blond out of her eyes. I kiss her on the forehead, and say, "You were right about Rick. I was really flying drones for him, took his cash, didn't say anything. He said he planned to tell the other kids, I think that there are five of us, but I'm the only one who figured it out. One of the missions, though, B. One of the missions was providing air coverage for these trucks. For a Pakistani security firm. They would bring in humanitarian aid or whatever, drive out of town, stop at a warehouse, pick up something else, and drive it back across the border."

"Drugs?"

"Yeah, opium." My voice is flat. Like roadkill.

"You have proof? I mean, did you record any of this?" he asks, words rising in pitch.

"Yup. Just about all of it. Ani backed it all up. She's recorded everything from the first mission on as a safeguard in case the whole UCS program crashed."

His pupils sort of narrow. He's thinking, fighting through whatever's going on inside so he can see, so he can sort through options. But he can't do it. Just can't. He leans back into the couch and I can see, can tell by that look, the look of euphoric emptiness, that he's not able to help. He's trying, but he just can't. Now when I actually need him, really need him to help me figure a way out of this, he's coming off of a high.

Have to think. Have to stay focused. We have to run. But that destroys Ani, her future, everything. Don't have much time, either. The apartment here is in Kelly's name, her parents are doctors or something in Milford and they cover the rent. Not wanting their baby to be homeless, I guess. But they'll find us here soon enough. Have to come up with a plan.

"We have to go to Canada," Ani says quietly. "See that guy who called you."

"The guy from the paper?" I ask, trying to remember his name. Damn. "Tim, Thomas, shit. B, what's the name of your friend in Canada?"

B looks at me, smiles. "Todd, Todd Sevier from the *Montreal Standard*. He's a great guy," B says, eyes off, out the window. "You should tell him everything. He'll cover the story, for sure."

"Ratting out Tidewater is going to help me how, exactly, B? They're already trying to kill me." I keep my hands clenched.

I look over to Ani, curled up around her laptop, and try not to think about how badly I'm ruining her life.

She says, "We have to get the word out there, Tyler. People have to know. This has to stop. The only way we can stop it is to go public."

"You can stop them." B's voice is a shadow of itself.

"By holding a big, neon target sign over my head?" I lower my voice. "Over her head? No thanks."

"We have to. We can get asylum." Ani's voice is taut, like a rubber band stretched too far.

"Asylum?" I say. "We're not refugees who lost our homes in a flood or something."

"No, but we *are* seeking asylum, Tyler. We can't go to the cops here because the people trying to kill us can just waltz into the jail and shoot us in the head. They have our government's permission to do whatever the hell they want and no cop in the world can protect us. We are sort of the definition of asylum seekers."

I don't want to go without her. Don't want to go anywhere without her. But I wish things were different. Wish there was a way to keep her safe.

"The border is too far. They'll catch us."

"We need a distraction, time," Ani says.

I say, "Can you look up how to declare refugee status in Canada?"

Her eyes widen, just a little, like a deer, then narrow, focus.

"We have to bring evidence, right, to Todd?" I ask.

"I've got plenty," Ani answers from her position on the couch, eyes never leaving the screen as her fingers fly. "Already sent a teaser to the *Montreal Standard* and to the *Washington Post*, Associated Press and Reuters. They'll be fighting over who gets the rest. Hopefully one of them will be able to figure out how to keep us alive."

Damn she's smart. If I live through this I am so going to marry her some day. Well, at least ask, anyway.

B closes his eyes. "Todd's a good guy, so good, he'll help you out if he can."

He's what you could have been, B.

"It's not enough for us to go public, Tyler. We have to stop the program," Ani says, voice quiet. "They're killing innocent people."

They're killing terrorists, too. I think. Don't think, don't defend Rick now. Can't defend someone who wants to kill me, who kills children. She's right. Mind racing through different options. Different ways to get to Rick before he gets to us. Hard. "Money?"

"Working on that." Her voice lowers. "I started looking into a way to stop the cash flow to the program a while ago. Or at least stop Rick from profiting off of it."

"Any luck?" I ask, angling myself against the kitchen counter so I can face her while I eat.

"I'm not sure if freezing or even emptying their accounts is going to do much to stop the program from running." Ani reaches for her glass.

"Stop the money, stop the program," B adds, making a sick, anguished noise. Testament to the boy that's only half here.

"No," I say, ready to vomit. Hate this. Hate seeing him like this. "Rick's program is just one very small piece of Haranco. Haranco itself is just an offshoot of Tidewater. Tidewater has hundreds of companies. If Haranco needed money, they would just borrow from one of their other companies to keep it going."

Ani puts down her glass. "But if we managed to freeze Haranco's assets then we would definitely get their attention. And freezing Rick's accounts might trip him up enough to slow him down, keep him from finding us so fast."

"How close are you to being able to cut off their cash flow?" I ask.

"Not very."

"No," I say. "There's an easier way to stop the program, and permanently."

They both look up at me.

"The drones," Ani answers for me, that brilliant, sexy smile spreading across her heart-shaped face. "We can crash the drones."

"Has he written you out yet?" I ask.

"He can try," she answers, fingers dancing over her keyboard. "But it's my program, and I gave it a virus. He can't keep me out for long."

"Why did you give your own program a virus?" Brandon asks.

"So I'll always have access. I can't imagine writing a program and then have someone else shut me out. I do it for everything I write, it's like keeping a safety line open just for me. A backdoor."

"Find an empty field, check the satellites. Just make sure you don't hit anyone," I add. Feeling just a little like we might survive this, it might all come out OK. "Can we do it from your laptop, though? Don't we need to use the Universal Control System?" I walk over to stand behind her, looking over her shoulder at the screen.

"I can do it from my laptop. Because I can get into the UCS from there." She taps some more keys. "Do you think we can make it into Canada?"

"They're going to be looking at the border crossings, right? And we need passports," I say eventually.

"We'll need passports," she says.

"Shit. Mine's at home. They're waiting for me to go home, I'm pretty sure," I say, trying to keep my anger down. Just scared, I guess.

"I have a passport," B says, eyes still closed as he wraps a blanket up around his shoulders. "Need it since they keep taking away my fucking license. Take mine, get into the country, then declare refugee status."

I shrug. We look enough alike, especially in those pictures, to pull it off, probably, but, "They'll be looking for any MacCandless. The second I cross, it'll send up some red flag and I'm sure I'll be dragged out back and shot or something. Besides, they'll be looking for her, too, and a MacCandless and a Bagdorian crossing into Canada at the same time... we'll be toast."

"Not if you declare refugee status at the border, man."

"Can't." Ani calls in from the other room, reading off the screen of her laptop, I'm sure. "The laws have changed. You can't declare refugee status at a land border crossing, only at a point of entry from the air or water."

"Shit," I say, mouth full, stomach trembling. "So that means what, we'd have to either fly in or take a boat? We can't fly, they'll never let us on a plane."

"The high-speed ferries out of Maine are closed for the season," Ani says quietly as her fingers pound the keys.

I take a swig of soda. "Can you ask for refugee status once you're in the country, though? I mean, you just have to get in, right?"

Ani checks. "Yes, once you're in you can, but your case will apparently be frowned upon if you enter the country with fake documents."

"We can roll in by kayak," I say, remembering our old family vacations in northern Vermont.

"What?" B asks.

"Lake Memphremagog, B, remember, we could go by boat. If the border patrol boats catch us, no big deal, we have real papers and we can ask for refugee status by boat, right?"

Ani's face brightens as she Googles. "Yeah, it's the only water crossing anywhere nearby. We can pop on a charter or something."

"No, the pilot will phone in our IDs when we step on the boat." I don't like the idea of going to Canada to bring Rick down. It's like throwing a rock then hiding behind your mom's legs, counting on her to protect you. But still, it's what we've got. Stay here and we're hit. "Do you have a passport?"

"No," she says quietly. "But I've got other forms of ID for once we get in."

"Remember when you, me and Dad kayaked out to that island on the lake? We got pulled over by border patrol, they helped us navigate our way back to the house?" I ask B, remembering being small and afraid, sitting in my dad's lap as he and B paddled around, water splashing up in my face.

"Yeah," he says, eyes distant.

"It'll be cold. But that's how we'll go," I say, voice firm. "We borrow a kayak, get in, find Todd, then ask for refugee status. Blow up Rick's program."

"And hope they don't catch you," B adds, voice a little unsteady.

"Yeah, and hope they don't catch us." I take a big bite of sandwich. "Well, and that the lake isn't frozen yet."

I look at B. He looks panicked, too. Really? Shit's coming to the breaking point and they both think that I'm the one to figure this stuff out?

"Brandon," I say. "Does Kelly have a car?"

"Yeah, of course."

"Right, well, when she gets home, I want you guys to get into her car, OK? Go someplace safe. I won't be able to think straight if I think that they could come after you." I hand him my bank card. "Drive south, west? I don't know, just anywhere but here. Find a new place, start over, someplace warm." He needs to get away from Kelly, she's no good. But I need him to drive far away. To get away before Rick finds him.

He stares at me. Just stares at me. Like he doesn't really see.

"No, you know what?" I say. "Go to the train station. Buy like six different tickets on like six different trains and then take a car. Then go by car someplace far away and I'll email you when we get across the border, OK?" He's still just staring. "B, you hear me? You listening?"

"Yeah." His voice floats away. "But it won't work. That'll buy you an hour or two, sure, but you need at least six, probably more like eight. Their technology is too good, Ty, they'll know it's a decoy."

I take B's phone off of the coffee table and walk into the bedroom to call Peanut and Alpha. Have to try. Have to at least give it a shot.

We head down to the street. B gave me his and Kelly's entire savings back at the apartment before we left. I don't want to know exactly how it came to be that they had four grand hiding in their mattress, but I take the money all the same because I have to. Ani and I are wearing like three thousand layers of clothes. Not too cold now in New Haven, but by the time we get to Vermont, out on the water, it's going to be absolutely freezing. Ani left twenty minutes ago, going to meet her roommate Christy at a coffee shop nearby, where she arranged to pick up Christy's car. She's going to let us borrow her car in exchange for Ani "fixing" her grade in organic chemistry. Not a bad girl, Christy. Kinda stuck up, but it works out for us that she doesn't really care about her stuff. Scary that Christy wants to be a doctor.

B keeps pumping me full of information, giving me more clothes, more money, shoving his passport at me just in case, telling me who to talk to, what to say.

Just for a second I forget about the marks on his arm, about the full bottle in the medicine cabinet, and he's the brother he once was. Makes my heart feel three times as big. Then he looks up at me and we both remember and I have to push it all back down again so I can focus. So I can survive this.

But I can't survive this, really. There's like no chance and he's here now and I say, "Why aren't you taking the medicine, B? You told me, you've always told me that you wanted to get better, to beat this. Now you're sick and maybe even dying and now people are trying to kill me and still you're sticking that shit up your arm."

His face drops, like a feather, like a boulder. "You have to understand, Ty, how hard it is. It's like the more I want to beat it, the more I need it. I've tried so hard, so fucking hard, and still it's winning."

"It's not a person, it's a drug! A disease, sure, but you are the one who's still choosing to do it. And what was that in there? I'm trying to figure out how to stop people from killing me and you're high?" My voice rises up like molten stone, "I needed you. I've always needed you and you just leave me to watch as you kill yourself. Expect me to sit back and watch. There's nothing I can do, is there? Nothing. I can't make you better, can't make you love me again."

"You're not being fair." He shakes his head, face red, bottom jaw jutting out.

"I'm not trying to be fair, Brandon, I'm trying to be your brother." My throat hurts, my head hurts, eyes hurt.

"I've tried so hard, so hard to beat this. To beat this for you, for Mom," he says, words garbled. "But I can't. You don't know, don't know what it's like. I'm not strong enough."

"Bullshit."

We walk in silence. Silence that's wound like livewire. Silence that says everything and nothing all at the same time.

We go down to the street. We walk together to where Ani's going to pick me up. Streets are pretty empty, no sign of suits. Or even nice khakis. Should be clear.

He says, "They won't stop, Tyler. They won't stop until they kill you."

"So?" I say, feeling draining from my arms, from my fingers.

"So let them think they killed you."

And then he meets my eyes. What is that supposed to mean? My heartbeat picks up. Ask no don't ask just walk just do this he's still pretty high and isn't making any sense is all.

He then turns to me, lips moving up a little in the corners. "You have your license?"

"Um, yeah. Just got it a month ago."

He takes a deep, halting breath. "Still have a copy of your permit on you? Library card?"

"Why do you need my wallet?" I pull it out, stomach contracting. Just to see, maybe he needs some of the cash back maybe he just wants to see if I'm using Dad's old one.

He opens it, looking at my library card, the pictures of us as kids that are stuffed in there from forever ago, the driver's permit and the new license. He hands the license back to me, and slips the wallet in his pocket. "Take this." He pulls out his own wallet and hands it over to me.

"No." My throat's tight. Like someone is grabbing onto it and squeezing and I don't know how to stop them. I don't like this. This is wrong. Very, very wrong. He can't be doing this he can't he can't he can't.

"Take it. Please." His voice wobbles and I slip my driver's license in my back pocket. My social security card is in my wallet, though, which he just took. Put in his pants. He opens the door to the car. Blue car, girly, probably Kelly's.

"Where are you going?" I ask, I know, but I can't. Can't let him...

"Going home, Ty." Tears. Tears redden his eyes.

My eyes burn, heart like a fist. "You can't... they'll have it staked out..."

"You need the time, Tyler. You'll never make it to the border without a diversion." The hair, he cut his hair to look more like me. Fuck. Fuck. Fuck.

"I've got a diversion. My cell phone is riding on the back of a Greyhound and my bank card is about to take a trip to Florida or some shit. Ani's, too, B, we don't..." Hell no.

"It's not enough. You know it's not. But if they think that they've got you, then you might have enough time to get to Todd." Tears falling, eyes begging, pleading, for what? Permission? Redemption? No no no no no. "You've always been the only one, you know. The only one who was there for me. You never once stopped believing in me, even after I had. You have to let me do this for you, Tyler."

The trees lining the street, dead and twisted and stuck into pools of dirt so old that it's gray, stuck in the middle of a sidewalk in the middle of a city where the cars and people and shops all line up to watch the world fall into itself. The trees seem to come together, hang closer, hang over where we're standing. So close to the street. So many people walking by. And none of them can stop this.

"No." I kick my foot into the ground and slap the wallet out of his hand. "No, fuck no I'm not going to let you do this, Brandon, you can drive out of here and find a new place and you can still get better I know that if you just…" The words come out frightened, barking.

"You have to let me do this for you." His voice is strong. "Let me have one thing, one choice that I can be proud of. Let me be your brother again, just this once."

"No." Deep breath. "No, no, no, no, no."

"Listen to me, this is not your choice, this is mine, I can't save myself anymore, Tyler." His hands grasp me around my face, pulling me towards him, forcing me to look him in the eyes. Blue and endless and wet. "But I'm going to save you."

Heart stuck, caught like a fly in my throat. "No, please," is all that comes out. Can't talk. Three thousand things to say. One syllable is all I get. "No."

His hands wrap around my shoulders, and he pulls me to him, hugging me. Words need to come out, I need to tell him, I want to tell him, I want to stop him but I can't do or say anything because everything seems to be moving around in my head at once.

"You get to Canada. Get to Canada with that girl. You bring this whole thing down around them. There's more in you than anybody ever sees, Ty. But I see it."

Oh no. Fuck no. This can't be happening.

Shit. Have to tell him, have to... "B," I call, voice broken, undone.

"There's no shame in dying for people you love, Tyler." He looks back. We stand there, staring at each other. Crying.

Three thousand things. Three hundred thousand things flow in the air between us as I look at him, my big brother, my hero since like forever until he fell. And now, everything else, the time I caught him smashing oxy, the time I found him lying unconscious on the floor of the bathroom, all that just disappears and all I can see is that kid, my hero, one last time.

But I can't get anything out. My eyes feel like they are bleeding and my heart is being hacksawed and my legs can't stay steady. But I can't get one fucking word from my head and out through my mouth. Not one.

"I know, Ty." He smiles. "I've always known."

He shuts the door and drives away.

CHAPTER 29

SATURDAY, NOVEMBER 3

TYLER

We drive Christy's Corolla three hundred miles up to Newport, Vermont. The worst ride ever. Long, quiet, waiting. Wondering if they found him yet. If he slipped out the back of the house when they came in, if he ran and is going to call. My only hope is that he flaked and pulled the junkie card, went to buy more H instead of doing what he meant to do. But I know that didn't happen. And I'm just waiting for the news. Flipping through channels on the radio, waiting, like they would run a broadcast of my brother's death. Like a junkie found shot in his house would make the news. Well, maybe, since we're in the burbs. Still.

Huge, racking thrusts of nausea pound on me. But I won't get sick. Can't. Don't have time. Need to drive. Need to drive faster. Every car, every truck behind us is a potential threat. Every guy on his way to work and every family on vacation sets me on alert. I don't think I can do this. Don't think this will work. But I have to try.

Have to try for her, for him. Shit. When did my life get so complicated? So wrong?

We left B's place around 7pm and we took the long way up, so it's like 1am when we roll into Newport. Looking behind us, I check to make sure we're the only car getting off at the exit. Only car rolling through town. Ani sees the place first. A place that rents kayaks and canoes, right on the lake. Closed for the season. Perfect.

We park in the center of town. Leave the car in front of some grocery store and hop out into the cold predawn air. Pulling on major backpacks, all that we own, the sound of the gravel crunching beneath our boots sounds too loud, like they can hear us.

We walk. It's not far, still, it feels good after such a long car ride and as I watch the clouds of frost around our breath decorate the still morning before us, my stomach trembles. We're close. Just have to get there. Stay focused. Steady. Faster. Walk faster.

The rental place is closed, of course. We find a two-person green kayak that isn't tied as securely as the rest and slip it out of its carrier and onto the bed of pine needles covering the ground. I write a note, apologizing for taking their boat, and leave a hundred bucks, figuring that's probably enough to cover the cost of it. I sign the first note, which, thankfully, Ani catches and makes me rip up and stuff in my pocket, so I write another one and slip that one along with the money up under the door.

"C'mon," I say and grab her hand.

●●●●

ANI

"Tyler... I don't know. What if this doesn't work?" I ask as I move towards the boat. He's carrying the awkward kayak over an outcrop of rocks and sets it near the water. The moonlight catches in his hair, and I can only see half of his face as he turns to me.

"Ani, look." He runs a hand through his hair. "We can't think like that. We have to do what needs to get done. Right now we're putting the kayak in the water, OK? So let's do that. Focus on that."

He's pushing the boat towards the water that sloshes around his feet just above on the shoreline. It's hard to see if his boots are actually submerged or not. It's hard to see how I got here, to see what I'm really doing.

What am I really doing? Mr Anderson's program is wrong, so wrong on so many levels, but why should we have to be the ones to bring it down? We could both lose everything. Am I ready to leave school, my mom, Julie, Dad, everyone, for what? What do I gain by doing this when I only see negative consequences? Mom won't see this as doing what's right, she'll see it as me being impulsive, see it as me falling for the wrong guy.

A big splash and a quiet curse from Ty indicate that now his boots are wet for sure. Oh God, is this right? Once I get in that boat there's no going back. If I cross the border then I have to finish this. "Ready?" he asks, standing in the quiet of darkness, starlight pooling in his eyes.

I look at the lifejacket he's holding out towards me and stare. I have to take it. If I don't, Mr Anderson will kill me, it's as simple as that. And right here, right now is a chance for me to live life on my terms, to write my own future, to write our future. "Tyler."

He looks up, voice gentle, "I know it's not comfortable, but you kinda have to wear it..."

"I love you."

Eyes wide, he says, "I... I..." He drops the lifejacket down by his side and wraps his hand around the base of my chin and kisses me. Slowly. His breath hot, the kiss is like silk, soft and decadent and real. He pulls back before I can part my lips, but his hand, strong and warm and tender, stays around my face and I push my cheek into it, wanting him to say the words, knowing that it's hard. "Love you," he says. The words sound like a prayer. He pushes his forehead into mine and drapes the lifejacket across the back of my shoulders. "Now get in the boat." He smiles.

The smile dies with the sound of tires screeching on the road behind us.

TYLER

"Duck!" I pull her behind the nearest rock. My heart's pounding so loud I'm pretty sure that they can hear it in the car. Depending on whether the car follows the lake road around, there's a good chance they'll see us on the other side. Her whole body shakes and I hold her but oh fuck what if it's that guy who was following me in New Haven and we're dead but can't think like that. We have to get the hell out of here.

It's cold. The rock is as cold as her hands and I rub them to warm them for her. We listen. Nothing. The car keeps on driving. Thank God.

I nod to her and stand up, legs stiff. "C'mon." Too cold to be doing this, but it's not far to the border and it's the middle of the night, so we might make it in unnoticed. Might make it.

We double-wrap our packs in the garbage bags we brought with us, grab the paddles, and push out into the lake. Ani's not so sure what she's doing. Thank God. Explaining how to kayak gives me something to focus on, something to do. She picks it up quick and we move out at a pretty good clip. It's cold, but the sound of the paddles cutting through the water and the waves beating on the side of the kayak is comforting, almost. The sound of good memories.

Lake Memphremagog is a deep glacial lake, and I tell her stories as we go, always with one eye up on the sky and the other searching, looking for that light of the border patrol boat. Telling myself that it's cool if the boat catches us, telling myself that it would be so miserably ironic if Rick launches a drone over the border and blows me out of the water. So I tell her the stories that my dad told me as a kid, about Memphremagog, the lake monster rumored to be living beneath our paddles, about the different fish I used to catch here, anything to stop my brain from spinning too much, to keep my arms moving even after they start to scream, to keep my eyes off the sky.

There aren't a lot of boats roaming around at night, but when we see one, we hide. Tuck ourselves down low in the kayak and hope the shoreline hides us. Hope that we're invisible under the moon. For every movement on shore I pray. Pray that it's not people or at least that they don't see us. Or they don't care.

Finally, as the sky brightens and we hide in the brambles along the shore from another large boat, hoping not to get turned in their wake, she asks, "Is that a town?"

I push off, looking out ahead of us, "Yeah, let's hope it's Magog."

We paddle over to a clearer patch of shore, legs aching as we disembark, and I practically fall over as she hugs me. "What do we do now?" she asks, voice breathless.

"Try and get to Montreal, I guess."

We take the bus. I sleep until Ani wakes me up, my head a blur of the sound of wheels and hydraulics. Cloth seats with those little rags draped over the top and emergency aisle lighting. What are those rags about, do they ever change them? Pointless. They started out white and now they're dirty from hair grease and drool. Stupid. Donovan Jones from the *Times* hasn't emailed. Whatever. We've got Todd, right? The conductor calls over the intercom that we're an hour outside of Montreal. Good. One hour to go. Wish the bus would go faster.

"I'm so sorry, Tyler," she whispers. Voice soft, like the kiss she leaves on my ear as she shoves her laptop onto my lap. The news reports that a body was found in my house. Found by the cleaning lady. Which is funny, because we don't have a cleaning lady. They're waiting until the family is notified before releasing any details.

My throat closes. Cinches up so tight. I shut my eyes against the visions of Brandon's last moments on earth.

If he was scared. If he regretted his decision. If it hurt. I squeeze my eyelids together, clamp them down quick and hard and press so that Ani doesn't have to see tears.

Have to get to Todd. Have to earn this.

Forty-five minutes later we roll into Station Centrale. I've been in Canada less than half a day and already the mix of French and English is driving me out of my head. Just seems like they can't make up their mind. Like they're teasing me.

My legs are stiff and I have to stretch them out and the place smells like diesel and stale piss. We're close. So close to getting to this guy, so close to being able to breathe again and feel like I can stop grinding my teeth and looking over our shoulder, looking at the other cars on the road like they bring nothing but death and the end. The end of me. Of Ani. Of us.

Ani walks off the bus first, grabbing her foot behind her back and stretching out her quads the second we get off the bus. I do it, too. Looking around. Watching the people. Talking on phones and drinking coffee and moving fast. Like they're important. Like they have somewhere to go. I grab Ani's hand and we walk into the main building.

Look at their faces. Watch. Keep her safe. Keep moving. Dude in the corner. Tall, dirty, floor-length duster and looks like he smells. He's watching us. But probably cool. Probably not one of Rick's. Can we make it? Can this possibly work?

My heart beats faster as we check out the map with the Metro stops and Ani tries to figure out how to get to

Todd's office. Watch. Careful. Old ladies. Group of them, smiling. Probably just came back from a casino. Cool. But behind them, behind them...

It's Rick. He doesn't see us. Yet. The whole building and its smells swirl around and seem to collapse in on itself until all I can see is him. And the distance between us.

Approximately one hundred feet. Back entrance. Have to split up. Save Ani. Stall Rick. "Ani, don't turn around."

She turns around. Shit. She gasps. "How? How did he find us?"

"No idea, but listen, don't panic. I have a plan." Shit, I need a plan. "See those old ladies over there? You're short enough, hide behind them and walk back towards the buses. Out the back door. They'll have it covered but they won't hurt you if you're surrounded by a mass of people, understand? Stay in the middle of crowds. Get out of here. Get to Todd's. Get there. Don't let them find you."

"But Tyler, I can't leave you." Her voice cracks open, and her eyes, oh man. I am so dead. She's so worth it, though.

"I'll be fine, just go." Rick's scanning the crowd on the level below us. Just a matter of time before he sees us. "Meet you there. Promise."

I kiss her, fast, hard, on the lips then push her a little, just a little, and nod to her as she walks. Walks through the door in a posse of old ladies. Please let her make it please I can't lose her, too. Please.

Looking down over the railing, he's talking to some old lady. Showing her a picture on his phone. Probably me. Has to be me. Think. Have to think. Two staircases leading down to his floor are on either side of me. Throngs of people, of tourists, all swarming past me. Great. Can't go down shooting. Don't have a gun. Or a plane, or a drone, or a plan.

I'm screwed.

My fingers go numb and my legs tingle but then I see them. The guys. Gay couple, probably. Oldish, playing with a video-camera. One is tall and bald on top with a funky goatee and the other is rounder but really well dressed and they are filming one another. Gesturing up at the walls that are covered in paintings. Great. Perfect. Hope they speak English.

My feet move. Each step having meaning, bringing me closer to either my salvation or my end. Probably the end. Shut up. Walk. Right foot. Left. "Excuse me, guys?" I start.

Thank God, they stop talking. They look at me. Half-afraid. Like they don't know whether I'm gonna make fun or ask where the bathrooms are. So been there. Rick is still surrounded by little old ladies. There's no way around him. If I go out the back door it'll lead him to Ani. Have to go out the front. Past Rick. "I was wondering if you could do me a favor?"

They look at each other, lowering the camera.

Well, at least they're listening. "See that guy down there, with the buzz cut? The one talking to the little old lady? I was wondering if you could film me when I go talk to him." Think of a lie, think of a lie. It comes so easy. "See, he's my dad and I've never met him before, so I was wondering if you could record it for me? I want to remember what he says and his face and all. Here, I'll give you my name and if you could just email it to me later. Can't believe I forgot my own video. Sucks."

Their faces melt. Soften. Totally cool. "We'd love to."

"Do you think you could even get sound from this far away, I mean, I don't want him to know we're being filmed because then he might not say what he really thinks, you know?"

"Oh, don't worry, he won't notice a thing," the larger one says.

I bet he won't.

Rick still doesn't see. But I bet he has his guys. Watching. Better not hurt these guys. I would feel so bad. I give them my email, knowing if something happens to me that getting into my email account would be easy for Ani, and they load it into their phones. Nodding my thanks, I try and look happy. Try and look like I'm not about to vomit.

Would he kill me right here? In front of everyone? Maybe. I walk down the stairs.

Right foot, left. Driving each foot down into the concrete. Feel it shudder up my leg. Strong. I can do this. If he shoots me at least it's on film. Breathe. He's not going to shoot. Not in public, anyway.

I hit the main floor. And he sees me.

He is so going to shoot me.

I stop about five feet away. "Hey Rick."

••••

ANI

What do I do? I have to get out of here quick and help Tyler. Brandon must have called Todd before they found him; it would have been easy enough from there for Rick to figure out that we wouldn't fly or even risk driving through a border crossing. I duck into the throng of old ladies and use them as cover until I see a door. It's probably a closet but I don't really need a lot of room, do I? The room is stuffed, filled with boxes of cleaning supplies and junk. I sit and open the laptop, quickly calling the Montreal police through the computer. Wrangling my fear until I can keep my voice steady, I tell them that there's a man with a gun in the bus station. Then I email Todd and let him know that we're here and that Tyler needs help. Listening through the door, I wait for the sound of people screaming, wait for the door to fly open and for the space to fill with a man and a gun. My heartbeat frantic, it hasn't happened yet, Tyler's fine, he'll be fine, just keep going.

Are people screaming? Tyler. Please don't be Tyler. No, just a toddler on the other side of the door, his mother. OK.

Taking a long breath, I go in for the kill. It took some doing, most of the ride through Vermont, in fact, to override Rick's block on the program. But it's my program. I built it. There's no way he could keep me out. I'm surprised he was able to block me for the full six hours that he did. Typing in the directive to the four other kids who are part of Rick's plan, I find that three are at their sim stations, flying. I hit the code and send three drones screaming out of the sky. Screaming out of the sky and crashing into desolate fields of poppies.

I peek out through the door and walk quickly, positioning myself in the middle of a tour group, and exit through the back doors. I stay with them all the way to their bus platform. Then I run.

TYLER

"Tyler." His voice is tight, guarded. I know he plans to kill me. I see the look of regret.

"How'd you track me?" Get him talking. Make him talk. Make him mad, make him blow up here and not in a car. Can't get in a car with him. Stay here. Stay public.

"I'm sorry to hear about Brandon. I know he meant a lot to you."

"Don't talk to me about Brandon" – saying B's name is agony, like the word weighs a thousand pounds on my tongue – "just tell me how you tracked me."

"Your brother's cell phone records. His last call was to someone here in Montreal. Figured if you crossed over the border you'd probably have to take the bus, since I know you didn't come through in a car." Rick searches my face for a reaction, his eyes looking into mine like he's trying to see. I don't care. Let him see how much it hurts. "I have to say that I'm impressed with you, Tyler. Sending Brandon to the house as a decoy, buying yourself some time. That requires moral clarity. You're a man of decision, sacrificing the weak to save the strong. These are exactly the kinds of decisions that we have to make every day in the real world. You're growing up. There's still a place for you with Haranco if you want it."

Brandon's dead. Dead. Grief grips my neck and I hate Rick. I hate him. Hate myself. Hate the fact that I want to scream and claw at him and at the same time I'm proud. Proud that I earned his respect. I'm sick. Something is wrong with me. But looking at him, looking at him not shooting, but instead beaming at me. He *is* impressed. It's written all over him and fuck if I'm not proud. I shouldn't be. Don't look. Don't look at his face. I ball my hands into fists, I look down. "You lied to me."

"I've never lied to you, Tyler."

"Yes, you have. I thought that I could trust you. I used to tell you everything, for years, you were the only one I could count on" – I take a deep breath – "and you were lying. The whole time."

"I can't stand dishonesty, Tyler. Tell me one time, one specific time, that I've been anything less than honest."

"There is no flight school. I checked."

"That's not true, it was being built, son, built around you, around your success." Rick takes a step closer.

I back away. "The game. The missions were real. I was flying Predator drones and killing real people and you never told me."

Rick looks around, glancing at the people around us, quickly, like he doesn't care. I can't see the guys with the camera. Please don't let him see the guys. Please, please, please.

"That wasn't a lie, an omission, maybe. I admitted it to you when you figured it out. Paid you, even. That's not the same as lying."

"The drugs, Rick. I was flying cover for drug dealers. You've turned me into something that you *knew* I hated more than anything." I straighten my back. "Does JSOC know what their money is doing? Or by not mentioning it are you not lying to them, too?"

His eyes tighten and he moves a bit closer. The crowds thin out. The guy manning the ticket booth closes his window with a shushing sound that echoes through the station.

"I'd rather not talk about these things here, and you know that I don't like knowing that you're hurt. We can talk about all of this somewhere else, work everything out. Now please hand over whatever information you have and tell me where we can find Miss Bagdorian."

"No." He reaches for something inside his pocket. My heart ticks up. Don't move. Don't show fear. Like with a dog. "It's too late, anyway."

"Really, how is that? Because from where I'm standing I see a fugitive who is transporting classified information. Releasing such information about our programs to a foreign government, even Canada, isn't just illegal, Tyler. It's treason, which makes you an imminent threat to the safety of our nation." He holds onto the word *treason*. "I'm authorized to stop you by whatever means necessary."

Shit. Is it really treason? Can't worry about it, now, though, it's too late. "You're going to have to shoot me, then. The information's already out."

The station seems to swell up around us, more people coming in to catch the next round of buses. A woman's voice calls some departures out over the intercom. Rick's hand moves in his coat. Cocking a gun. I just feel it. I know that gun, too, it's the one I used at the shooting range. Remember the way it felt in my hand. The way he smiled when I hit the targets. My chest tightens. He raises his eyebrows at me and looks broken. Devastated. He is so going to kill me. Drag me out back somewhere. Throw my body in a dumpster. *Rick. Rick* is going to kill me. Of all the fucking people.

"It's on Twitter," I say and he stops. Shock painting his face white. "See, I sent my friends a copy of our little talk in the dining room. You knew I was recording, it, right? Told them to put it out on the web if they see ambulances or police or whatever on the way to my house. A body being pulled out of my house was on the news, you know. Alpha lives right down the block from me, I told him to watch for it. So it's out. Facebook, Twitter, the blogosphere. It'll be everywhere in a matter of hours. Oh, and the drones should all be gone by now."

"Drones?"

"Crashed. Done. Gone."

"That wasn't a smart move." His face tells me that it was, though. It just closes in on itself, like he's about to implode. Please let Alpha and Peanut and Ani do what they're supposed to. Please, please, please. The intercom sounds again and I turn, I start to walk away. "I'm afraid that you're coming with me, Tyler."

"Nope. Don't want to. Sorry." I take one step back.

"Only cowards run." His words are taunting, mean. Not his usual style.

"I'm not a coward." I take another step back. "Cowards shoot people in the back. I've made my decision."

"You're a spy right now, Tyler, a *terrorist*. Leaking information about government operations is a crime. You're leaving this station in my custody or not at all." His words are flat. Thin. Like he doesn't want to mean them.

"Later." I turn, I walk.

It's quiet. I don't even hear it over the noise from the station. But I feel it. Pain. Pain bursts in through my back, just beneath my shoulder and spreads out and everywhere and it burns and oh my God this hurts so bad and I fall to the ground, force knocking me forward. It's warm and it hurts and I can't catch my breath to scream. Voices, but not mine. Loud. "Hey, that guy just shot his kid!" Filters in through the growing haze. Like my head is getting wrapped in layers and layers and layers of white gauze. I open my mouth and my hands claw at the dirty tile floor and I get no sound. There's a scream. Lots of screaming. From the men with the camera. From the people around me. I hear them. Feet stamping and people dropping things and a pair of ugly white sneakers stopping in front of my face. Someone pushing into my shoulder and telling me to hold on and that everything's going to be OK.

But I know a lie when I hear one.

The hallway is packed. Green, I think. But all I see are the tiles of the ceiling as they pass. The lights. Flat panels of fluorescent badness hit my eyes and I want to close them.

But there's too much to see. Like if I close them now they won't open again. Noise comes from everywhere and nowhere specific all at once. Tubes. Beeping. Smells like plastic and the super-clean zing of oxygen coming to me from the mask. Ani's got my hand. Slowly my eyes adjust a little and I see people in suits and uniforms and even a few dresses speaking in English and French and it's so loud. The lights change. Ani's hand is gone. The lights look like big flowers that are pulled right over the top of me. Someone tells me something in French, then everything, everything fades away.

CHAPTER 30

MONDAY, NOVEMBER 5

TYLER

A small window looks out over Montreal's skyline, mountains to one side, river to the other, millions of people sandwiched in between. The beeping is softer now. The steady pulse of one of the many machines they have me hooked up to. Damn, I hurt. Don't want to admit it to Ani, though. Try to just be happy that I'm still alive and not think about the tube running up beneath my ribcage. Reinflating my lung. Stupid surgeries. The bullet went in through the back, just beneath my shoulder blade and clipped my lung. I look out the window, trying to feel like I'm someplace else, at least until all the smoke in my head clears. I'm not really ready for visitors. Well, people other than Ani, anyway, but here they are. There's a policeman and everything.

Some guy, maybe Todd, sits in a large wood chair, pillowed with pleather, too large for the small room. He pulls his eyes off of his phone when he hears me move. I'm young, covered in dirt, bullet hole in my body, smelly,

I'm sure. I can't blame him for looking at me like I just walked off a spaceship or something.

"Hello there. Welcome to Canada." The cheer in his voice is not entirely sincere, you can hear the annoyance in its undertones.

"Hey," I say.

"I've called the authorities. Tyler, you understand this: they will record your claim of refugee status and make sure that you are given your temporary permits."

"Yeah," I say. Ani called him from the bus station right before we got on the bus for Montreal. From a pay phone. The pleather on his seat just looks awful. Almost looks slimy. Gross.

"So, what do you have for me?" he asks, not in an aggressive way, eager, sure, but not nasty.

Ani looks over to me, handing him the first hard drive.

I ask, "Are we on record?"

"Yes," he says. He has red hair. Red hair and bright blue eyes. His manner is open, smart-looking, I guess, non-judgmental. "Let's start with your name."

"My name is Tyler MacCandless," I say as Ani hands him another hard drive from her backpack. I look him dead in the eye as I say, "I've killed one hundred and sixteen people."

Including my brother.

"Can I look at this now? Do you mind?" he asks, reaching around the back of the bad chair for his briefcase. They really have to update that chair. Looks awful.

What if this isn't enough? What if he can't read the drives? They don't believe me? They send us back. We'd be traitors. I nod.

He exhales, a low, long sound, and plugs the hard drive into the computer he takes out of his bag. After a few minutes watching the gun camera footage of a drone piloted from my bedroom, he looks up, first at me, then Ani. "This is unbelievable." Is that good? Bad? "I'll sponsor you both for asylum myself," he grins. "Mr Anderson has some pretty long arms, but we should be able to find a way to keep you safe."

The two guys standing against the wall move closer to the bed and start going back and forth with Todd in rapid-fire French, and I squeeze Ani's hand, tight. "Where's Rick?"

"They didn't catch him, Tyler. They chased him out of the bus station, but they didn't catch him. His face is all over the news. For some reason they think that he's your father, and they have the video of him shooting you on every major Canadian news network." Ani rubs her small fingers over the back of my hand. Sound from the video must not have come through. That's OK, though, we have plenty of evidence on the hard drives, the flashes, on the cloud. "You're lucky to be alive."

Not lucky. Rick was in the military. If he wanted to kill me, he would have, would have shot me in the head. Why didn't he kill me? That question's gonna keep me up at night.

"We will have to contact your parents. But in the meantime, can we put you both down as students? Or do you have any skills that would qualify you as skilled labor?" the policeman asks.

The policeman is named Laurent, or so says his badge. He pours me a cup of water from a pitcher.

The pitcher is a horrible shade of pink. Like old salmon. "Hey, can I use your phone to call my mom?" I ask, and Todd pushes me his cell across the table.

Ani looks at Laurent and declares herself to be a student.

"And you?" he asks, watching me move my leg back and forth beneath the covers. Need to move. Need to get out of this bed and just move. Hate this stupid bed.

"I think I'm qualified as a skilled laborer," I say, drawing weird looks from Todd and Laurent. "I'm really good at piloting drones."

A little while later, Ani's sleeping on a cot pulled up next to my bed, curled up on top of the covers in a really weird position. I feel weak.

A doctor walks in. Her name tag says something long and French-ish that I'm never going to be able to say right. But nobody has cared, yet. Canadians are pretty nice.

"How are you feeling?" she asks. She's round and kind and wearing one of those shirts that are just tragic. Her brown hair is pulled up high into a ponytail, and she starts to prod at me. Taking my blood pressure and stuff. She's trying to be careful not to wake Ani. It's dark outside. Must be late.

"OK, I guess." It's true. I'm alive. Mom knows I'm safe, though. I had a hard time understanding her when we spoke on the phone. She couldn't stop crying. I've got Ani, though, and Rick hasn't tried to visit me in the hospital yet, which is good.

She pulls an IV out of my arm, pushing gauze into it quick so it doesn't hurt so badly. After a few general doctor-like questions, she hands me a little cup. Two pills. Familiar pills.

"What are these?" I ask, staring at the pills.

"Your new pain medication. We can't keep you on the morphine any longer."

"But what are these?"

"Oxycontin. Should help you with the pain as you recover."

"No. I'm not taking these," I say and all I see is Brandon, like me, sick and broken and hurting. And this is how it all started. No. Fucking. Way.

"But–"

"Can't you just give me like a super-dose of Advil or something? Please," I say, not wanting to hear how my voice wobbles and how my eyes sting and how much I miss B. How much I want him right here.

"Alright. I'll order you Toradol injections, it's like ibuprofen, only stronger. But it may not take care of all of your pain, Tyler. Your injury is very serious."

"It's OK." I lean my head over, looking over at Ani's sleeping face. "Pain's not fatal."

CHAPTER 31

MONDAY, NOVEMBER 19

ANI

"Julie?"

"Oh, hey babe, what's up?" Julie sounds like she's still half-asleep. She shouldn't be, it's past one out in LA.

"Nothing." Well, that's not exactly true, is it? "I'm just calling to make sure you and Mom aren't worried."

"Worried? Why would we be worried, what's going on?"

"A lot, actually." She doesn't know. Mom didn't tell her? I take out millions of dollars' worth of weaponry, Haranco's all over the news and she doesn't even know. She doesn't even call? I mean, the Haranco story has been the top headline for two weeks. Even Dad managed to call – and he's in jail.

"Sorry, Ani, I went to this banging party last night and then I went back to Andre's place. Have I told you about Andre? I was dating his roommate, Shane, but then Andre and I met and it was, like, *real*, you know?"

"I'm in Canada, Julie. My boss tried to kill me. I created a virus to hijack the drones I put online and then I crashed them into some field in Afghanistan. But don't let me ruin your week or anything. Have fun screwing Andre. I have to go." I press end and look out the window of our room in Todd's apartment at a city full of people. People with friends and sisters and boyfriends and problems. I wonder if all families are like this: messed-up somehow.

Tyler's talking with Todd in the small kitchen, I can hear the sound of his voice traveling down the hall and echo around the small room with the old metal bed and the lace curtains. I put the phone in my bag, wondering if all this is worth it.

As I walk into the kitchen, I see Tyler, sitting at the far end of the small table, and when he looks up, his words stop mid-sentence, and his lips pull up into the hint of a smile. He looks at me like I am the only thing in the world worth seeing. And *that* is worth everything.

CHAPTER 32

WEDNESDAY, AUGUST 14

TYLER

They let us back into the US. It's nuts. I never thought that they would and it took endless battles with lawyers and whatever but we were declared whistleblowers or something and allowed to go back home. I hated the aftermath. The news. The Twitter shitstorm that Peanut and Alpha unleashed the second they thought I was dead. They did great. Who needs the *New York Times* when you have friends like them?

The trials. So many months of just torture. The endless reels of tape and of my mission and of grainy pictures of Rick and me together taken on my webcam and then the video from those guys in Canada that seemed to play nonstop on like every news channel ever.

Something inside me hurt when I saw Rick's face on the news under the banner WANTED. Ached. Just a little. I know he cared. If he didn't he would have shot me in the head. It's not like he hasn't killed people before.

He knows how it's done and he chose to shoot me in the back, out through the chest. High enough so he wouldn't snag my heart, off to the right to miss the trachea. He knew what he was doing.

He's MIA, still. Knew they wouldn't catch him. Ani's trying, following some kind of money trail, but he's been at this kind of stuff for so long that if anybody knows how to disappear, it's Rick.

Althea didn't know. At least they say that they didn't know. Just like Tidewater disavowed any knowledge of what exactly its subsidiary Haranco was really up to. Haranco declared Rick a "rogue agent" and swore he worked alone on this. Ani believes that. She also believes her friends over at Althea. Which is fine. The country, JSOC, Congress, everybody seems to believe all of them, too. Except for me.

Not that I'm trying to be a dick, but how do you own a company and not have any idea what it does? It just doesn't make sense, is all.

Ani's back in school. Yale wouldn't drop her. Apparently, they have fellowships for kids who are partway through school and can't pay. We're back in Connecticut. Mom's here, too. Gets nervous now if I leave her sight for too long. She's in counseling. I go sometimes, too, when she gets on my case about it. I can't take the drugs for the ADHD. I tried, I just flake out and don't remember so it doesn't do me any good, anyway. It's cool, though. Ani has me running whenever my thoughts won't clear and it's better.

The Air Force wanted me. Crazy. Turns out Rick's assessment was true. It does take three pilots to fly a single drone. Althea created a great system, just like the sim, and I let them hire me as a consultant, show them how to use fewer pilots to fly more drones. They really want me to fly them for real, though. But I'm done with that.

I'm back in school, at a community college, and during the day, well, I'm a firefighter. I hooked up with a division of fire and rescue that flies actual planes over forest fires and keeps watch. Sucks sometimes, when nothing is happening or when we're called out to an accident, when people don't make it. And it's not as cool as flying fighter jets or anything, but hell, it beats jail. Or Canada. The people were awesome but it was really freaking cold.

Do I miss B? Every day. Some days it hurts so bad, with the guilt, with thoughts of him alone in that house, that I can barely function. But other days are OK. Days when I try to cook something for dinner that doesn't taste like ass or when Ani and I just go for a run that lasts forever or days when we just sit by the pool in the sun are good. Really good. B is still there, still with me, in my head and in his favorite movie lines or whatever.

But finally, for the first time I can remember, my life is moving forward. I jump as Ani slams the door behind her. Is she back from class already? Throwing down her bag, she comes over to sit next to me on the couch. She leans her head back, sighs. "Ready to get schooled at *Skyreach*?"

I grab two controllers. She's dreaming. I own that game. "Hell yeah."

ACKNOWLEDGMENTS

There is no way I am going to be able to list by name all the people I have to thank for their help in the journey of bringing this book to print, but I will try my best. My first shout-out is to my readers, without you guys, there would be no book.

Thank you to Joe, who talked me out of writing a choose-your-own-way book about shape-shifting zombie supermodels and insisted that I write this book instead. He is the best husband I could have asked for, the one who's willing to help me litter the dining room table with notecards full of "turning points" and "exciting incidents" and doesn't mind spending thirty hours in the car with me playing the "what-is-TL-going-to-write-next" game. Love you.

To my kids, who give me purpose.

To the incredible Kristan Higgins. Not only is she a New York Times/USA Today bestselling author, she is funny, kind, and generous. She's helped me navigate the sometimes scary, always exciting world of publishing, and I can't thank her enough.

To Joanne. A friend like her is a treasure beyond all imagining. The world's best beta-reader. She is the first person I call about everything, my second pair of eyes and ears, who is not afraid to tell me what's what. My life and my writing never would have gotten to where it is without her.

To my incredible agent, Jenny Bent, for believing in me and my work, and for giving this journey her all. And to the whole Bent Agency, especially Molly, the best agency team around.

To the Strange Chemistry crew, especially my amazing editor Amanda, for taking a chance. And to the rest of the Chemistry Set, particularly Ann, Sean, Bryony and Christian, for being such a supportive bunch.

People say that things like this take a village, in my case, it feels more like a tri-state area. My sister Holly, friends Christina, Liz, and Nicole, I love you and couldn't have done much of anything without all these years of love and support.

My amazing and loving family, who helped talk me off ledges and held me up when I was down... or as was the case after my parents' death, didn't have money for food or anyplace to live. I know I was young, but I am thankful for you all every day. Thank you for sacrificing so much to step up. Especially Grandma G., Cindy, Robert and William Badrigian, Grandma F., Uncle George and Aunt Carol and Douglas, Scott and George and their families, the Spencers and everyone else in the family.

To CTRWA, the best writers group ever. Thank you for never talking down to me when I was a new writer with nothing more than a laptop and a dream. Thank you for giving my practice pitch an F (and helping me turn it into *the* pitch) and thank you for being there every step of the process. Especially to Peter Andrews and his wonderful How to Write Fast tips, which have become words I live by, and for being a great friend. There are so many of you to thank that this section will be over fifteen pages if I list out everyone's name, but you are all loved and appreciated.

To my Texans, especially to Eddie Prislac and his mad web-designing skills. To my crew from Spring, especially my teachers, thank you. And my CT friends and cheerleaders, especially Sarah D., the Taylor clan, the Girard-Menchettis, and Mr. Hagan and everyone at the Y, Master Gary's kickboxing and Good Shepherd Church. And thanks to God.

To my friends from BMC, especially Kim and Amanda and Ginger and Heather and Lauren and Em and well, everyone. Being around brilliant women is good for the soul.

ABOUT THE AUTHOR

T L Costa is a graduate of Bryn Mawr College and has a Masters of Teaching from Quinnipiac University who taught high school for five years before becoming a full-time mom and writer.

She has lived in Texas, New York, New Jersey and Spain. Currently, she lives in Connecticut with her husband and two children.

"Death, kissing and a smoking hot mystery boy:
what more could you ask for?"
Amy Plum, author of Die For Me

AudioGO▶
The home of BBC Audiobooks

If you liked reading this book, you'll love listening to it as an audiobook, and the rest of the AudioGO range too!

AudioGO has over 10,000 titles available as CDs and downloads including Young Adults, Sci-Fi and Fantasy and more.

Use this **£5 free voucher** on anything from the AudioGO range.

Simply use discount code **OSPREY14** at **www.audiogo.com/uk** by December 2013.

MORE WONDERS IN STORE FOR YOU...

- ◆ Gwenda Bond / BLACKWOOD
- ◆ Kim Curran / SHIFT
- ◆ Sean Cummings / POLTERGEEKS
- ◆ Cassandra Rose Clarke / THE ASSASSIN'S CURSE
- ◆ Jonathan L Howard / KATYA'S WORLD
- ◆ AE Rought / BROKEN
- ◆ Laura Lam / PANTOMIME
- ◆ Julianna Scott / THE HOLDERS
- ◆ Martha Wells / EMILIE & THE HOLLOW WORLD
- ◆ Christian Schoon / ZENN SCARLETT
- ◆ Cassandra Rose Clarke / THE PIRATE'S WISH
- ◆ Gwenda Bond / THE WOKEN GODS
- ◆ Kim Curran / CONTROL
- ◆ Ingrid Jonach / WHEN THE WORLD WAS FLAT
  (AND WE WERE IN LOVE)

**EXPERIMENTING WITH
YOUR IMAGINATION**

strangechemistrybooks.com
facebook.com/strangechemistry
twitter.com/strangechem